Praise for Sharon Sala's
Blessings, Georgia series

"Eng...ood."
—.........y You

"A ha...and
cheer...

—*Harlequin Junkie* for *You and Only You*

"Sala once again shows why she is a master of the romance genre...an amazing story by a true storyteller."
—*RT Book Reviews* for *I'll Stand By You*

"Blessings sure sounds like a great place to put down roots."
—*Fresh Fiction* for *Saving Jake*

"There are not many authors who can write a story with such depth and emotion, but Sala excels and shines... Sala is magical!"
—*RT Book Reviews* for *A Piece of My Heart*

"With plenty of danger and passion, Sala will have readers flipping the pages."
—*RT Book Reviews*, 4 Stars for *The Color of Love*

"A strong and positive second-chance romance that fans of Robyn Carr and Susan Wiggs will enjoy."
—*Booklist* for *Come Back to Me*

the WAY
BACK to *you*

Also by Sharon Sala

Blessings, Georgia

the WAY BACK *to* *you*

SHARON SALA

sourcebooks
casablanca

Sourcebooks and the colophon are registered trademarks of Sourcebooks.

Published by Sourcebooks Casablanca, an imprint of Sourcebooks
P.O. Box 4410, Naperville, Illinois 60567-4410
(630) 961-3900
sourcebooks.com

Printed and bound in the United States of America.
OPM 10 9 8 7 6 5 4 3 2 1

We all have a need to belong to someone somewhere. Even if our lives are about always being on the move, the knowledge that we have a place to call home is what grounds us.

Many of us take a wrong turn on the road of life and have a hard time finding our way back to center.

Home does that for me. But not necessarily back to where I was born, or where I was raised. It's the people we're tied to, by blood and by love, that keep us rooted in the reality of life.

I dedicate this book to all the lost ones who finally find the people they are meant to love.

CHAPTER 1

THE ENTIRE FORTY-FIVE YEARS OF SULLIVAN RAINES' existence crashed and burned when his mother died, but it wasn't from grief. It was the adoption papers—his adoption—that he found in his parents' safety deposit box, along with the will he'd gone there to retrieve. In shock, he'd dropped the will off at the lawyer's office and taken the papers and a box of photo albums he'd already rescued from his parents' home back to his apartment. In going through the box, he found an envelope with a letter, and a silver chain with an ornate cross hanging from it.

I'm sorry we never told you. This belonged to your birth mother. She left it for you.

The rest of the day was a blur, and the ensuing days up to the funeral weren't any better. He kept replaying vignettes from his past, remembering the times he'd asked his parents why his hair was black and straight when they were both blonds. And how did he get so tall when they were both short? They'd always laughed it off, blaming ancestors or recessive genes, and he'd bought it.

He was still going through the house, moving things he wanted to keep into a storage unit and getting the rest ready for the upcoming estate auction. In the evenings, he would go through photo albums, remembering the events and seeing anew the marked differences of his appearance within the family.

Some pictures were taken at parties, like the one he had at the skating rink for his thirteenth birthday. He grinned at the clothes they were wearing and started eyeing the faces to see if he could remember all the names. One photo stood out from the others because it was him holding hands with a girl out on the floor of the skating rink. They both smiled and waved at the camera as they skated past his dad, who was the family photographer. Her name was Missy, and she was the first girl he kissed. He'd had the biggest crush on her most of that year, but then her family had moved away. When school started that fall, she was gone, and life moved on.

After that trip down memory lane, Sully put the albums up.

The evidence of his adoption was impossible to ignore, and the differences in appearance between him and his family finally made sense. Even though his parents had been wonderful and loving, this lie was huge, and he didn't know how to get past it.

The adoption papers stated he was the baby of a teenage girl named Janie Chapman. He found out later that his parents knew her because she had lived on their street. Although she'd signed the adoption papers the day he was born, the accompanying letter he found stated that she actually lived with Joe and Dolly Raines for the first six months of his life, nursing him, caring for him in their house while they worked, and then one morning she was gone.

Sully couldn't get her out of his head. She'd carried him in her belly for nine months, nursed him for the first six months of his life, then disappeared without an explanation?

He needed to know why, and the few details he had were what was on his original birth certificate.

He had her name, and where and when he was born. Boone County Hospital in Columbia, Missouri, on June 4, 1974.

Since that was all he had to go on, he chose one of the ancestry sites and took a DNA test. After the results arrived, he hired a genetic researcher named Marilyn Bedford to see if he had any blood relatives registered in the system.

Within two weeks, she found genetic links to a branch of Chapmans, but the only one on the family tree who was still living was a distant cousin.

After a couple of emails back and forth between them, Sully learned the cousin had never met Janie Chapman, didn't know where she was, or if she was even still alive. All the cousin remembered was hearing her mother talk about the scandal Janie had caused when she got pregnant, and that the last piece of mail the family had received from her was years ago and had been postmarked from somewhere in Texas.

Sully was still thinking about where to go next when he got one last email from the cousin. It was the return address for Janie Chapman that she'd found in one of her mother's old address books. She apologized for the oversight and wished him well. He typed Grapevine, Texas, into Google search to find the location, then packed a couple of suitcases.

And on a gray and stormy morning, Sullivan Raines drove out of Kansas City, Missouri, driving away from one storm into another that had been fed by a lifetime of lies. He drove straight down I-35, through Oklahoma and into Texas, with steady intensity, stopping only for food and fuel.

Sunset had long since come and gone by the time Sully reached Grapevine, and then he began looking for a place to stay. After settling on a hotel and getting into a room, he dumped his luggage, cleaned up, and went downstairs to the restaurant to eat. His waiter arrived within a couple of minutes and took his drink order, giving Sully time to scan the menu. The waiter came back with the tall glass of sweet tea and took his order for chicken-fried steak with all the trimmings.

Sully took a long drink and then glanced around the busy dining room, eyeing all the older women with more than curiosity, looking for glimpses of himself in their faces, and not for the first time wished he wasn't on this journey alone.

His one stab at marriage had lasted eight years before she cheated on him with his best friend. The breakup had been ugly, the divorce even more so. After that, although he'd had a few relationships that went nowhere, he'd never been tempted to try it again.

All of his close friends were guys he knew from work, but now that he was no longer on the job, it was difficult to stay in touch. For a fireman, timing was everything, and the timing in Sully's life was off-kilter. He needed roots. He might be kidding himself that finding his birth mother would fill the hole in his life, but he had to give it a try.

His food finally came. The chicken-fried steak was crispy on the outside and tender on the inside, and the white gravy studded with peppercorns was as good as the gravy Captain Lawson made at the station.

Sully went back to his room later, showered, set his alarm for 8:00 a.m., and then crawled into bed.

The next thing he knew, his alarm was going off, and sunlight was coming through a gap in the curtains over his window. Anxiety lent speed to his morning routine as he showered, shaved, and dressed. After he checked out, he grabbed a coffee and a sweet roll from the Starbucks kiosk in the lobby and headed out the door. His first step to the beginning of this search was entering the address the cousin had given him into his GPS.

He set out, easily following directions, only to discover after twenty minutes of morning traffic that there was now an apartment building on that location.

Marilyn had given him a list of suggestions as to where to search, so he googled the address of the city hall in Grapevine, and with some help from one of the clerks, discovered a marriage license for Jane Chapman and Bryan Jackson, and divorce papers for the same couple less than two years later.

At that point, Jane Chapman Jackson showed up nowhere else in Grapevine. Sully wondered if she might have left Texas altogether, so he called Marilyn.

"Hello, Sully. How's it going?" she asked.

"It's going. The address I had for her is no good, which figures because it was so many years ago, but I did find a marriage license for her and a man named Bryan Jackson, then divorce papers for them less than two years later."

"Good job," Marilyn said. "Let me have the details, and I'll see if I can track her down elsewhere. It may take a couple of days."

"No problem, and I appreciate your help. I'm sticking around here until I hear from you again."

"Then I'll get right on this. You'll be hearing from me soon," Marilyn said.

As it turned out, Sully was in Grapevine for three days before Marilyn Bedford called him again, this time with news that she'd found another connection to Jane Chapman Jackson. The reason it had taken a while was because Jane Jackson married again in Mobile, Alabama, to a man named Robert Carter.

So, Sully packed up his bag, checked out of the motel, and headed for Mobile. He arrived just as the tailwinds of a hurricane were passing through the area and found a safe place to ride out the storms that followed it. But even after the storms had passed and the weather cleared, he had not been able to find a trace of Janie anywhere. Just as he was giving up, he got a call from Marilyn.

"Hello, this is Sully."

"Sully, this is Marilyn. I have a bit of information that may help you. Jane divorced Robert Carter about six years after their marriage in Mobile."

"Again? Wow, she doesn't have a very good track record with husbands," Sully said. "Do you know where she went from there, or if she's still somewhere in Mobile?"

"I don't know where Jane went, but her ex, Robert Carter, never left Mobile. I have a phone number for him. Maybe he would have further information for you. Do you want it?"

"Absolutely," Sully said, and took down the number. "Got it, and thank you, Marilyn. I'll stay in touch."

"Okay, and if I find anything more, I'll let you know."

They disconnected, and Sully immediately called the number Marilyn had given him. No one answered, but Sully left a message and his number on voicemail. All he could do was wait to see if Carter called him back.

It was just after eight that same night when Robert Carter called.

"Hello, this is Sully."

"Mr. Raines, this is Robert Carter returning your call. So you say you're looking for my ex-wife."

"Yes, I am, and call me Sully. My interest in your ex-wife is personal and very important to me. I only recently discovered that I was adopted, and according to paperwork I found at my parents' house, I know for certain that your wife, Jane, was Jane Chapman, my birth mother. You're her second ex-husband, and I'm having trouble finding new leads. By any chance, do you know where she went when you two divorced?"

"Well, well. You're something I didn't know about. As for where she went, all I know is what she said she was going to do. She was looking for a place to live to start a new life, and she wanted to do it in Georgia. She found a place called Blessings on a map and said that was the sign from God that she was looking for. I got one piece of mail from her about a week later. She'd found a key to my old trunk in her jewelry box and mailed it back to me. The return address was 104 Brigade Street, Blessings, Georgia, and I never heard from her again. I want you to know that our divorce was mostly my fault. Jane was a good woman, and I didn't do right by her. I wish you success in your search. Sorry I wasn't more help," Carter said.

"No, this is perfect and I really appreciate it," Sully said, and hung up, then sent Marilyn a quick text.

Last known destination for Jane was 104 Brigade
St., Blessings, Georgia. See what you can do with
that.

He got ready for bed, packed everything but what he
was going to wear the next day, and fell asleep dreaming
that, one way or another, Blessings would be the end of his
search.

He overslept, woke up late, then had a tire going low that
he had to get fixed before he could leave. Getting a flat fixed
turned into buying a new tire, and finding the right size
turned into an all-day search. By the time he found the tire,
then got it mounted, the sun was going down. Frustrated
by the day, and hungry, he went to eat dinner. The logical
choice would have been to stay over another night, but after
coming out of the restaurant, he made a knee-jerk decision,
entered Tallahassee, Florida, in his GPS and left Mobile on
I-10, heading east.

He drove with purpose, stopping only when necessary. It was well past midnight when he finally arrived in
Tallahassee. He found a motel on the outskirts that looked
clean and safe enough and fell into bed without changing
his clothes.

He woke up to find a text from Marilyn with a brief
message.

No record of Jane Carter at that address. It must
have been a rental.

Disappointed, he washed up and was gone by 7:00 a.m.,
this time heading north toward Georgia on I-95. He had

Blessings entered into his GPS, and if nothing went wrong, he should pull into town around midmorning.

It was a little past noon when Sully passed the city limit sign and drove into Blessings. The highway he was on had turned into Main Street, and he began checking out all the businesses as he drove through town. The police station was on Main, as were a hair salon, a pharmacy, a florist, and some kind of exercise place.

He'd read a few months earlier that a few of the Piggly Wiggly supermarkets were closing, and there was evidence of that right here on Main.

The Piggly Wiggly sign had been taken down from the top of the building housing a supermarket, but the little pig logo was still evident. Obviously, someone was running it. Being the only supermarket in a town this size, it should do a good business.

There was an eating establishment called Granny's Country Kitchen a bit farther up the street, and from the number of vehicles in the large parking lot, the food they served must be good.

Sully knew Janie was no longer at 104 Brigade Street, but he was curious to see what was there and entered the address into his GPS.

He found Brigade Street and drove slowly past the houses, looking for that number. There was a huge gathering a few houses down on one side of the block, and people were going in and out of what looked like a new build. *Maybe it was a housewarming party*, he thought, and kept on driving without any luck, which told him this was going to require checking in at City Hall for land records and deeds.

He wondered if Jane had remarried again, and would be checking to see if another marriage license had been registered. He also had the library and old newspapers as more places to search.

The more he drove, the more he noticed what looked like high-water marks on the sides of commercial buildings. He knew Hurricane Fanny had just hit this part of the East Coast and it appeared the town was still in various states of recovery.

He made a random choice of streets and left Main to drive through another part of the residential area. Again, he saw more houses in different stages of storm repair. He thought about the windstorms and the floods and tornadoes he'd grown up with in Kansas that brought their own level of devastation and destruction. But wind was wind, and water was water, and no matter how it was delivered, he empathized with what the people had endured.

His whiskers itched, and he'd been in his clothes two days. The first thing he wanted was a place to stay so he could clean up and change clothes.

Another search on Google revealed his choices for an overnight stay in Blessings were either a motel or a bed-and-breakfast. He chose the Blessings Bed and Breakfast and found it easily enough. When he pulled up and parked, the appearance of the two-story home with a wraparound porch was immediately appealing. He was glad he'd chosen here instead of the motel. He got out, grabbed his luggage, and walked inside. The woman standing behind the registration desk smiled when she saw him walk in.

"Welcome to Blessings. I'm Rachel Goodhope."

"Nice to meet you, ma'am. I'm Sully Raines. I need a room for at least a couple of days, maybe more."

"Certainly. Is it just you, sir?" Rachel asked.

"Yes, I'm alone," Sully said.

Rachel went about getting him registered and then led the way up the stairs to his room. He stood aside as she unlocked the door and walked in, turning on lights as she went.

"The bathroom is just to your right," Rachel said. "There's a stocked mini-fridge in the cabinet next to your closet and a house phone on the bed stand. If you need assistance or have a question, just press the number 9, and either I or my husband, Bud, will answer. Breakfast is served from 7:00 to 10:00 a.m. There are several good places to eat your other meals in Blessings. I personally recommend Granny's Country Kitchen. It's on Main Street, so you can't miss it. There's also Broyles Dairy Freeze if you want fast food, or there's a barbecue joint. It's small, but the food is really good. I hope your stay here in Blessings is a pleasant one," she said, and gave him the room key.

"Yes, ma'am. Thank you. Before you go, may I ask you a quick question?"

"Of course," Rachel said.

"Do you know a woman named Jane Carter, or have you known of anyone by that name ever living here? She would be in her mid-sixties by now."

Rachel thought a moment, then shook her head. "No, I don't, but I didn't grow up here. If you go to Granny's for lunch, ask Lovey Cooper. She's lived here for years and owns

Granny's. At one time or another, everyone in Blessings has eaten there."

Sully grinned. "Thank you, I will."

After she left, he unpacked his things, then stripped and headed to the shower. He stepped beneath the hot spray with his shampoo bottle, then after his hair was washed, proceeded to scrub from the top down. When he was through, he got out and wrapped a towel around his waist, then moved to the sink to shave, dripping water on the thick, fluffy bath mat as he stood.

The mirror had fogged over from the heat of the shower, so he wiped it clean, then paused and stared at himself in the mirror.

He'd seen that face every day of his life and never once doubted his identity, even though his black hair, the Roman shape of his nose, and the classic curve to his jaw were nothing like either of his parents'. He leaned closer, staring intently into his own brown eyes as water dripped from equally dark lashes. If he had to guess, at least one of his parents might have been part Middle Eastern, or maybe from any one of the Mediterranean cultures. Not knowing even the most basic of things about them left him feeling lost.

"Who are you?" Sully muttered, then shook off the feeling and plugged in his electric razor.

The simple act of removing the dark stubble on his face was calming. Even though he didn't know where he'd come from, he was restoring order to his appearance. For now, it was enough.

Once he was finished, he towel dried his hair and got dressed. The last thing to go on were his old Justin boots. They were a little worn at the heels but familiar, and right now he needed all of the grounding he could get.

He pocketed his room key and headed back downstairs, then out to the parking lot to his car. He hadn't had anything to eat but fast food for a couple of days, so the idea of a sit-down meal was enticing.

The sun was bright, the sky clear as he drove back toward Main. Since he'd left home in a storm, he took the good weather as a positive sign.

He was just turning onto Main Street, eyeing the traffic in the distance ahead of him and watching for the sign to Granny's Country Kitchen, when all of a sudden, a car came speeding out of a side street and T-boned the car ahead of him. The impact was so hard, it sounded like an explosion. Glass flew as the car spun and stopped, facing the opposite direction. He got a glimpse of a woman behind the wheel, and then steam and smoke began coming out of both cars. Old work habits kicked in as Sully stomped on his brakes, put the car in park, and jumped out running.

Melissa Dean had been at the shop all morning, overseeing the installation of a new dry-cleaning machine. Her employees were excited to get it and eager to learn how to use it. By the time Melissa left, they were all in the back getting firsthand instructions from the installers.

She glanced at herself in the rearview mirror as she backed away from the curb, liking how the pale-lavender eye shadow she was wearing accentuated her green eyes. And she was still liking the chocolate-brown color of her hair and the shoulder-length cut. She'd come a long way from the drab woman who'd worked at Bloomer's Hardware.

Growing up an only child in Missouri, she'd never imagined herself being unhappy. She'd always had friends, some more special than others, but there was never a shortage. Her parents moved away from Kansas City when she was in junior high, and she later met her husband, Andy, during her last year of junior college.

They married within six months of his graduation from Missouri State and had a few happy years together before he died. And that's when she'd put her life on hold. She hadn't meant to, but over the years, being a widow had become her identity. A recent windfall in her life had changed all that, for which she would be forever grateful.

She glanced at the time as she put the car in gear and tried to remember what she had at home in the way of leftovers. There was leftover baked ham, but beyond that, she couldn't remember and decided to go to Granny's to eat instead.

Today was Monday, which meant the Curl Up and Dye was closed, and she was thinking about giving Ruby a call to see if she wanted to join her for lunch. But then she glanced at the time as she braked at a stop sign and decided it was too late for that spur-of-the-moment call.

She turned right onto Main, accelerating slowly, and was just getting ready to turn left into the parking lot at Granny's when a car came out from a side street without stopping, ramming into her at full speed.

The impact threw her against the door, then yanked her back as the car spun around in the opposite direction. Her seat belt kept her from being thrown out as the driver's side door flew open and then slammed itself shut from the momentum of the spin. Glass had already shattered as the airbags deployed. Steam and smoke began coming into her car from somewhere beneath the dash, along with tiny fingers of flames.

For a few seconds she was so stunned by what had just happened that she couldn't think, but then smoke began to billow up inside the car, and when she saw flames coming out from beneath the hood, she panicked and reached for her seat belt to get out. To her horror, it wouldn't unlatch.

"No, no, no, God help me," she mumbled, and then began trying over and over to unlatch it, even pulling and tugging on it without success.

She didn't know she was screaming until someone yanked open the driver's side door.

CHAPTER 2

SULLY WAS RUNNING AT TOP SPEED AND WITHIN TEN YARDS of the car when he saw the flames and heard the woman's screams. Without hesitation, he yanked the door open and felt for her arm. She jerked at his touch but stopped screaming.

"Lady! Can you move?" Sully asked.

Melissa couldn't see him, but she could feel his hands on her shoulder.

"Help me! It's on fire!" she cried.

The tone of his voice was more urgent now. "I know! I see it. Can you move?"

"Yes, yes, but my seat belt...the latch... I can't get it open."

She felt his weight against her as he leaned across the steering wheel. She felt him fumbling for the latch, and then suddenly she was free.

"Put your arm around my neck," Sully said, and when she did, he slid one arm beneath her legs and the other around her body and pulled her out. The moment they were clear of the car, he tightened his hold and turned and ran—straight toward the parking lot at Granny's, trying to get as far away from the wreck as he could before it blew.

All traffic on Main Street had stopped, and people were coming out of the businesses. Sirens were blasting, announcing the approach of emergency vehicles. People were getting out of their vehicles, and the man who'd hit her was out of his car and sitting on the curb a short distance away.

And then the wreck exploded into flames, sending

shrapnel-like pieces of metal flying in all directions and burning debris up into the air. It went up, and then it began to come down, sending onlookers running for safety.

Sully stumbled from the impact of the blast at the same time he was hit on the shoulder by a sharp, burning blow.

The woman was coughing and struggling to breathe. He had to get her out of this smoke, so he kept running straight to the front door of the restaurant. But now, burning debris was also coming down from above them. He was only yards from the café when the door flew open and an older woman ran out.

"In here! In here!" she cried, and he leaped across the threshold with the injured woman in his arms.

———————————————

Granny's dining room was doing business as usual up until the wreck. The sound of crunching metal and screeching tires was impossible to miss. At that point, diners began getting up and running to the windows to see what had happened.

Lovey was up front at the checkout counter when she heard the impact. She jumped up from her seat and pushed the curtains aside to look out just as the cars exploded into flames.

"Oh my lord!" she gasped, staring openmouthed at the huge plume of smoke and fire shooting up into the sky.

And then she saw a man running across the street and into her parking lot with a woman in his arms, with burning debris falling down around them.

With no time to waste, Lovey ran out from behind the counter and opened the door only seconds ahead of them.

"In here! In here!" she shouted, and then stepped

outside long enough for them to run past her before duck-
ing back inside.

The man was in the act of laying the woman down on
the bench seating in the lobby when Lovey saw her face.

"Oh my God! It's Melissa! She's bleeding!" she cried,
and then saw a scorched and bloody spot on the man's back
and realized he'd been hit by some of the debris. "Mister,
you're bleeding, too," Lovey said.

Sully didn't look up. "I'm okay. Will you please call 911
and let them know one of the victims is in here?"

"What did you say?" Lovey asked.

Everyone who worked at Granny's was well aware Lovey
had lost complete hearing in one ear.

Mercy Pittman, who did all the baking at Granny's,
had come out of the kitchen with most of the others in the
dining room when the explosion happened, and she'd followed Lovey into the lobby. When Lovey didn't hear what
the man asked for, Mercy tapped her on the shoulder.

"I've got it," she said.

Lovey nodded.

By now, business inside the dining room and the kitchen
had come to a complete halt. Waitresses and customers
alike were all trying to wedge their way into the small lobby
to hear and see.

Sully was assessing the woman's condition, checking out
the small cut on her forehead, then checking to see if there
were others.

"Ma'am, show me where the pain is worst," he said.

Melissa's eyes were burning so badly that she wouldn't
open them, but she was locked in on the sound of her rescuer's voice, responding to everything he was asking.

"My head and my neck, I think."

"Try not to move or turn your head, okay?" he said.

Melissa's heart skipped in sudden fear. Head and neck injuries often led to bigger problems, and there had been no time to immobilize her before he pulled her out of the car.

"Can you move your legs?" he asked.

Melissa responded again.

"Good job," he said, then began feeling up and down the length of her arms and legs for signs of broken bones.

"My eyes burn so bad," she whispered.

"Can someone bring a wet cloth for her eyes?" he asked.

Lovey pointed. "Wendy, go get one from the kitchen."

"Yes, ma'am," the waitress said. She ran out of the lobby and returned carrying a wet linen dinner napkin. "Here you go," she said, handing it to Sully.

"Thank you," he said, then reached for the injured woman's hand. "Melissa. Your name is Melissa, right?"

"Yes."

"Feel this? I'm going to put it across your eyes."

The soft tone of his voice was as gentle as the touch of his hand as he unfolded part of the napkin and laid it across her face. A soft moan was all she was capable of making, but it was one of relief.

Melissa wanted to see him—the man that went with the voice—and after patting the wet cloth against her eyelids, and letting the cold water seep beneath the lids, she was finally able to open her eyes. Her vision was still a little blurry, but what she did see was a good-looking man with very black hair and kind eyes.

For a few timeless seconds, their gazes locked.

Greenest eyes I've ever seen, Sully thought, and then knelt beside the bench because his head was spinning. His throat burned, likely from smoke inhalation, and the pain in his shoulder was increasing.

"Are you okay?" Lovey asked.

"Yes, ma'am. Just feeling the smoke," he said.

Before Lovey could respond, the door opened, and a couple of firemen stepped inside.

"Miss Lovey, we're going up on your roof to make sure none of that falling debris caught anything up there on fire."

"Oh my goodness," Lovey said, and ran outside with them to look. When she came back inside, two EMTs pushing a gurney were right behind her.

After making a cursory check of Melissa's condition and applying a neck brace, they loaded her onto the gurney and wheeled her out to the waiting ambulance.

Sully slipped out when the EMTs arrived and jogged back across the street to his car. It was still running, the keys in the ignition and the door wide open. He slid in behind the steering wheel, then shut the door and took a deep breath.

For someone who'd just left the Kansas City Fire Department, this was a hell of a way to start retirement. When he saw an ambulance leaving the scene, he followed it to the ER. His shoulder hurt like hell, and he was pretty sure whatever had hit him was still in it.

Melissa was in shock. The ambulance ride had felt surreal, and even after they transferred her from the gurney to a bed in the ER, she couldn't believe this had happened. People were all around her as they began assessing her condition, talking to one another and then asking her rapid-fire questions about what hurt and what didn't until her head was spinning.

She had the headache from hell. Her eyes were burning, and it hurt to breathe in too deeply. She didn't know if it was from smoke inhalation, the impact from the steering wheel, or a combination of both. She still didn't know who'd hit her, and she didn't know the man who'd saved her life. But a short while later, as they were taking the portable X-ray machine out of her room, she heard his voice again. This time it was coming from the room next to hers, and she was immediately curious.

"The man who saved me is in the next room, isn't he?" Melissa asked.

Her nurse, Hope Talbot, hesitated to answer.

"I'm not sure who's there, honey. I can check for you in a few minutes."

"Thank you," Melissa said. "Do I have a concussion? Can they tell if I have internal injuries from the X-rays?"

Hope noticed a little bit of drying blood in Melissa's ear and wiped it out with a swab to make sure she wasn't bleeding from the ear.

"Just a stray bit of blood from that cut on your head," Hope said, then checked the gash on Melissa's forehead that they'd just glued shut. "The test results will answer your questions, honey. Rest for now, and if you need me, remember to just ring this buzzer, okay?"

Melissa nodded, but as soon as Hope left her room, she swung her legs out of bed and sat up. It wasn't as easy to move as she'd thought, and she had to steady herself until the room quit spinning. But as soon as she felt able, she slipped off the bed and headed next door.

The door was open, and the man who'd saved her was shirtless and sitting on the side of the bed. Dr. Quick was cleaning a cut on his back. The man wasn't talking or moving, but his hands were clenched into fists, which meant he was likely hurting.

Melissa's head was pounding as hard as her heart. Every muscle of his upper body was taut and lean, but she was too dizzy to admire the scenery and knocked to get their attention before walking into the room.

Everyone turned to look—including Dr. Quick, who immediately frowned—but Melissa was looking at the stranger, and the longer she looked, the more puzzled she became.

"Do I know you?" she asked. "You look so familiar."

Sully was staring at her eyes again.

"My name is Sully Raines."

Melissa frowned. "I knew a Johnny Raines from Missouri."

Sully's dark eyes widened as he remembered them calling her Melissa.

"Melissa? Missy, is that you?"

Melissa gasped. "Yes! Oh my God, Johnny! What are the odds of this happening? Where did you come from? Why are you in Blessings? You just saved my life. Thank you from the bottom of my heart!"

Doctor Quick pointed toward the door.

"You're not supposed to be out of bed," he said, but Melissa didn't even acknowledge his remark.

Sully smiled.

"I dropped the Johnny for Sully when I was in high school. As to why I'm here, it's a long story."

"Are you just passing through?" Melissa asked.

"Not exactly," Sully said.

Before Melissa could ask anything more, Hope had her by the arm.

"Here you are, Melissa Dean. I thought you had better sense," Hope said. She took Melissa by the elbow and led her back into her room and settled her back into bed. Then she raised both of the guardrails and pulled up the covers. "How do you feel?" Hope asked.

Melissa wasn't going to admit that she was dizzy and glad to be lying down again.

"Oh my God, Hope! You don't understand! I know him! I grew up with him. He's the first boy I ever kissed, and I haven't seen him since I was thirteen! He saved my life, Hope. I had to say thank you."

Hope brushed a lock of Melissa's hair away from her forehead as she smiled. "That is amazing, and I understand the quirks of fate better than most. But you two will have to catch up on old times later. You don't want to make yourself worse by passing out, okay?"

"Yes, I promise. I won't get up on my own until you guys are through checking me out."

Hope left, and Melissa tried to rest, but the longer she lay there, the more she began to hurt. She was verging on tears when Sully appeared in her doorway.

"Hey," he said.

"Hey," Melissa said, noticing for the first time how tall he'd become.

"I'm leaving now, but I'll be in town for a couple of

days. If you get to feeling better, maybe we could meet at Granny's for coffee. I'm at the Blessings Bed and Breakfast. Just leave me a message if you're up to it."

"I will. I promise. I'm sorry you were hurt, but thank you again for today. I would have died if it hadn't been for you."

Sully blew it off. "I'll take the pain for the pleasure of running into you like this. Do what the doctor tells you," he said, and then he was gone.

Melissa smiled and closed her eyes. The next time someone came in the room, it was Hope and the doctor. He moved to the side of her bed.

"How do you feel?" Dr. Quick asked.

"I hurt all over," Melissa said.

He nodded. "As you should, and I hear you had quite a rescue."

"I couldn't get out of the car," she said, and started crying. "I thought I was going to die, and then this man appeared out of nowhere. The car was full of smoke. I could barely see him, but I clearly heard his voice. He didn't panic. Not once. Now I've found out I knew him. I grew up with him."

"Your old friend was just what the doctor ordered when you were hit," Dr. Quick said. "He's a recently retired fireman."

Melissa was still marveling at his appearance. "Fate sure does throw in some life twists."

"Agreed," Dr. Quick said. "Now about you. Nothing is broken, but you likely have whiplash, and there is some serious bruising on your chest area, although no broken bones. You have the one cut on your forehead where you hit the window, but we glued it shut, and it should heal nicely. We got a few glass shards out of your hair, but Hope is going to make sure we got them all before you leave the ER. Are you still experiencing dizziness?"

"A little," Melissa said.

He nodded. "That's the concussion. You have a choice. Stay here overnight, or go home and get someone to stay with you. I know where you live. Is your bedroom upstairs?"

She nodded.

"If you can, stay downstairs, at least for tonight until you see how quickly you recover your balance and mobility."

"I can. There's a bathroom downstairs, but all my clothes and toiletries are upstairs."

"That's easily remedied with help," Dr. Quick said. "So what is it? Stay here, or call a friend?"

"I don't know who to call," Melissa said. "I have friends, but I don't have girlfriends. Not like that."

Hope patted her arm. "Yes, you do. My shift ends at three this afternoon, and tomorrow is my day off. I'll stay through tomorrow until you're given an all clear. But for now, I'll call someone to come pick you up and take you home. They'll stay until I can get there, okay?"

Melissa started crying again.

"Don't cry, sugar," Hope said. "We've got this."

Dr. Quick left the room as Hope was raising the head of the bed to comb through Melissa's hair one last time. She was nearly finished when Chief Pittman appeared in the doorway.

"Melissa, do you feel like talking to me a minute?"

"Yes," she said.

Hope smiled at her. "I'm through. I think you're good to go here. I'm going to make some calls, and I'll talk to you soon. She's all yours, Lon."

"Thanks," Lon said. "Oh, hey, Hope! Are you guys still coming to dinner Sunday?"

"Are you kidding? Do you have any idea how cool it is to have a brother-in-law who's the chief of police and a sister who can cook like Mercy does? We wouldn't miss it," Hope said.

Lon gave her a thumbs-up and moved up to Melissa's bedside.

"What do you remember about the accident?" he asked.

"I never saw the car, and I didn't know what had happened until after my car stopped spinning. Who hit me?" she asked.

"Niles Holland," he said.

Melissa's lips parted in shock. "Niles—the president of the country club—Holland? What happened?"

"Yes, that Niles."

Melissa gasped. "You aren't serious? Was he hurt? Oh my God. I'm sorry to hear this."

Lon frowned. "You don't apologize for anything. He got himself out of the wreck, but when the cars exploded, I'm sorry to say he was killed by flying debris."

"Oh no! Poor Barb. This is terrible," Melissa said, and started tearing up again. "This whole day has become a reality check on how fast life can change."

Sully was still smiling as he drove back to the bed-and-breakfast to change into clean clothes. He couldn't believe the woman he'd pulled out of that wreck was Missy. She held a special place in his heart, and he couldn't wait to talk to her again.

But when he walked back into the B and B, his condition caused something of a stir.

"What on earth happened to you? Are you all right?" Rachel asked.

"I witnessed a pretty bad wreck on Main Street and wound up pulling the woman who got hit out of her burning car. I'm okay. Just got cut by some burning debris as I was carrying her away."

Rachel gasped. "Oh my lord. I heard what sounded like a big explosion about an hour or so ago. Was that it?"

"Yes, ma'am."

"Who was the woman?"

"Melissa Dean. The weird part of all this is that I know her. We were kids together in Missouri, before she moved away."

Rachel smiled. She loved stories like this. "What a coincidence!" she said. "But is Melissa okay?"

Sully nodded. "She's going to be. She got hit pretty hard, and I'm not sure about the extent of her injuries, but nothing appeared to be life-threatening."

"Oh no! Bless her heart!" Rachel said. "I'll have to make sure to take her some food tomorrow. Likely she'll be all sore and laid up for a while. Did you hear who it was who hit her?"

"No, I didn't."

"Then I'm guessing you didn't make it to Granny's, did you? You must be starved."

"Actually, Granny's is where I took her until the burning debris was no longer an issue. I'm going to get clean clothes and go back."

"If you don't feel up to it, I'd be more than happy to

make some lunch for you here. I have plenty of roast beef to make you a sandwich, and peach cobbler for dessert. Bud's on his way home. We'd love to have you eat with us. That way you could rest up and go to Granny's for supper later."

Sully hesitated. The offer was tempting. "My back is pretty sore. If you're sure it's okay, I will take you up on the offer."

"Perfect," Rachel said. "You go clean up. Bud and I always eat in the kitchen, and you're the only guest here at the moment. It will work out perfectly. When you come down, just go through those double doors at the end of the dining room."

"Yes, ma'am, and thank you again."

"Please, call me Rachel," she said.

Sully nodded, then took the stairs up two at a time and let himself into his room. Once again, he was back in the shower, washing away the blood and the choking scent of smoke. The small wound on his back had also been closed with glue after they'd removed a small piece of metal and cleaned it up. He showered in lukewarm water, patted his back dry, and put on more clean clothes. At this rate, he was going to be looking for a place to get laundry done.

As he came downstairs, he heard dishes rattling, then voices, and followed the sounds into the kitchen.

"Come in, come in!" Rachel said. "Sully, this is my husband, Bud. Bud, this is Sully, the man I was telling you about."

Bud came forward smiling and quickly shook Sully's hand.

"Good to meet you," Bud said. "Sounds like you've had quite an introduction to Blessings. It's not normally this exciting. Have a seat at the table. Lunch is almost ready. Hope you're hungry. These open-faced roast beef sandwiches are the bomb, and so is the gravy that goes on them. Rachel is taking french fries out of the deep fryer right now. Would you rather have coffee or sweet tea?"

"Sweet tea, please," Sully said.

The food appeared moments later, and as soon as they sat down, Bud reached for the ketchup for his fries. When he did, Rachel rolled her eyes.

"Peasant," she said.

"Snob," Bud fired back.

Then they laughed at each other as Bud began shaking ketchup all over his fries.

"Rachel thinks gravy should go on the fries that come with these sandwiches," Bud said.

"Bud puts ketchup on everything, which is a slight blow to my ego, considering I'm supposed to be this great cook," Rachel countered, and then winked at her husband.

Sully laughed. "Pass the ketchup, please," and proceeded to do the same thing that Bud had, which sent Bud and Rachel into peals of laughter.

"I guess that settles it," Rachel said. "When in Rome… and all that. Will someone pass *me* the ketchup, too? Oh… and save room for dessert. It's peach cobbler à la mode."

Sully took his first bite and then rolled his eyes in delight.

"This is amazing. The meat is so tender. What kind of bread do you use for this?" he asked.

"Different kinds," Rachel said. "This is toasted and buttered sourdough bread."

"I'm going to remember this," Sully said. "We all had to take turns cooking at the fire station when I was still on the job. Those guys would love this food. Rachel, you are an amazing chef."

Rachel beamed, pausing a moment to watch two men wolfing down her food like they'd been starving. The satisfaction of knowing people loved her cooking was a huge part of the reason she enjoyed owning the B and B.

Once lunch was over, Sully went upstairs to rest and fell asleep, dreaming about the wreck.

The dream was on a loop in his head—his own kind of eternal hell. In the dream, he knew it was Missy in the car and he had not been able to save her. He was hearing her screams over and over in his head when he woke.

He groaned as he got up, and walked to the windows. The day wasn't as sunny as it had been earlier, and he wondered if the weather was supposed to change.

His shoulder was aching, and he remembered the minifridge was stocked. He opened the cabinet to see what was in it, and then grabbed a Mountain Dew and opened it. He took one drink, then got a couple of over-the-counter pain pills out of his travel bag and washed them down with another swallow.

Sully hadn't counted on his search for his birth mother being dangerous, but the throb in his shoulder reminded him of how close he and Melissa had come to dying. He wondered how she was right now—whether she was still in the hospital or if she'd gone home.

Then out of the blue, he wondered if she had someone to go home to and was surprised at himself for even going there. He'd come looking for the woman who'd given birth to him, not to renew a teenage crush, even if she had grown into a beautiful woman.

He did smile, though, remembering her defiance of rules. Seeing her walk into his room determined to say thank you, even if she had to get out of bed to do it. Staring down the doctor who chided her for being out of bed was evidence of a woman bent on doing the right thing, and the plus was finding out they knew each other.

He was curious about her and her life. Maybe she'd call and take him up on that cup of coffee. It was something to look forward to—a relaxing break from the tension of his search. He'd meant to go to the local courthouse this afternoon and search the property deeds and marriage licenses. And there was the local paper he intended to research as well, which likely meant a trip to the library. But he'd only arrived today. Thanks to the unexpected drama, he was too sore to do anything but hang out, and there was always tomorrow.

CHAPTER 3

WHEN RUBY BUTTERMAN SHOWED UP WITH AN orderly behind her, Melissa was beginning to shake from the shock of what had happened.

"Thank you for doing this," Melissa said when she saw her walk in.

Ruby patted her cheek. "No thanks are needed, sugar. That's what friends are for. My car is already at the door, and this fine young man is going to give you a ride in his wheelchair." Then she glanced up at the orderly and frowned. "Tommy, have you been cutting your own hair again?"

Tommy grinned. "Yes, ma'am. Is it that bad?"

Ruby rolled her eyes. "Just make an appointment and get yourself into the shop so one of us can fix that mess."

He laughed out loud. "Yes, ma'am. I sure will."

"Good. Now let's get Melissa into this chair so I can take her home. Are there pain meds to go home with her?"

"Yes, ma'am. They were called in to Phillips Pharmacy," Tommy said.

"Good enough," Ruby said.

A few minutes later, Ruby and Melissa were on their way to the pharmacy. Although the burned-out cars had been towed away and debris cleaned up from the streets, the black marks from the fire were still visible on the pavement.

"I still can't believe all this happened," Melissa said.

"Girl, I know just what you mean. It doesn't take but a heartbeat for your world to change. Are you okay, or do you need to lie back? The seat reclines."

"I'm okay," Melissa said. "It's not far to the pharmacy, and it's not far to get home."

A couple of minutes later, Ruby reached the pharmacy and parked.

"You just sit tight, sugar," Ruby said. "I won't be long." She was out of the car and inside the pharmacy in seconds.

Melissa leaned against the headrest and closed her eyes. Now that she was out of the hospital, she could almost convince herself that all of this was a bad dream, except she hurt all over—and Niles was dead, and Johnny Raines had just saved her life. It was going to take a bit to get used to thinking of him as Sully, but she was so sorry about Niles. He was one of the town leaders and president of the country club. Only a few months earlier, he had been elected to the town council, and now he was gone.

She was still blinking back tears as Ruby returned with the meds and a bottle of water.

Ruby opened the water and then handed the prescription to Melissa. "Take two pills now," she said. When Melissa shook them out in her hand, Ruby handed her the water and watched her swallow them.

"It says not to take them on an empty stomach. Do you have food at your house?" Ruby asked.

Melissa started to cry.

"What's wrong, honey?" Ruby asked.

"I debated with myself as to whether I would go home for lunch, or go to Granny's. If I'd just gone home, none of this would have happened."

"Or...if Niles hadn't run through a stop sign and hit you, it wouldn't have happened," Ruby said.

Melissa sighed. "You're right. I guess there's no way to make sense of an accident, and yes, there's food."

"Okay, then. We're off," Ruby said, and backed away from the curb.

Melissa was quiet all the way home and still couldn't quit shaking.

Ruby frowned. "As soon as I get some food in you, you need to rest."

When they pulled up in the drive at Melissa's house, she breathed a quiet sigh of relief. The sight of home had never been so welcome.

Ruby walked her inside, afraid to let her go for fear she'd fall, but Melissa felt better just being here.

"I'm going to the bathroom," Melissa said.

Ruby nodded, then pointed into the living room.

"Why don't you take the recliner to sit and eat. It will be easy for you to hold a tray in your lap, and you'll be more comfortable with your feet up," Ruby said. "I'm going to your kitchen to make you some food."

Melissa didn't argue about any of it, and a short while later she was in the recliner, eating a sandwich Ruby made for her from the leftover ham, with a glass of milk on the table beside her.

"Drink some of the milk, sugar," Ruby said.

Melissa took a few sips, then kept eating, alternating bites with sips of milk until she was too full to eat any more.

Ruby covered her with an afghan she took from the back of the sofa, then carried the tray back to the kitchen. By the time she came back, the pain pills had kicked in, and Melissa was asleep.

"Bless your heart," Ruby said softly, and then sat down on the sofa, kicked off her shoes, and stretched out. It wasn't long before her eyes grew heavy and she, too, fell asleep.

Granny's Country Kitchen was particularly busy tonight. After the devastation of losing a beloved member of the community, and the rescue of another by a passing stranger, the conversations among the diners were more or less on the same subject.

Since Lovey had played a small part in providing shelter for Melissa and her rescuer, everyone wanted her take on what had happened. So far, she had been reassuring everyone who came in that her roof had escaped fire damage from falling debris, and that no, she didn't know the stranger and hadn't even caught his name. She'd been so wrapped up in finding out Melissa Dean had been one of the victims of the crash, and then with the anxiety of hearing the firemen warn her of the fire danger to her roof, the stranger had slipped out of Granny's and was gone before she knew it.

Nearly everyone knew by now that it was Niles Holland who'd caused the wreck. The horrible irony was that he'd escaped with minor injuries only to be killed shortly thereafter by flying debris. His death brought a third victim into the picture—his grieving wife, Barbara. It was a sobering day in the little town of Blessings.

Then, to everyone's delight, the hero of the day showed up for supper.

Lovey was at the front counter when the door opened. As usual, she looked up with a ready smile, recognizing the hero of the day. Then her eyes narrowed thoughtfully, trying to figure out why he looked familiar.

"Welcome back," she said. "You look a whole lot different without the blood and smudges. Are you okay?"

"Yes, ma'am," Sully said.

"Good to hear. By the way, I'm Lovey, and I own Granny's. You've been part of the conversation tonight. You saved one of our dearest residents, and for that we are so very grateful."

"Just call me Sully, and it was pure coincidence that I was there when it happened."

"So, Sully, are you dining alone?"

"Yes, ma'am."

"Then come with me and brace yourself. I'm about to introduce you to some of Blessings finest. And just so you know, your meal is on the house."

"Thank you," Sully said. "Your place came highly recommended. I'm staying at the Blessings Bed and Breakfast, and both Rachel and Bud sang your praises."

Lovey smiled as she picked up a menu and led him into the dining room.

Sully was admiring the woman's silver-white hair and guessing she stayed fit from the nonstop flow of her job.

Diners glanced up to see who Lovey was seating, and then looked again when she stopped and whistled an earsplitting note to get their attention. To Sully's delight, the room immediately went quiet, which led him to believe this wasn't the first time she'd done this.

"Everyone! This is Sully, the man who saved Melissa's life!"

The room erupted in cheers, clapping, and smiles. Sully had no choice but to respond. He waved and nodded to the people complimenting him as they moved through the dining room, and as they passed Peanut and Ruby's table, Peanut stood up.

"Welcome to Blessings, Sully. I'm Peanut Butterman, and this is my wife, Ruby. If you're not set on dining alone, we'd love to have you join us."

Sully smiled. Meeting a man named Peanut Butterman could not be overlooked, and the smile from the pretty woman seated at the table was echoing her husband's invitation.

"How can I turn down such a warm invitation?" Sully said. "I guess I'll be sitting here, Miss Lovey."

"Good choice," she said, and laid the menu at the empty chair. "His meal is on the house, Peanut. Y'all enjoy." She hurried back to the front as Sully sat down.

"Thank you for the company," Sully said.

"Of course," Peanut said.

A waitress appeared to take his drink order, and when she was gone, Peanut pointed to the menu.

"We'll be quiet long enough to let you read the menu for what you want to eat. Whatever you choose, you won't be disappointed."

Sully scanned the dinner options and immediately settled on fried catfish just as his waitress appeared with his sweet tea and a small basket of fresh biscuits.

"Have you decided what you want to eat?" she asked.

"The fried catfish dinner," he said.

Ruby reached across the table and gave his arm a brief pat.

"While you butter up one of those wonderful biscuits, tell us what brings you to Blessings," she said.

"Are they that good?" Sully asked.

"Just butter it and take a bite," Peanut said.

Sully wasn't going to argue. A hot biscuit was a hot biscuit, so he broke one in half, put some butter on it, and took a quick bite. He knew when the bite started melting in his mouth before he had a chance to chew that he'd stumbled on a winner.

"Wow," he said.

"Told you," Ruby said. "Now do tell us what brings you to town."

Sully had already taken a second bite, chewed, and swallowed it before answering.

"Actually, I'm looking for someone. A couple of months ago my mother died, and while going through personal papers, I found out I'd been adopted. It came as quite a shock, and within days I decided to search for my birth mother. It's been a journey, and the latest information I have is an old letter with a return address from here in Blessings."

Ruby's eyes widened, and Peanut was immediately intrigued. He couldn't imagine not knowing something like that.

"I'm a lawyer," Peanut said. "I've dealt with all kinds of custody battles, and with social services when kids were abandoned or unwanted, but I've never come across someone on a birth-parent search. Are you having any luck?"

"I started out with more info than some have," Sully said. "My birth mother's name was Janie Chapman, but she was Janie Carter by the time she got here. She signed me over to my adoptive parents on the day I was born, but here's where the story becomes bizarre. She came home from the hospital with them, and for the next six months she nursed me and took care of me while my parents worked. Then one day when they woke up, she was gone. I want to know what happened. Why she left so abruptly. Why she had to give me up. Who my father was. You know...all the usual questions."

Ruby was verging on tears. "That is such a tragic story. I can't imagine what could cause her to leave so abruptly after bonding with her own baby for six months."

Sully nodded. "That's one of my questions, too. What triggered her sudden flight? I submitted a DNA sample to an ancestry site, then hired a researcher to help me run down facts. She's been on the search with me from the start. Even though I knew my birth mother's name, I've learned she married twice in subsequent years. I don't suppose either one of you knew a woman by that name? She would be in her early sixties by now."

"I run the hair salon called the Curl Up and Dye on Main Street," Ruby said. "I don't know anyone by that name, and if she still lived here and had not remarried, I would know her."

"I don't remember anyone by that name, either," Peanut said.

Sully nodded. "Not surprised. But I'm not giving up. I still have several places to check out here, and I'll keep asking around. Maybe my researcher will find a new clue somewhere. I'm not quitting until I get answers."

Before the conversation could go further, their food came and they began to visit as they ate. While talking about the accident, Ruby mentioned Melissa.

"I'm the one who took Melissa home from the hospital. I stayed with her until midafternoon, and another friend is staying with her tonight."

Sully smiled. "There's a bit of synchronicity with my rescue. We realized at the hospital that we'd grown up together in Missouri. Her family moved away right before I turned fourteen, so having that connection was a surprise."

Ruby clapped her hands. "I love reunion stories! And I don't know anyone more deserving of joy than she is."

Sully frowned. "About Melissa. You said you took her home and someone else is staying with her. Doesn't she have any family here?"

"She has no one but herself," Ruby said. "You know what, Sully? I believe in things happening for a reason. And whether you find your mother here or not, I believe you were led here to Blessings to be the angel Melissa needed today. Have you two talked?"

"Just briefly in the ER when we finally recognized each other," Sully said.

"Today notwithstanding, she is quite a survivor," Peanut said. "She was widowed at a young age and had been living a very simple life here that bordered on poverty. She'd worked at Bloomer's Hardware ever since she moved here, around twenty years ago. She used to clean house for an old man named Elmer Mathis to make extra money to make ends meet. Earlier this year her boss let her go so he could hire a nephew. She was angry, and with good reason, but in a panic too, trying to find another job.

"Then Elmer passed away and left everything he owned to her, and it was a godsend. Her situation has drastically changed since then, inheriting his laundry and cleaning business, his money, and the grand old home that she'd cleaned for so many years. It would have been a tragedy for her life to have ended at any cost, but it would have been such irony, considering her financial troubles were finally over."

Sully was quiet. Knowing her story gave her even more substance than he'd already witnessed. He couldn't wait to talk to her.

As Niles Holland's body was being removed from the scene of the accident, Lon thought he noticed the scent of liquor on him, but with all the smoke, it was hard to tell. He wasn't one to let suspicion slide and turned to his deputy.

"Ralph, take a camera to the impound yard and check out the inside of Niles's car. See if there are any signs of empty cans or bottles…anything that might indicate he had been drinking."

"Yes, sir," the deputy said. "Although there's no telling what's inside that car after the explosion and the fire."

"Well, we didn't pick up any beer cans or bottles around here after the explosion, so if it's not still in the car, I'm going to assume there wasn't anything. But if there is an empty liquor bottle or empty beer cans, it will confirm my suspicions. Just check it out and take pictures, regardless. If he had been drinking, it will show up in the autopsy report."

"Yes, sir," Ralph said, and headed for his cruiser.

Lon still had to notify Barb Holland. The Holland residence was at the far edge of Blessings, and he needed to tell her before someone else beat him to it.

Workers from the city were sweeping up glass from the street as Lon got in his cruiser to make the notification. He took the short route to their house by going past Blessings High School and then up through the neighborhoods until he reached the west side.

The Holland home was a two-story Tudor with formal landscaping all across the front of the property. Lon turned up the driveway and drove to the house, parked, and got out. This was the absolute worst part of his job, but it had to be done. He reached the house and rang the doorbell, then waited.

Barb Holland was going through the house with a large garbage bag, removing the empty beer cans and the occasional empty liquor bottle, making certain all remnants of her husband's secret vice stayed a secret before the cleaning ladies came tomorrow.

She didn't know where Niles had gone, but she suspected to the club or the golf course. Those were his two favorite hangouts. She moved from their bedroom to the media room to clear out the trash cans and the empty bottles at the wet bar, then made a sweep through the den.

She was on her way down the hall when the doorbell rang. Now she was in a quandary. She could hardly drag the garbage to the door with her, and on impulse, she ran to the kitchen with it and tucked it in the pantry, then hurried back, smoothing down her hair before she opened the door. The last person she would have expected to see was the police chief.

"Good morning, Chief. What can I do for you?"

Lon took off his hat. "Morning, Mrs. Holland. May I come in?"

Barb frowned. "Why…uh, yes, of course," she said, and stood aside as he entered, then shut the door behind him.

Now they were standing in the foyer, and the silence was worrisome.

"What's going on? Did I forget to pay a parking ticket?"

Her lame joke went nowhere, and the look on the chief's face was scaring her.

"Mrs. Holland, I'm—"

"Please, call me Barb," she said.

Lon sighed. "Barb, I'm afraid I have bad news."

Barb gasped. "Is this about Niles?"

"Yes, ma'am, and—"

She groaned. "I knew this would happen one day. I mean, he took chances every time he got behind the wheel. He was driving and drinking, wasn't he? Please don't charge him publicly. We'll gladly pay the fine."

Lon's heart sank. Barb had just confirmed their suspicions and didn't even know it.

"Barb…ma'am… Niles had a bad wreck. He was speeding when he came off a side street onto Main without stopping and hit Melissa Dean as she was driving past."

Barb gasped and then staggered.

Lon caught her. "Where can we sit?"

She pointed down the hall, and Lon led her into the first room on the left. He seated her on the sofa and sat in a chair facing her.

"How bad were they hurt?" Barb asked.

"He hit her hard enough that it spun her car all the way around in the other direction. He managed to get out of his car and was sitting on a curb a short distance away, but Melissa's car was burning and she was trapped."

Barb shuddered. "Oh my God, please tell me she didn't perish!"

"Had it not been for the quick thinking of a passing stranger, she would have died. He got her out and far enough away before the car blew up."

Barb was shaking. "Is Melissa okay?"

"She has some injuries, none of which are life-threatening."

"Thank God," Barb said. "What about Niles?"

"I'm so sorry to tell you that he died at the scene from flying debris from the explosion."

Barb screamed, and then covered her face and started sobbing.

"Is there someone I can call for you? You shouldn't be alone," Lon asked.

"Was he drunk?" she asked.

"That will be determined during his autopsy," Lon said.

"Oh my God," Barb whispered. "Everyone is finally going to know."

Lon was a little startled that Barb's first concern was people finding out her husband had been driving impaired rather than about his death.

"Did he drink a lot?" Lon asked.

She nodded, and sat for a few moments in silence, wiping her eyes and gathering her senses. Finally, she looked up at Lon and asked, "What do I need to do?"

"Nothing. You don't have a part in the investigation. When Niles's body is released, you will be notified. At that point, you will be free to begin planning the funeral. Is there anything I can do for you before I leave?" Lon asked.

She shook her head.

"Then I'll be leaving," he said. "If you have any questions or need help, don't hesitate to call. Again, I am sorry for your loss."

Lon left the room, walked back down the hall, and let himself out.

Barbara heard the door open and close, but she couldn't bring herself to move. It didn't seem real. She didn't remember if she'd even said good morning to Niles when they woke up. He'd gotten up and poured himself a drink, and she'd rolled over and gone back to sleep. They'd been married almost thirty years, and this was how it was going to end. She was heartsick.

"Oh, Niles, you fool. Leave it up to you to go out in a blaze of glory! I can't keep your secret any longer. Once that autopsy comes back, everyone will know. I'll bury you, but I'm not staying to be talked about. I can't be that wife. This was going to be our forever home, but I don't want it without you."

Once the news got around, people would be calling, so Barb made herself get up and go back to the kitchen. She got the sack she'd stashed in the pantry and carried it out to the garbage bin. All the metal and glass clattered as she dropped it inside, but as she shut the lid, it dawned on her that she would now be responsible for getting the garbage to the curb. For a woman like Barb, it was just another blow to her ego, and the humiliation was just beginning.

Barb Holland's life of indulgence was coming to an end.

Men from the club who had played golf with Niles were

already speculating among themselves about what caused him to drive so recklessly. She knew this because Retta Durrett, one of her friends from the club, had come calling this evening and felt it her job to inform Barb that Niles was becoming a topic of gossip among their circle.

The comment struck Barb to the core, especially after seeing the glitter of satisfaction in Retta's eyes when she'd said it.

Barb lifted her chin, her own eyes brimming with tears, and fired back.

"So, Retta, you said people are gossiping about my husband. Do you mean the same kind of gossip that you felt the need to share with me just now?"

Retta Durrett's face turned red. "Now, Barb, I didn't—"

Barb interrupted. "Yes, you did. So just hush your mouth, because you've said enough already. Surely you don't expect me to throw my hands up in dismay, as if I didn't already know my own husband's strengths and weaknesses. However, since he just died in the wreck he caused, I hardly see the need for you to speak of this at all—unless, of course, your intention was to hurt me?"

"No way, Barb, I only wanted to warn—"

"Consider me warned. Now I suggest you take your Spanx-bound ass out of my house. I'm glad I've already made the decision to move back home to Dallas after the funeral. I don't need my husband's name to belong to country clubs anywhere there. I am a Texan by birth and a direct descendant of Stephen A. Austin and Sam Houston. We come from two of the first families in Texas, and I am already accepted and valued. See yourself out. I'm busy," Barb said, then turned her back on Retta, leaving the woman with no option but to leave.

Barb waited until she heard the door open and close, and then the sound of Retta's car as she drove away, before she lost it. The conversation had been crushing, and Barb was still in a funk hours later. The later it became, the more her phone continued to ring. She let the calls all go to voice-mail and took herself off to bed.

CHAPTER 4

MELISSA ACHED IN EVERY MUSCLE AND WAS BECOMING stiffer by the hour. Hope had arrived as promised, and Ruby went home. At that point, Hope began moving Melissa's things to the downstairs bed and bathroom, per doctor's orders, then began to care for her as if she'd never left the hospital.

As soon as Melissa was comfortable in bed, Hope called her sister, Mercy, and asked her to bring food from Granny's by the house before she went home.

An hour or so later, Mercy was at the door.

"You are a lifesaver," Hope said as she took the big sack of food Mercy gave her.

"It was no problem. And just so Melissa knows, your supper is on Lovey," Mercy said.

"Did you include some of your yummy biscuits and pie?" Hope asked.

Mercy laughed. "Yes, and please give Melissa my love. I'm so sorry she was hurt, but very grateful she's going to recover, and much easier than you did."

The conversation turned serious. "I would not have recovered at all if you hadn't responded to that call," Hope said.

Mercy nodded. "And I would still be waiting tables at the Road Warrior Bar in Savannah and would never have known you existed."

"All things happen when they're supposed to," Hope said, and gave Mercy a quick kiss on the cheek. "Thanks again for bringing this by."

Mercy let herself out as Hope carried the food into the kitchen, then went back to the bedroom.

Melissa was watching television with the sound on mute as Hope walked in.

Melissa looked up. "Did I hear someone at the door?"

Hope nodded. "Lovey sent supper, and Mercy brought it by. Are you hungry?"

"Yes, but I don't want to eat in bed. I'll get up."

"Awesome. Moving will help keep you from getting so stiff. I don't know what she sent, but it's in the kitchen."

"I'll wash up," Melissa said.

"I'll wait. We can walk to the kitchen together," Hope said as Melissa got out of bed.

Hope set out a pair of house shoes, and Melissa stepped into them when she came out.

Hope smiled. "Now let's go see about supper."

As soon as Melissa was seated at the kitchen table, Hope poured her a glass of sweet tea, then got out plates and flatware before taking out the containers.

"Looks like fried chicken, mashed potatoes and gravy, green beans, and biscuits. Do you think it will hurt to chew? You have a pretty-good-sized bruise on your jaw."

"I don't know, but I'm about to find out," Melissa said.

Hope grinned. "Do you have butter in your refrigerator?"

"In the door," Melissa said, and began removing the lids from the containers.

She scooped out a serving of mashed potatoes and gravy, then a serving of green beans. She chose a chicken thigh from the assortment of pieces and held out her plate so Hope could put a buttered biscuit on it.

After getting Melissa comfortable, Hope sat down across the table from her and made her own plate.

"Girl time is always good," Hope said. "You need to come out to the farm sometime. I'm not as good a cook as Mercy, but I haven't killed anybody yet."

Melissa grinned.

"So, what do you think about your hero Sully Raines? I hear you two grew up together," Hope said.

Melissa looked up. "What do you mean?"

"He's obviously good-looking, and you told me he asked you out for coffee. Are you going to take him up on that?"

Melissa blushed. "I don't know, but he's probably married. It feels weird even thinking about it. I have not had a date since Andy died."

Hope paused. "Seriously? How long has that been?"

"I guess about twenty years," Melissa said.

Hope's eyes widened. "Honey! You were so young! Why not?"

Melissa shrugged. "At first it seemed like I would be cheating on Andy. I didn't want anyone but him, and he was gone. We had planned on moving to Blessings, so I kept to the plan and moved on my own, only to realize I was in a strange place alone, and with people I didn't know. After that, time just slipped away from me."

Hope leaned forward. "That was then, and this is now. I'm a person who believes there's no such thing as a coincidence. I always think it's a God thing. Like when my sister and I found each other again. If I hadn't been in that wreck and needed a blood transfusion, the rare blood directory would not have called Mercy. And if she had been living far-ther away than Savannah, she wouldn't have arrived in time. Synchronicity. When the universe is perfectly aligned for something special to happen."

Melissa shrugged. "Never thought of it that way. I do want to talk to him though. Hope I feel better tomorrow."

"I predict you're going to be fine," Hope said. "And don't let a few bruises stop you. I mean…you've both shared part of your childhood, and now a life-threatening experience. It shouldn't be that hard to share coffee and conversation. Anyway, think about it. Do you want sec-onds on anything?"

"No. I couldn't finish all this," Melissa said.

Hope arched an eyebrow. "Oh, so this means you don't want any pecan pie?"

"No, that's not what it means at all," Melissa said. "It means I was just saving room for pie."

Hope grinned. "I thought so. Do you want me to make coffee to go with it?"

"Not for me," Melissa said. "I'll stick to sweet tea tonight."

"Me too," Hope said. "Just keep your seat. I'll get the dirty dishes off the table and bring dessert. It won't take but a couple of minutes."

"You're the best," Melissa said.

"Why, thank you, honey. Next time you see my husband, I want you to remind him of that."

They both laughed and then settled into a comfortable conversation as the meal ended on a sweet note.

Ruby was at home, making a list of everything she needed to reorder at the salon. She'd written down everything she could think of, and before she went online and placed the order with the beauty supply in Savannah, she needed to call Vera and Vesta to see if they needed anything. She knew it was late, but she also knew the sisters' penchant for watching old movies on the classics channel and rang their number.

Vera was in the kitchen popping corn, and Vesta was in the living room sobbing. Niles Holland had been her customer for as long as she could remember. Normally, he came twice a month to get a haircut, and tomorrow morning would have been his day.

Vera did Barb Holland's hair, and Vesta knew Barb would be coming in to get it done special before the funeral, whenever that was.

The fact that Niles had caused his own demise made it even harder for Vesta to think about. He'd always been so full of himself, but he'd been a good customer and a friend, and she was going to miss him.

When her cell phone rang, she quickly blew her nose, cleared the tears from her throat, and answered. "Hello."

"Hey, Vesta, it's me."

"Oh hi, Ruby. What's up?" she asked.

"I'm about to put in an order to the beauty supply in Savannah. Do you or Vera need anything?"

"Oh...I do for sure. I'm out of the little permanent papers, and I need two Easy Wave perms. Also, some of that shampoo we use for the lavender-haired ladies in town."

"Oh, right! I need that, too. Thanks for the reminder. How about Vera?" Ruby asked.

"Wait a sec and I'll ask." Vesta jumped up from the sofa and hurried into the kitchen and handed her sister the phone. "It's Ruby. I'll tend to the popcorn," she said.

Vera nodded and took the phone. "Hi, Ruby. You're up late."

"I know. I'm about to get online and put in an order at the beauty supply in Savannah. Do you need anything?"

"Yes, I do," Vera said, and began naming off products, while Vesta stood at the microwave, waiting for it to ding and stealing a quick sip of her sister's Coke.

The microwave went off. Vesta took out the bag of popcorn, tore it open, and dumped it in a bowl, then poured herself a glass of Coke as well, and waited for Vera to get off the phone.

Seconds later, Vera ended the call, turned around and dropped the phone in the pocket of Vesta's bathrobe, and picked up her drink.

"Let's hurry," she said. "Our movie is about to start."

"I know, but I'm not in much of a movie mood," Vesta said.

"Why? What's wrong?" Vera asked.

"Tomorrow morning would have been Niles's appointment day. I'm just sad that he's gone and Barb is now a widow."

Vera paused. "Oh. I hadn't remembered that. I guess Barb will be making a special appointment now before the funeral."

Vesta nodded. "That's what I was guessing."

Then Vera took the bowl of popcorn out of Vesta's hands.

"Come on. We planned on watching that movie, and so we're gonna watch it," Vera said.

Vesta frowned. "But it will make me cry, and I don't like to cry."

"It's good for your energy and your chi to release

emotions," Vera stated firmly, and sailed out of the kitchen with her drink in one hand and the popcorn in the other.

Vesta glared at her twin. She'd been the bossy one when they were little, and nothing about her personality had changed.

"I still don't like to cry," Vesta muttered.

Ruby had just finished entering everyone's orders. As soon as she hit Send and printed off a copy of what they'd ordered, she logged out and went to bed.

Peanut had fallen asleep in bed with the remote in his hand. Ruby slipped it from his fingers, turned off the television and the lights, and crawled into bed.

The moment she did, he rolled over and slid an arm across her waist without opening his eyes.

"I love you, too," Ruby whispered, and then got teary, thinking of how Barb Holland must feel tonight in bed all alone.

Lovey did her last walk-through in the café, making sure all the appliances in the kitchen had been cleaned and turned off, and checking to make sure the back door was locked. Then she retraced her steps through the dining room, turning off lights as she went.

She paused in the doorway and looked back at the empty tables and chairs, picked up the deposit bag on the way out, and locked the front door as she left.

One more stop and then home, she thought as she got in her car and headed to the bank. The stray tomcat she always fed there was sitting beneath the night deposit, patiently waiting for its supper.

"Good evening, you ratty old thing," she said, and tossed out the little piece of ham she'd fished out of the garbage for him.

He grabbed it and ran into the shadows as she put the money bag in the night deposit, then headed to Ruby's little cottage.

Lovey was grateful for the quiet as she let herself in. It was already almost 11:00 p.m., and Granny's would be open by 6:00 a.m., which meant the kitchen crew showed up for work around four thirty, and she always arrived to open up.

Even though her injuries had healed, she was having to pace herself to get through a day. It was as if her body had worked so hard to keep her from dying that there wasn't as much left of her as there used to be.

"First thing is a nice, hot shower and then into a nightgown and bed," Lovey said.

She went into the bathroom and turned on the water to let it get hot, then began undressing. The water was steamy by the time she got in, and she stood beneath the spray, letting the jets massage out the aches and pains of the day.

A short while later, she was in her nightgown, walking through the house, checking locks here just as she'd done at the café. She took a bottle of water back to the bedroom, put it on the nightstand, then pulled back the covers. After stacking some pillows behind her back so she could watch a little TV, she got into bed and opened the water to take a drink.

She'd long since gotten over feeling sorry for herself that she was living on her own. She'd tried marriage more than once and, after her last husband died, had given up on the institution altogether. Some people were meant for marriage, and some weren't.

Lovey had been fine on her own when she was living in her own house, but she was a little lonesome here. She thought it was because she was surrounded by other people's things.

She missed her keepsakes from home and the pictures hanging on the walls. She missed her little library of books, and her stash of old DVDs that she watched on Sunday evenings. She was grateful for this cottage, but she would be glad to get home.

She fell asleep with the show still on, woke up sometime after 1:00 a.m. and turned it off, then rolled over and went back to sleep.

Sully woke abruptly, then lay motionless for a few moments, wondering what he'd been dreaming. But whatever it was, the memory was gone.

He glanced at the clock. Seven thirty, which meant breakfast was waiting whenever he got downstairs. The thought of coffee was enough to get him up. His shoulder was stiff, but it wasn't hurting nearly as much as it had yesterday.

He quickly showered and shaved, then planned out his morning as he dressed. First to the courthouse, then to the library.

He could smell the coffee and the wonderful aroma of

something sweet baking in the oven as he went down the stairs. Bud was behind the front desk, taking a reservation, but he waved at Sully as he passed by on his way into the dining room.

There was a young couple at one of the tables. They must have arrived last night after he went to bed. They didn't acknowledge him past a glance as he moved to the sideboard where the breakfast buffet had been laid out.

Rachel came out with a plate of bacon to replace the one that was nearly empty, and smiled at Sully when she saw him.

"Good morning, Sully. Were you able to rest last night with that sore shoulder?"

"Yes, very well. It feels better today, too. This all looks so good. I can't wait to dig in."

Rachel smiled. "Then enjoy, and I hope you have a good day with your search."

"Thanks. Me too," Sully said.

He picked up a plate and dipped out a big spoonful of scrambled eggs, then a serving of grits, added a pat of butter on top of them, then several slices of bacon, and one of the warm cinnamon rolls iced in a white sugar glaze. He set the food at his table, then went back for coffee before he sat down.

As he did, he paused a moment, looking at the food and thinking about how the guys from the station would so decimate the buffet on the sideboard. On impulse, he got back up with his cell phone and took a picture of the food-laden sideboard, then sent it to a couple of his friends before going back to his table.

Rachel paused in the doorway of the kitchen to glance back and make sure everything was in order. The young couple had informed her and Bud last night when they checked in that they'd eloped. The young woman had flashed her newly acquired wedding ring, and after congratulating both of them, Bud had taken up a bottle of wine and two glasses after settling them in their room.

Rachel glanced at Sully and saw he was reading something on his phone as he ate. She smiled and was starting to go back in the kitchen when he laid down his fork and began texting, smiling as he did it. Before, she'd only spoken to him face-to-face, but now she was seeing him in profile, and as he suddenly threw his head back and laughed at a reply he'd just received, the hair stood up on the back of her neck. The moment of déjà vu was startling, which was weird because they'd only met yesterday. Then it hit her. He reminded her of someone she knew. Someone here in Blessings!

Oh my God. I must know his mother! But who does he remind me of?

Hope was used to getting up early, so she was already dressed and in the kitchen making coffee before daylight. After putting it on to brew, she peeked into the bedroom to check on Melissa, who was still asleep, and was in the kitchen when her phone signaled a text. It was from her husband, Johnny.

It's lonesome in bed without you. How's Melissa?
Duke and I send her best wishes and swift healing.

Hope smiled. She'd missed Johnny last night, too. Her

brother-in-law, Duke, was another story, but she was used to his clueless, often brash behavior. As soon as the coffee was done, she poured herself a cup and went into the living room to watch the early-morning news.

About an hour later, she thought she heard Melissa moving around and ran back into the kitchen to get her a cup of coffee.

Melissa had dreamed of the wreck all night. In one dream, Niles kept trying to apologize while Sully was pulling her out of the car. The last dream was her husband, Andy, telling her to be happy.

She woke up with tears on her face. She hadn't dreamed of him like that in a while, and the message he gave her was curious.

She got up, eased her way to the bathroom, and when she came out, her hair was brushed, her teeth were clean, and she was thinking about getting into the shower. She was still debating about that when Hope knocked on the door, then came in with a cup of fresh-brewed coffee.

"Here you go, honey," Hope said.

Melissa reached for it gladly.

"Thank you so much."

"Absolutely," Hope said. "So how do you feel?"

"Sore, of course, but better. I'm not dizzy anymore. Not even when I first get out of bed. I still have the headache from hell, but I haven't had pain pills since midnight."

"I'll get you some," Hope said. "Let the coffee cool a bit. I'll get you some water to take the pills."

Melissa set the coffee down and then sat down on the

side of the bed and shook two pills out into the palm of her hand as Hope came back with the water. Melissa took the pills, then scooted to the back of the bed, using the headboard for a backrest.

"I'll bet Johnny missed you last night," she said.

Hope grinned. "Of course. He already sent a text this morning, and he and Duke sent their best wishes for swift healing."

Melissa smiled. "That's so sweet. Tell them I said thank you."

"I will," Hope said. "After you've been up and moving about a bit, I'm going to call Dr. Quick with my assessment of how you're doing and see what he recommends."

"Thank you, again," Melissa said. "I rested so much better here than I would have in the hospital."

"I know. Even when people really need to be there, it's hard to find comfort in the constant noise and lights, not to mention the repetitive poking and prodding. So, what sounds good for breakfast?" Hope asked. "I saw pancake mix and cereal, and there's still cold fried chicken and pecan pie."

Melissa grinned. "You may think this is weird, but I think the cold fried chicken sounds way better than breakfast food this morning. Actually, eating it cold is one of my favorite ways to eat fried chicken."

"Then when you get dressed, just wander on down to the kitchen. I'll get out the leftovers, and you can put whatever you want on your plate."

"Deal," Melissa said. "I'm going to enjoy this coffee first, and I'll be there shortly."

As soon as Hope was gone, Melissa picked up her phone and called the bed-and-breakfast.

"Blessings Bed and Breakfast. This is Bud."

"Bud, this is Melissa Dean."

"Melissa! It's good to hear that you are up and about. How are you this morning?" he asked.

"Beyond being sore all over, not too bad," she said. "I'm calling because I need you to give Sully Raines my phone number. I owe him a cup of coffee, for sure, so if you would give him my cell number, he can call at his convenience. I'm going to be home all day."

"Okay, I'm ready to write it down," Bud said.

Melissa gave him her number and thanked him, then took a sip of her coffee. The warmth going down her throat felt good, and the idea of seeing Sully Raines again was even better. Even if it was just a moment between two old friends.

Bud started to take the message to Sully, when Rachel, who'd overheard the conversation, slipped it out of his hand.

"Let me," she whispered. "I'll tell you later."

Bud shrugged. He loved his wife, but she was a drama queen, and he could only imagine what she was up to now.

Rachel sashayed through the dining room straight to Sully's table. He was finished with breakfast and reading something on his phone.

"Excuse me, Sully. I have a message for you," Rachel said.

Sully laid down his phone as she handed him the slip of paper. The moment he saw who it was from, he looked up at her and smiled.

"Thanks a lot," he said. "And by the way, breakfast was great."

Rachel beamed. "Thank you," she said.

Sully got up and left the dining room, unaware that Rachel was staring at him.

The newlyweds had already gone back to their room, and Bud was bussing tables.

"So what's the big deal?" he asked as Rachel began helping him clear up.

Rachel spoke quietly. "Something about Sully struck a chord this morning. For a few seconds, I saw a resemblance between him and someone I know. I just can't put my finger on who it is."

Bud's eyes widened. "You mean, the mother he's looking for?"

She nodded. "I think so. Wouldn't it be amazing if I figured it out?"

Bud grinned. "Yes, it would be amazing."

When he started into the kitchen with the cart full of dirty dishes, Rachel called out to remind him.

"Remember not to put the Blue Willow plates into the dishwasher."

"Yes, ma'am," Bud said, and rolled his eyes. Like she hadn't told him that every time they'd used them for the past however many years.

Upstairs, Sully was gathering up what he wanted to take with him this morning, and as soon as he had it all together, he sat down in the overstuffed chair by the window to call Melissa.

Hope was on her phone in the kitchen, speaking with Dr. Quick, and Melissa was sitting in the living room finishing her last cup of coffee and reading the morning paper. She knew most people these days read everything on some kind of technology, and she'd tried it all out, but she liked the leisure and feel of a real newspaper best.

There's something to be said for familiarity, Melissa thought as she leafed through the pages, looking for the ad she ran daily. And there it was. Mathis Cleaning and Laundry, and the address, phone number, and hours.

Once she was satisfied it was okay, she went back to the first page and began reading the stories. She had just turned to the second page when her cell phone rang. She put down the paper to answer it.

"Hello."

And just like that, Sully's voice was in her ear.

"Good morning, Melissa. How are you feeling today?"

Melissa felt her face flush and rolled her eyes that it was happening.

"Not too bad. I hope you rested well," she said.

"Yes, I did, thanks."

"Listen, Sully, if you still want to have coffee, why don't you just pick a time and come here? Just give me a call beforehand. I make decent coffee, and I have most of a pecan pie from Granny's left from the food she sent over here last night."

Sully was grinning and glad no one could see him, because he felt like he was thirteen again, trying to make small talk with a pretty girl.

"That sounds perfect. I have some research to do this morning at the courthouse and also at the library. How about I give you a call later and see if you're still up to a visitor?"

"Works for me," Melissa said. "Happy hunting."

"Thank you," Sully said.

Melissa shivered a bit as they disconnected.

"Oh, Andy...that just felt like I agreed to a date," she whispered, and at that same moment she remembered her dream. *Be happy*, he'd said. Maybe this is what he'd been trying to say.

A couple of minutes later, Hope came back and gave her a thumbs-up.

"Dr. Quick says you're cleared for simple tasks. No heavy lifting. No working big projects. He suggested you spend today just lying around or napping. And to order in any food you might want and don't try to cook. Try to stay off your feet. If your headaches persist beyond the pain pills he gave you, he wants you to go see your regular doctor."

Melissa breathed a sigh of relief. "That's wonderful, Hope. Now you can go home. You still have most of your day off, and I don't want you to wait on me to start enjoying it. I can't thank you enough for all you and Ruby did for me yesterday, and the fact that you stayed over was going above and beyond."

Hope leaned down and hugged her.

"Honey, this is what friends are for. I'm glad you're better, too. I'll go pack my bag. Johnny will be happy, for sure."

CHAPTER 5

SULLY'S FIRST STOP HAD BEEN TO SEE IF ANY MARRIAGE licenses had ever been issued to a woman named Jane Carter. He gave the clerk a search window from the current date going back thirty-five years, but the search had been futile.

He'd gone straight from there to property records and, with the help of one of the clerks, spent the next hour and a half looking to see if anyone named Jane Carter had ever owned property in Blessings.

It was nearing 11:00 a.m. when he walked out of the courthouse. He paused on the steps and looked out across the grounds, wondering if Janie had ever stood here. Would she have been scared? Would she have been sad, feeling defeated by the turn of events in her young life?

"Where did you go, Janie? I'm looking for you. Have you ever gone looking for me?"

A church bell began ringing somewhere, and he still had newspapers at the library to tackle, but that would take hours, maybe even a whole other day. He was in the mood for a break, and seeing Melissa again would be the break he needed.

He pulled out his phone and called her.

Melissa was in the kitchen making a fresh pot of coffee when her phone rang. She knew before she looked that it was likely to be Sully.

"Hello."

"Hey, it's me. Are you still in the mood for a visitor?"

"Yes," she said. "I'm just making a fresh pot of coffee. Do you have my address?"

"No. Go ahead and give it to me."

Melissa gave him the address and a brief description of the house, and as soon as they disconnected, she went straight to the bedroom to brush her hair and check herself out. There was no need putting on makeup, because it wouldn't hide the obvious, but she did put on a little lipstick.

She was straightening up the living room when her doorbell rang. She gave the sofa pillows one last pat, then went to the door.

"Hi, Sully. Come in," Melissa said, and stepped aside.

Sully walked in with a small bouquet of flowers.

"A little something cheery for your day," he said.

Melissa beamed. "Dutch irises are one of my favorites. Walk with me. We'll have coffee in the kitchen, if that's okay with you."

"Absolutely," Sully said, and watched when she stopped in the dining room to get a vase.

"I'm going to put these in water. Have a seat," Melissa said, then went about filling the vase and arranging the irises before carrying them back to the dining table.

"I love these flowers. They remind me of perfect little orchids. I can't remember the last time anyone gave me flowers," she said, and then went to the kitchen.

"I gave you a corsage before the Winter Ball."

She looked back at him and grinned. "I remember that! My dress was black, and the carnations were white with a silver bow. I felt so stylish."

Sully grinned. "I remember thinking how it suddenly made you look like an older woman, which probably scared the crap out of me."

Melissa laughed. "And now I am an older woman."

"You're the same age as me, so that doesn't count. And you need to sit down," Sully added. "I didn't come here just so you had to wait on me. Is there anything I can do to help?"

"You can pour the coffee if you'd like. I set out two mugs. Cream and sugar is already on the table. Would you like a piece of pecan pie with it, or is it too close to lunch for you?"

Sully shook his head. "Nothing ruins my appetite, but if it did, I'd gladly sacrifice one lunch for pecan pie."

Melissa was surprised at how easy it felt to be with him. And she'd been so nervous.

"Then I'm going to set the pie on the table, in case you feel the need to have seconds."

"Which saves me the embarrassment of having to ask," he said.

Melissa smiled to herself as they sat, and for the first few seconds, each went about doctoring their coffee to suit them before cutting into the pie.

"I asked you at the hospital if you were just passing through. Are you married?" Melissa asked.

"Divorced years ago," he said. "I had an impromptu dinner last night with two people you know. Peanut and Ruby Butterman. Peanut told me you'd been a widow a long time."

"A bit over twenty years," Melissa said. "You told me your reason for being in Blessings was a long story. Wanna elaborate on that?"

"Sure. The more people who know why I'm here, the better chance I have for getting answers."

"So why are you here?" Melissa asked.

"I'm one of those people that you see on TV. The ones who never knew until their parents had passed that they were adopted. I recently found that out about myself, and I'm looking for a woman named Janie. She was my birth mother."

Melissa gasped. "I cannot imagine what a shock that must have been. It's also unusual that adoptive parents keep that a secret. It must feel like your whole existence was a farce. Are you finding leads? What led you here, of all places?"

Sully began to explain, and Melissa sat while her coffee got cold and she lost her taste for pie. She sat motionless, listening to his story and watching the changing expressions on his face. When he finally stopped talking, it seemed to Melissa as if he had visibly relaxed. As if sharing the tale had lessened the burden of his truth. She leaned forward and, without thinking, put her hand over his.

"I don't know how to react. Part of this is intriguing, like a wonderful secret just waiting to be revealed, and part of it is so sad I want to cry."

It was the warmth of her hand and her voice that cut right through the drama of his story.

"Thank you," he said.

"What if you never find her?" Melissa asked.

"Then I will assume it wasn't meant to be. But if I do, I hope she's someone who will want to get to know me, because I have a thousand questions for her."

"What do you know about your birth father?" Melissa asked.

"Absolutely nothing, but I'd like to at least know his name," Sully said.

Melissa couldn't help thinking about Sully moving on and never seeing him again. "What are you researching here next?"

"The newspapers. I'm assuming I will find the old issues at the library."

"Yes, and they're on microfiche, if you can believe that. In this day of technology at the speed of light, we're still using the old ways. You'll be flipping through those old records for hours. Too bad you don't have help. I'm pretty sure there's no one but the librarian on duty, which means she wouldn't have time to help you much."

"That's okay," Sully said. "I have nowhere else to go and nothing else to do."

"You said you retired from the fire department. You're really young for that."

"I put in twenty-five years. In fireman years, multiplied by the number of fires, I'm as old as Methuselah."

Melissa had a sudden vision of all the dangers he must have escaped during that time.

"I didn't think of it like that," she said.

Sully grinned. "I get a pension, but I do plan on finding another occupation. I was considering it when my mother died. And then this search began, and I've let everything else slide."

"With good reason," Melissa said. "If the going is very slow at the library, I wouldn't mind helping you out a bit tomorrow. I mean, it's just sitting, right? And looking for a name, right?"

The offer surprised, then touched Sully. It was a sweet and generous thing to suggest.

"I don't think watching those screens flipping past would be very good for the two-day headache you're working on."

"We'll see," Melissa said. "If I feel better tomorrow, and you're still at it, I'll let you know. I've delayed you far too long. But your company was wonderful, and I got selfish."

She stood up, giving Sully permission to leave gracefully as she walked him to the door.

"Thank you again for the flowers and the kindness," Melissa said.

"Thank you for being the wonderful listener that you are. I didn't realize how alone I'd been feeling. And if you still want to, and you feel like it, I would love help going through thirty-plus years of back issues of the local paper," Sully said.

Melissa beamed. "Perfect. We'll talk tomorrow, okay?"

Sully started to reach toward her, then stopped.

"I very much want to hug you for being a much-needed friend, but I don't know where it's safe to touch you."

Without thinking, Melissa pointed to her right cheek.

"A safe zone," she said.

Sully's dark eyes flashed, but the heat in them was there and gone so fast she didn't notice as he leaned over and very gently kissed her cheek.

"Thank you," Sully said.

Melissa's heart was pounding, but she managed a smile.

"You are most welcome. I have a good feeling about your story, Sully. I think it will have a happy ending."

"From your lips to God's ears," he said. "I'll call you in the morning. Rest well, and thank you for everything."

He was out the door and gone before Melissa could respond. She stood in the doorway until he'd driven away, then shut the door and went back to the kitchen to clean up the cups and pie plates.

All in all, this might have been the best day she'd had in the last twenty years.

Sully went back to the courthouse to see the property records for the county. It was always possible his birth mother had wound up buying land and moving to the country. But after more hours of looking, he gave it up and left. He went to Broyles Dairy Freeze on the way back to the B and B, bought a couple of burgers and a shake, then sat in the car to eat them.

He'd forgotten to tell them to leave off the pickles, so he sorted through the first burger and pulled them off. As he did, he remembered that when he and Missy ate together in the school cafeteria, she always ate his pickles. He hadn't thought of that in years, but seeing her again was bringing back all kinds of memories.

He finally finished, tossed what he didn't eat into the garbage on the way out, and then decided to drive around Blessings for a while. He wanted to see what it was about the little town that made Melissa come here and then stay so long.

As he drove through residential areas, anyone who was outside when he drove past turned and waved. They didn't know him, but they smiled when they did it. That was nice. The houses were mostly well kept, although he could see there were plenty of them still in stages of repair.

There were kids playing on the school playground, and parents were at the field house, picking up their boys from football practice. His wife had never wanted kids when they were still young enough to have them, and then they divorced, and that dream had ended with the marriage. Now, he'd have to marry someone considerably younger to start raising a family, and he didn't want someone considerably younger anymore. In fact, he hadn't thought about a steady woman in his life at all until seeing Melissa again.

The sun was going down by the time he got back to the B and B.

Bud was at the front desk when Sully walked in.

"Evening, Sully. Have you had a good day?" he asked.

"Yes, I have. Didn't make any new discoveries about my search, but the day was still good."

"Awesome... Oh... Rachel baked chocolate chip cookies this afternoon and left some for you," Bud said, and pulled out a plate of cookies covered in plastic wrap. "Enjoy."

"Thanks," Sully said. "I sure will."

He went upstairs with the plate, kicked off his shoes, washed up, and then got a cold bottle of pop from the minifridge, took the cookies with him to bed, and settled in to watch some TV.

Two hours later, it hit him that this was going to be his life. No more dividing his time between the station and an apartment. No more roughhousing with the guys. No more buddy time at the weight benches. The only life he'd been living was now behind him, and beyond this search, he had no other plans.

Later, he showered and shaved and this time pulled back the covers before he sat down on the side of the bed to call Melissa.

Melissa was just getting out of the shower when her phone rang. She wrapped herself up in a bath towel and ran to answer.

"Hello."

"Hey, it's me. I just wanted to tell you how much I enjoyed spending time with you today and to wish you a good night."

Melissa was grinning from ear to ear. "Thank you. I loved spending time with you, too. Did you find any new leads?"

"No."

"I'm sorry," Melissa said. "Just remember I'll help you tomorrow if you want."

"Rest well, and I'll check on you in the morning, if it's okay with you."

Melissa laughed, and the sound rolled through him like silk against his skin.

"Of course it's okay," she said. "Call anytime."

And then the connection ended, and Sully put his phone on the charger, got in bed, and turned out the lights. He pulled up the covers, and within minutes he was asleep.

The sound of a siren woke Sully up the next morning, and he was out of bed, his heart pounding with adrenaline, before he remembered he wasn't at the station anymore. But hearing a siren before daylight had him wondering what was going on in Blessings.

He glanced at the clock. It was just after six. He could smell coffee wafting up from downstairs and could do with a cup of that right now. However, it was too early for breakfast, and he wasn't dressed. There was a one-cup coffee maker and an assortment of flavors on the cabinet above the mini-fridge, so he chose one of those, filled it with water, slid the empty coffee cup into place, and started it before going into the bathroom to shave. By the time he was finished, so was the coffee. He carried it with him to the window and watched what was left of the sunrise as he took his first sip, wondering if Janie was somewhere in the world, watching it, too.

Later as he was dressing, he began rethinking the wisdom of calling Melissa to help. Selfishly, he would love to spend the morning with her, but he'd had a concussion before and remembered the headache that had come with it being pretty rough and lasting a couple of days. And with that memory firmly in place, he talked himself out of calling.

Then five minutes later, she sent him a text.

My headache is barely there. I would be happy to help.

He grinned. She'd taken the decision out of his hands by offering, and he couldn't think of one good reason to tell her no, so he sent her a text.

Pick you up around nine.

The day was suddenly a whole lot brighter as he hit Send and went down to breakfast with a bounce in his step. He noticed the young couple was absent, but three older women had arrived. He nodded at them as he entered, then paused at the sideboard to talk to Bud.

"What was the siren about so early this morning?"

"I was listening on the scanner, and I'm pretty sure they had a woman giving birth in the ambulance on the way to the hospital."

"That's great. A new baby in the world," Sully said, then thought of his birth mother, knowing when the baby was born she was giving him away.

"Morning, Sully," Rachel said as she came out of the kitchen. "Belgian waffles fresh from the waffle iron. Whipped cream and a mixed-berry compote, or warm maple syrup."

It was against Sully's personal beliefs to refuse waffles.

"Don't mind if I do," he said, then picked up a plate.

"Are you going to do more research today?" Bud asked.

"After breakfast," Sully said.

"Then good hunting," Bud said, and took the coffeepot over to the table to refill the cups for the trio of ladies.

A few minutes later, Rachel came back out with more hot waffles. She put them on the sideboard, then paused, eyeing Sully when he wasn't looking, trying to figure out who he reminded her of. She was still staring when Bud came by and shifted her focus.

"Hey, honey, I just registered a family of four. They're putting their things up in the room and will be back down for breakfast soon."

"What are the ages of the kids?" she asked.

"Oh, both teenagers for sure."

"Then the menu on the sideboard should suit them all."

After texting Sully, Melissa still had a few calls to make, and this one she dreaded. She had yet to call her insurance company to let them know what had happened, because after she did, they would have to contact the responsible party, which in this case would be Barb Holland. She hated to add to what Barb must be going through and felt sorry that she was left to clean up her husband's mess.

But the good that came out of Melissa finally making the call was finding out a rental car would be furnished as part of the perks of her policy.

With that checked off her to-do list, she gathered the garbage to take out before Sully arrived and headed out the kitchen door.

After Sully finished breakfast, he ran upstairs to get his notebook.

"Still on the search?" Bud asked as Sully came down with his keys in his hand.

"Yes. I'm going to the library today."

"I wish you good luck," Bud said.

"Thanks. Maybe today will be the day," Sully said, and was out the door to go pick up Melissa.

His heart skipped a beat as he pulled up in the driveway. The anticipation of seeing her again made him feel like a teenager on a date. He was halfway to the door when she came out of the house with a purse on her arm and a smile on her face. She waved, and he waved back.

He thought as she walked toward him what an elegant woman she'd turned out to be. Classic features. A calm demeanor. And her clothing choices were timeless. Dark pants, a pale-pink long-sleeved shirt, and black flats. The smile on her face overwhelmed the bruises.

"Morning, sunshine," Sully said as they met on the brick-paved path.

"*Buenos días*," she said. "Remember Spanish class?"

He laughed. "I do now! Lord, I hadn't thought of that in years. The teacher wouldn't let us speak anything but Spanish in the class."

Melissa grinned. "I remember you told the teacher you were *infernó*…when you meant *enfermo*."

Sully grinned. "Yeah. Something I'd eaten in the lunch-room. If I remember right, I wasn't the only one to get sick that day. You have a wicked memory."

"Oh, girls always remember stuff about their first love."

"And boys are so hormone-driven at that age with the girl they are crushing on that the only thoughts in their heads are when they might get a chance to kiss her."

"As I remember, we had quite a few of those chances," she said.

"Not nearly enough," Sully said as he slipped a hand beneath her elbow and walked her to the car.

As soon as she was inside, he got in. Now they were together within a confined space, and the easy conversation had stalled. He glanced at her. She was looking at him.

"I don't think I mentioned how beautiful you look," he said.

A faint-pink flush spread across her cheeks, but she shook her head at him and smiled.

"Thank you. You certainly know how to make a woman forget about the purple bruise on her face."

"What bruise? I don't see a bruise," Sully said, then winked as he started the car.

With Melissa pointing out the way, they soon arrived at the library.

"This is nice," Sully said as he parked beneath the shade of the widespread limbs of an old oak.

"It's been here about as long as Blessings has," Melissa said. "They have a fairly new librarian. Her name is Gina Green. So let's get this party started. Here's hoping we find a lead for you today."

"Here's hoping," Sully said.

They got out, and a couple of minutes later, Melissa was introducing him.

"Gina, this is Sully Raines, an old friend of mine who's on a search to find his birth mother. Sully, this is Gina Green."

"It's a pleasure to meet you, Sully. How can I help you?" Gina said.

"The pleasure is mine," Sully said. "I need to see some older issues of the local paper, going back at least thirty years to start."

"They're going to be on microfiche," Gina said. "Follow me back here to the readers. I'll show you how to access and load them. Try not to get them out of order."

"Yes, ma'am," Sully said.

Gina set Sully and Melissa up with the first rolls of microfiche, showed them how to switch them out, and then left them to it.

"Here goes nothing," Sully said as they began with issues over thirty-seven years back, which was when Robert and Janie Carter parted company.

They kept changing rolls of microfiche and reading,

until they'd gone forward through five years of papers. At that point, Melissa quietly got up to go to the bathroom, and Sully was so focused on reading that he didn't realize she was gone until a few minutes later. He looked toward the bathroom, then shrugged and kept reading until he saw how much time had passed since she left.

He got up to go check on her, but saw her curled up on a sofa in the reading area, sound asleep. He walked over to where she was lying to feel her pulse. It was as steady as her breathing.

He stood for a few moments looking down at her, remembering how mesmerizing her green eyes were when she watched him, and thought of the awkwardness of their first kiss. They had gotten better at it as the year progressed, but she'd moved away before it went any farther. He couldn't help but think what might have been, and even let himself wonder what the possibilities were of having a relationship now.

Before his imagination took him any farther down the road to "what if," a tear rolled from the corner of her eye and down the side of her nose.

Ah dammit. Don't cry, honey.

The urge to reach out to her was strong, but the bruises on her forehead and cheek were vivid reminders not to touch. Shoving a hand through his hair in frustration, Sully sat back down and read ten more years of newspapers before he turned off the reader.

CHAPTER 6

SULLY HAD HIT ANOTHER ROADBLOCK. BLESSINGS WAS a small town. If Janie Carter hadn't been mentioned during the first fifteen years after her arrival, he doubted she was still there. He felt defeated, and he hadn't heard from Marilyn to see if she'd found any other leads.

It was already after 2:00 p.m. He was getting hungry, and he imagined Melissa was, too. He went to the sofa where she was sleeping and gave her a gentle shake.

"Melissa, it's me, Sully. Time to wake up."

She opened her eyes, then rolled over on her back and looked up.

"Is it time to go?"

He nodded.

"Did you find anything?" she asked.

"No. I'm beginning to think she didn't stay long enough to make an impression." He held out his hand. "Get up, sleepyhead, and I'll take you to a late lunch at Granny's."

She grabbed his hand, and within moments she was upright and staring at the small scar on the underside of his chin.

"How did that happen?" she asked, tracing the shape with the tip of her finger.

"I slipped on ice when I shoveling snow off my mother's driveway a few winters back."

"Ow," Melissa said. "We don't have much of that kind of weather here."

"I wouldn't mind trying out weather like that," he said.

The comment was intriguing, but she didn't respond. Instead, she finger combed her hair.

"Is my hair sticking up anywhere?" she asked.

He smoothed a little bit down over her left ear and winked.

"You're good to go," he said.

They thanked Gina on their way out and were blasted with the midafternoon heat as they walked to the car.

"Good thing you parked in the shade," Melissa said.

"And it's a good thing we're leaving now, because the shade is abandoning us."

He started the car the moment they were in and rolled down the windows at the same time he turned on the air-conditioning.

"This will get cool in a few seconds," he said, and off they went.

They hadn't gone far when Melissa suddenly cried, "Stop!" Before Sully knew what was going on, she was out of the car and running into the alley they'd just passed.

He jumped out to follow her, and the moment he turned the corner into the alley, he saw her holding an old man's hand and walking him back toward the street. When she signaled for Sully to stay there, he stepped back. As they neared the sidewalk, he could hear what she was saying.

"It's okay, Billy. I know where you live. I'll take you home."

The wisps of white hair on the old man's head were awry and twisted. His shirt was gray and buttoned all the way to the neck, and the red suspenders he was wearing were holding up a pair of brown pants. He was barefoot and crying, and Melissa kept patting his hand as they walked. They were almost to the street when Sully heard a commotion and looked up.

A man and woman came out of a house on the run. Their expressions were frantic as they paused just outside the gate to their yard to look up and down the street. The woman started shouting, "Dad! Dad!"

"Here!" Sully shouted, and pointed down the alley, just as Melissa and the old man emerged.

"Look, Billy. There they are! Mona sees you. She's going to take you home."

"Need to go home," Billy said.

"I know, sweetheart. Mona's going to take you home."

Sully's heart went out to the couple. His mother hadn't known anyone the last two months of her life, and she was bedridden. He couldn't imagine what that would be like with an elderly person with dementia who was still ambulatory.

"Oh my God, Melissa! Thank you," Mona said.

"How did you find him?" her husband asked.

"I just happened to look that way as we drove past the alley. He was all the way at the other end when I caught up with him."

"Want to go home," Billy said as his daughter hugged him.

"I know, Daddy. Hold my hand, and I'll take you there."

Like a child who trusts those who love him most, he took her hand and let them lead him away.

"Oh my lord," Melissa said as she thrust a shaky hand through her hair. "Being responsible for an elderly parent like that would be a living nightmare."

"You always did have a tender heart. Good job," Sully said quietly, and hugged her. "Come on, there's a cool car and a late lunch waiting for us."

Melissa sighed. "That's not the first time Billy got lost. This has been happening off and on for almost a year. They're going to have to face the fact that they can no longer keep him safe, if they keep him at home. We all know Billy, and we look out for him."

"People who live in Blessings are truly blessed," Sully said, and reached for her hand as they walked back to his car. They rode the rest of the way to Granny's in silence.

Sully pulled up into the parking lot and killed the engine. "Are you okay?"

"I'm fine," Melissa said.

"If you're not up to a public outing, just say the word and we can get this to go."

Melissa frowned. "I know how I look, but I long ago quit caring about that. None of what happened to me was my fault. I'm hungry. Let's eat."

Sully laughed. "I'm beginning to remember why I fell so hard for you back in the day. You weren't just a pretty girl. You had sass."

Melissa sighed. "'Had' is the operative word. I traded sass for guts and somehow got over being afraid to live on my own after Andy died."

"We are a sorry pair," Sully said. "I'm at a dead end with my search, and life has bounced you around like a rubber ball. Maybe those biscuits waiting inside will make both of us feel better. Let's go make friends with some food."

Peanut was sitting in the outer lobby waiting for a to-go order and talking to Lovey when they walked in.

"Melissa!" Lovey cried, and came out from behind the register to greet her.

Peanut stood up and shook Sully's hand.

"Girl, it's good to see you up and about," Lovey said.

"And I need to thank you for the food you sent to the house after it happened. It was wonderful."

"You're welcome," Lovey said.

"How's that search going?" Peanut asked.

Lovey frowned. "I'm sorry. I don't hear so good anymore. What search?"

"I'm searching for—"

Before Sully could finish, a loud bang came from the kitchen.

Lovey groaned. "Even with my bad hearing, I heard that. Sorry. I need to see what happened," she said, and off she went, calling out to one of the waitresses. "Wendy! Two customers are waiting to be seated," she said, and kept going.

Wendy hurried to the lobby. "Your order is nearly ready, Mr. Butterman," she said. Then she smiled at Melissa and Sully and grabbed two menus. "Follow me," she said.

"Could we have a booth, please?" Sully asked, as they entered the dining room.

"Absolutely," Wendy said, and seated them at the closest one and took their drink orders, leaving them to check out the menus.

It was almost 4:00 p.m. when Sully took Melissa home.

As they were getting out, Melissa looked toward the house.

"There's a note on the door," she said. She pulled it off as they went inside. "It's from Ruby and Rachel."

"Rachel Goodhope?" Sully asked.

"Yes. She and Ruby are bringing some food by around six. Yay. I won't have to figure out what to cook tonight or tomorrow."

"You have really good friends here in Blessings, don't you?"

"Yes. This is home."

Sully ran a hand down the side of her face, lifting a stray strand of her hair from her cheek. "Your parents aren't still living, are they?"

"No, they're not. They both passed when I was in junior college. Dad died of cancer, and six months later Mom died of a heart attack. I always said it was because Mom was so heart-broken without him. They didn't even live to meet Andy."

Sully's heart hurt for her all over again. "I'm so sorry." Then he sighed. "I keep saying that, don't I? You might not need a hug, but I need to hug you."

Melissa saw the empathy on his face, and she was begin-ning to like the hugs. She walked into his open arms and wrapped her arms around his waist.

Sully felt her body curve to fit his and fought the longing for more.

One hug led to a kiss on her forehead, and then a kiss on her cheek, but Melissa was the one who turned her head and caught the third one on her lips.

It lasted longer than it should have, but it wasn't enough. Sully reluctantly ended it, then cupped her cheeks, looking long and hard at the flush on her face and the glitter in her eyes.

"Is this a place we want to go?" Sully asked.

She didn't hesitate.

"Yes."

"You sure you're not confusing gratitude for something else?" he asked.

Melissa frowned. "I've been grateful to a whole lot of people in my life, but I never wanted to kiss them. However, if none of this plays into your plans, just say so. I'd like to think another man might love me some day, but I don't need it to survive."

Sully's gut knotted. He wasn't sure what had happened, but it felt like she'd just climbed back over that wall behind which she'd been living.

"Don't, Missy. I wasn't rejecting you. I was protecting myself. It's hell to be attracted to someone who doesn't share the same feelings."

Melissa suddenly shivered. "Are you attracted to me?"

A slight smile shifted the contours of his face. "I guess I am. So how does that fit into your schedule?"

She grinned. "I can move some things around."

He laughed. "There's that sass, and thank you for making time for me. How does your day look tomorrow?"

"While you're waiting on your researcher for new leads, I could use a ride tomorrow."

"I happily volunteer," Sully said, and grinned.

Melissa poked a finger against his chest. "Don't make fun. The need is real. I have to get a new insurance card, so I can get my driver's license replaced, so I can rent a car. They'll take another picture when they replace my license. Just look at me! Women fret about their hair and makeup when they have to renew their license. I have a purple face."

"As soon as the bruises fade, you can get the purple-face picture replaced. And since you're in the business of washing and cleaning clothes, and I have clothes needing to be washed, how about I pick you up tomorrow. You take me to your laundry so I can drop off my stuff, and I'll take you anywhere you need to go. And if some kissing and hugging happens between the two of us during the day, we'll just enjoy the heck out of it."

Melissa grinned. "I know a good deal when I hear one. I'm in."

Sully laughed. "Awesome. Clean shirts and a hot babe in the seat beside me. What time do you want me to swing by?"

"Anywhere between eight and ten okay?"

"Yes," he said.

"Thank you, Sully…so much."

He brushed a kiss across her lips. "It's all my pleasure," he said, and then he was gone.

Melissa locked the front door and went back to the kitchen. It felt so good to do things for herself again that she put a load of laundry in to wash, cleaned the downstairs bathroom, and was sitting in the living room with her feet up when her doorbell rang. She saw Rachel's car in the driveway, and Ruby's car right behind it, as she hurried to the door.

"Hello, hello!" Ruby said.

"Evening, honey," Rachel added. "Lead the way to the kitchen."

"This is so thoughtful," Melissa said as the girls set their boxes on the kitchen table and began taking out covered dishes.

"I brought lasagna and a small tossed salad. You'll need to add dressing. There's also a meat loaf and some scalloped potatoes you can freeze," Ruby said.

"I brought a loaf of homemade sourdough bread, some orange breakfast scones, and a loaf of apple praline bread. There's also a mini-cheesecake. Just right for two," she said, and winked.

"I have no idea what you mean," Melissa said, which made the girls laugh.

"I'm heading back," Rachel said. "We're really having an influx of guests right now. Besides Sully, I still have three elderly ladies, but they'll be checking out after breakfast tomorrow, and another couple due tonight, so I need to prepare for all that. Enjoy your supper. I'll let myself out."

She hugged Melissa, and then she was gone.

Ruby saw the happiness on Melissa's face and knew Sully was responsible.

"I've known you a long time. I don't think I've ever seen you happier."

"Sully and I go back a long way. He's easy to be with, and you are a wonderful friend. The best people in the world are living in Blessings."

After Ruby left, Melissa locked up the house and headed for the kitchen. She took out a serving of lasagna, then put part of the food in the refrigerator and part of it in the freezer, and tossed the load of laundry into the dryer.

When she finally got around to eating supper, she reheated the lasagna, added salad and a glass of iced tea, and ate it in the living room while watching the evening news.

When it came time to go to bed, she went upstairs to her bedroom to spend the night. The sooner she resumed her normal routine, the better she would feel.

She stripped in front of the full-length mirror on the

bathroom door, turning first one way and then another, checking the bruising she got from the wreck.

Her shoulder was still sore from hitting the door, and her chest was sore from the seat belt. But nothing was broken, and she was blessed to be alive.

She thought of Sully again and shifted her perspective to how her body would fare in his eyes. She'd always been lanky. Long legs and arms attached to a less-than-sexy body. There were no voluptuous breasts, just a handful apiece, as Andy used to say. When she was younger, people used to say she looked like actress Sandra Bullock, but she never saw it. All she'd seen were dark hair and green eyes.

Sully, however, had grown from a really cute teenager to a drop-dead sexy man with a body to match. And after seeing him without a shirt in the ER, it was easy to understand how he had been strong enough to pick her up and run. Staying fit had to have been part of his job.

She turned away from the mirror and headed to the shower. A short while later, she came out with her nightgown on and her hair still damp from being washed. She checked to make sure the security alarm was on, then set her alarm clock and got in bed.

The sheets were cool, but soon warmed by her body. The softness of the bed eased her aches. She fell asleep and dreamed of the time before, when Sully was still Johnny, and life was good.

Up just after daybreak, Melissa was getting ready for the big day ahead of her and excited she was spending part of it with Sully. She was trying not to dwell on how attached she was becoming to his presence. There was no guarantee that any of the attraction they were feeling toward each other would go anywhere but in and out of bed. But she was thinking about it.

With a little bit of mascara and choosing what to wear with an eye on comfort and style, she'd picked a yellow cotton-knit pullover to go with straight-legged jeans, and reminded herself that her next hair appointment would also be the day for a touch-up on the color. She'd already had all the breakfast she wanted and had a to-do list. All she needed now was her ride.

Sully woke up to a text from Marilyn, telling him she had reached a dead end on the search, but if he had any more leads to let her know and she'd run them down. It was a disappointing message, but he sent her a text with a thank-you and a reminder for her to invoice him what he owed her, then went to shower and shave.

Spending the morning with Melissa was way more fun than going through microfiche all day. If he was honest with himself, there was no need to choose between Melissa and a task that went nowhere. She was a draw all on her own. Even if he never found Janie, he'd found someone from his past who once meant the world to him. The attraction between them was still there, and he was hoping for more.

He was feeling good about the day as he went down for breakfast. The three little old women were still there, but there were bags in the lobby. They must be leaving today.

"Morning, Sully. What's going on today? More hunting?" Rachel asked.

"Not for a while. I've reached a dead end, and so has my researcher. I'm not happy about it, but I didn't expect it to be easy. However, I'm going to be Melissa's driver for the morning, so that's a plus."

Rachel smiled. "Enjoy the day. There are buckwheat pancakes on the buffet, along with maple-flavored sausage links and scrambled eggs cooked with a little Gruyère cheese grated into them."

"Sounds great," Sully said, and went to the buffet as Rachel filled the coffee cup at his table and moved on.

A short while later, he left the B and B with his car keys in hand, thinking about the way Melissa's eyes crinkled at the corners when she laughed. Yep, she was under his skin, and it was a comfortable fit.

As he drove to get her, he passed the house where the old man with dementia lived, and wondered how they were faring. He thought back to how quickly Melissa had reacted, and how anxious for her he'd been when she jumped out and ran. It was hard to believe all those years were between what they'd been and who they were now, because it felt as if he'd known her forever.

He got to her house and rang the bell.

She appeared in the doorway within moments. "Come in. I need my shoes and a little lipstick, and I'll be ready to go."

Sully came inside and shut the door. "Wait a second," he said, and took her in his arms. "I thought about this all night. So before you put on lipstick, may I have a proper good-morning kiss?"

Melissa threw her arms around his neck, homing in on his mouth with abandon, but whatever she'd thought it would be turned into something she hadn't dared dream.

His arms went around her; his lips opened up beneath hers. Within seconds, she'd forgotten lipstick and bare feet and was lost in the fantasy of being bare beneath him. One kiss turned into another, and then another, until on instinct, they both stopped and stepped back in unison.

Sully's heart was pounding. It was all he could do not to pick her up and head for the nearest bedroom. They weren't there yet, but he still had a need to touch her, so he cupped her cheek instead.

"That is one damn fine greeting," he said.

Melissa shivered. "Uh...I..."

"Don't explain it away," Sully said, and brushed one last kiss across her lips. "You're dynamite and lightning hiding there in that quiet woman's body. Now go get yourself put back together, love. I'll wait for you here."

"My things are in there," Melissa said, pointing to the nearby living room. She went in and put her shoes on, added a little lipstick, then dropped it in her purse.

She paused in front of a mirror to check out her appearance. Looking at herself was like looking at a stranger. She didn't know who the hell that woman was, but she liked her.

She tapped the mirror with her fingernail. "Just hold that thought," she said softly, and left the room.

CHAPTER 7

Sᴜʟʟʏ ᴡᴀs sɪᴛᴛɪɴɢ ɪɴ ᴛʜᴇ ᴄᴀʀ ᴡᴀɪᴛɪɴɢ ꜰᴏʀ Mᴇʟɪssᴀ to come out of the car rental agency. He'd picked her up two hours earlier, and that good-morning kiss was still on his mind.

When they dropped his clothes off at the cleaners, he saw another side of Melissa as she shifted into owner mode. She introduced the employees and showed him the new dry-cleaning machine they'd just installed. He could tell the employees really liked her and were all sympathetic about what had happened to her.

He and Melissa had gone next to the insurance company, then to replace her driver's license, and now here to rent a car. It was the last stop, and he didn't want it to be over. When she came out smiling, dangling the keys in the air with the owner of the rental agency behind her, he got out.

The rental agent went over the details and inspection of the car with Melissa before going back inside. She mumbled something Sully couldn't quite hear, then patted the trunk of the car and giggled.

"What's so funny?" he asked.

"I just told her she has a nice butt."

"I'd tell you the same thing, but it might be mistaken for sexual harassment, so you can pretend you didn't hear that come out of my mouth."

Melissa laughed, and as she did, Sully had his first

glimpse of the Missy he'd known—the happy, bubbly girl who was always the first one to laugh at herself.

Sully grinned. "You made a nice choice," he said, eyeing the late-model white Ford Focus.

"It's new enough to be reliable, which works for me. You are now officially released from further chauffeur duties," Melissa said.

He frowned. "But what if I don't want it to be over?"

She thought of the good-morning kiss. "What do you have in mind?"

"Nothing dangerous, I assure you. How about I follow you back to your place to leave the car, then we'll have lunch. We can figure it out from there."

"I'd love it," Melissa said.

She got in the car and headed home, smiling all the way at the sight of the car behind her.

By the time Sully reached her house, he had a whole new idea about lunch. She was already out and locking her rental car when he pulled up. There was a bounce in her step as she got in.

"I had a thought about lunch," Sully said. "Does Blessings have a good place to have a picnic? The day is so pretty, I thought maybe we could find a shade tree somewhere and eat there."

"I would love to do that!" she said. "There are great picnic tables at the park."

"Do we want to get something to go from Granny's, or go to the supermarket and get stuff from there, or get something from the Dairy Freeze? It's fast food, but—"

"Oh, the Dairy Freeze for sure," Melissa said. "I love their chili dogs and fries."

"I've had burgers from there and they were good, but I forgot to tell them to leave off the pickles. When I was taking them off, it made me remember you always ate the pickles off my burgers."

Melissa laughed. "I'd forgotten all about that. That's back when you were still Johnny. But I'm used to Sully now, and it fits you."

"Then the Dairy Freeze it is," he said, and drove up the street a few blocks, then pulled into line at the drive-through.

"This is such fun," Melissa said. "Thank you for this."

"No, thank *you*. Being around you has made me realize what I've been missing out on in life. I have friends, but I didn't have anyone that I spent time with like this."

"I can't fault you for that," Melissa said. "I have friends here, but no matter how many times I was invited to things, I rarely went. I had crawled in such a deep hole that I had no idea how to get out."

The line began to move, and they were soon at the window ordering their food. After it arrived, they took off to the park with Melissa directing the way.

"This is nice," Sully said as they parked and got out. "That table is in the shade. Is it okay with you?"

"Absolutely," Melissa said.

She took some of the extra napkins to wipe off the table-top and benches, then Sully took out the food.

"A chili dog and fries for you. Fries and cheeseburgers, minus pickles, for me. Here's your chocolate shake and my vanilla shake. Enjoy!"

They ate a few bites, and then conversation started as they began playing catch-up on each other's life.

"Tell me about your wife," Melissa asked.

"Ex-wife," he said, and shrugged. "Her name is Karen. She's on her third husband, last time I heard. We didn't fit. I got over her a long time ago. Tell me about Andy. He had to be a smart guy to be with you."

Melissa smiled. "Andy was smart and quiet. He liked being home, so there wasn't a lot of partying or hosting dinners. But we were happy." She glanced off into the trees for a moment, then added, "And then he died."

"Was it an accident?" Sully asked. "I mean, you two being so young and everything."

Melissa shook her head. "No, it was a brain aneurysm. The doctors said it was something he'd been born with. No warning. No way to prevent it or treat it."

"I'm sorry. That's rough," Sully said.

Melissa nodded. "Yes, it was. I didn't deal with it well, as you can imagine. I withdrew. Literally. Coming here to Blessings was my saving grace. I don't know what it is about this place, but nobody suffers in this town for long. Once they learn someone had a hardship, the town sort of pulls together to make it right. And quite often, Ruby and Lovey are the ones who organize us all. They're like fairy godmothers. Always looking for a way to bring happiness."

"That's an amazing tribute," he said.

"It's an amazing place to live," she said.

A little bird flew down to the other end of their picnic table and began to chirp.

"We have company," Sully said.

A couple of minutes later, it was joined by two more, perched in the tree over their heads. She pointed up into the branches.

"He's calling in his buddies. Probably hoping we'll leave a few crumbs," Melissa said.

"Then we don't want to disappoint them," Sully said, and pulled a piece of bun off his last cheeseburger and crumbled it onto the ground.

Melissa added a few french fries to the feast as she and Sully gathered up their trash. She got up to stretch her legs as he carried the sacks to a nearby trash bin, then came jogging back.

Before she knew it, he'd swung her off her feet and into his arms. She laughed at the unexpected joy.

"You're my dessert," he said, and gave her a quick kiss before putting her down. "Do you have business to tend to this afternoon?"

"No. What do you want to do?"

"I want you to show me around. Show me where you used to live. Where you worked. Show me where Peanut and Ruby live. Where Lovey lives. I am getting to know the people, but seeing where they live always says a lot more."

"I would love to," Melissa said, and slipped her hand in his as they walked back to the car.

The first place she took him was across the tracks to the other side of town to point out the little house she used to live in.

As he pulled over to the curb, he felt the stark absence of *home*. There were no flower beds, no landscaping. Just a small white house with a gray roof. Nothing over the front door that even pretended to be a porch, no garage, and no carport. Just a driveway that stopped beside the house.

"It's the one with the black Toyota in the driveway. A young couple lives in it now. It's a rental. I never thought I'd be able to buy a house, and then Elmer Mathis passed away, leaving everything to me. It was a life-changing gift I will never take for granted."

Sully held her hand as she talked about losing part of the roof once in a tornado, and when the water heater went out and flooded the whole kitchen.

"You want to know the irony of this? My landlord was Niles Holland. The man who ran into me. I liked him."

"In a small town like this, I can see how that would happen. I'm sorry," Sully said.

"Okay, enough about me. As you can see, we're on the poor side of town. If you'll go back toward Main, I'll show you where Peanut and Ruby live."

And so they drove, and Melissa talked, and little by little Sully began to feel the vibe of the place in a whole new way.

"I already showed you where Lovey is living now, but it's not her home. It belongs to Ruby. Lovey is just living there while hers is being remodeled. Her home was severely damaged during Hurricane Fanny. If you'll take a right at the next corner, then go two blocks down, I'll show you."

"Got it," Sully said, following her directions, then saw it before she'd even pointed it out. "Is that it? The one where the carpenters are working?"

"Yes. They had to put a whole new front on the south half of the house. There used to be a huge tree in her yard there where that backhoe is parked, but the hurricane blew it into that side of the house. The horrible part was that Lovey hadn't boarded up the little window in her bathroom, and the town was flooding, so she went into the bathroom to look out the window. She was worried about how close the floodwater was, and as she was looking out, the tree hit the house, pushing all of that inward, right where she was standing.

"Glass was everywhere, and the hurricane-force winds that were now blowing straight into the bathroom blew the door shut, leaving Lovey badly injured and unconscious on the floor. She came to later with the rain in her face, bleeding and in horrible pain. The roar of the wind was so strong and so loud that during the time she was trapped, she lost hearing in one ear. Her arm was broken, her shoulder injured, and she was cut all over and couldn't get out."

"Trapped?" Sully said.

"She couldn't open the door against the force of the wind."

"Oh my God," Sully said. Now he was looking at that house with a different view, imagining Lovey fighting for her life.

"How did she get out? With no power, how did anyone even know that had happened?"

"It's a crazy story. As it was told to me, Elliot Graham, an elderly man who lives here, had a vision. People say he's something of a psychic, and so far none of his predictions or warnings have been wrong. Anyway, Elliot had a vision that she was trapped and in danger of dying. Somehow he got word to the right people, and the police chief found out, and then someone else was contacted who owns a dozer service. In prep for after the storm passed, he had his biggest dozer here in town at his house.

"When the chief told him about Lovey, he left the safety of his own house and made his way to the massive dozer, drove it through floodwaters to this house, and then managed to get inside the house without blowing away. He figured out she was inside the bathroom, and when he shouted at her, she shouted back. He couldn't open the door, so he chopped his way into the bathroom with a hatchet to get her out.

"He'd found her, but the danger was only half over. She could barely walk, so he carried her out into the storm, somehow got them both up inside that huge dozer, and took her to the ER. He saved her life. His name is Johnny Pine, and he's twenty-two years old. That's the kind of people who live here, Sully. He's only one of a half dozen I could name right now, men and women, who have saved lives and made differences in the way people live."

Sully was speechless. He'd lived a life of rescuing people, and he knew the guts it took for a person to put their own life at risk for someone else. He was in awe, and the more he thought about it, the more convinced he was that this was the place he wanted to live for the rest of his life.

"Thank you for today," Sully said.

"I loved doing this with you," Melissa said.

"Are you ready to head back?" he asked.

"Sure," she said.

She dozed off on the way back, then woke when Sully pulled into the drive.

"Want to come in for coffee? I have all kinds of food that Ruby and Rachel brought over, remember? And some of Mercy's pecan pie left, as well," Melissa said.

"If you're sure you aren't too tired, I'd love to," Sully said.

"I'm not too tired for you," she said.

They got out together, went up the walk side by side, and then into the house. The cool interior was such a reflection of Melissa—peace personified. It felt welcoming. And it was beginning to feel like a place he could call home.

"Make yourself comfortable. Bathroom is just down that hall if you want to wash up. I'm going to take my things upstairs. I'll be right back," she said, and then gave Sully a quick kiss before running up the stairs.

He took her up on the offer to wash up. After he came out, he began wandering through the first floor, looking in all the rooms, marveling at the rich wood features, the wide-plank hardwood flooring in some rooms and white marble tile in others that went well with the elegance of the draperies and furnishings. He couldn't imagine how it must have felt for her to go from that little box of a house where she was living to this place. It must have felt like moving into a palace.

He was in the kitchen, looking out at the rock walls surrounding the perimeter of the back property. The trees were huge, and the shrubs were tall, bushy, and looked like they'd been there since the house was built.

He recognized the crepe myrtles and the rose of Sharon bushes, but there were others he didn't know. He wondered if she did any gardening herself, or if someone did it for her. Then he heard her coming through the hall and turned around just as she entered the kitchen.

"Well, what do you think of the place?" Melissa asked.

"It suits you. It's beautiful, elegant, even graceful, like you."

Melissa stammered, a little taken aback by the unexpected compliment as she went to the counter to start the coffee.

"I can't take credit for any of it except the clean part. I cleaned this house once a week for Elmer for the past fifteen years. He wanted it just like his sweet Cora left it, and so that's what we did."

"Cora was his wife?" Sully asked.

Melissa nodded. "But she'd already passed before I knew him." She measured coffee into the filter, filled the carafe with water, then poured it into the tank and started it to brew. "What sounds best to you? Cheesecake, pecan pie, or a slice of apple praline bread?"

"Oh wow, that's a hard decision to make," Sully said.

"Then I guess I'd better get out all three and let you sample all of them."

He grinned. "I won't say no."

She smiled. "You still have that sweet tooth, don't you?"

"Yes. The way I like sweets, I think I must have a whole mouthful of sweet teeth," Sully said.

Melissa pointed to the cabinet. "Dessert plates are in the first cabinet on the right on the second shelf. Forks in the drawer below."

So while she was getting out the desserts, Sully got down the plates and brought them to the table.

She went to get cups, then joined him at the table. They were as comfortable together as if they'd been doing it for years.

"This is nice," Sully said as she settled in the chair across the table from him.

"The desserts? They do look amazing."

"No. I meant you—me—together like this. You're so easy to be with. I'm surprised some man hasn't already snatched you up, but selfishly, I'm glad he didn't."

"I wasn't snatched because I was not available for snatching," Melissa said, and cut a couple of slices of the apple praline bread, then moved to the pie and cut a couple of slices there, too.

"And now you are?" Sully asked.

She licked a sticky spot on her thumb. "Only for you," she said. "If it was anyone else, I wouldn't have given him the time of day, even if he'd saved my life. You and me here in this place is because we have history. A good history. A history I trust. And a little love history, even if we didn't go past first base."

Sully's thoughts were spinning. "Now that we're long past the age of consent, would you be interested in seeing what second or third base are like?"

She looked up at him and grinned. "What happened to home runs?"

Sully laughed. "I wasn't going to push my luck."

"Don't ever sell yourself short," she said.

"I'll remember that," Sully said, and when she cut the mini-cheesecake in half, he held out his plate.

Melissa noticed the coffee was ready and got up to get the carafe and filled their cups before setting it back on the stand.

"Cream or sugar?" she asked.

"I drink it black," he said.

"Are you a fan of flavored coffees?" Melissa asked as she sat back down.

"Not so much. You?"

"I like mine black, as well." Melissa ate another bite, then paused. "What happens when your search is over?"

"What do you mean?" Sully asked.

"I mean, will you be going back to Kansas City?"

"Only to pack up my stuff," he said.

"Are you moving?" Melissa asked, trying not to be too inquisitive.

Sully reached across the table and grabbed her hand.

"Girl, stop playing around. You know where I want to be. There's nothing in Kansas City for me anymore. I want to be near you. I want to make Blessings my home."

The joy in her eyes spread across her face.

"If you want to be *near*-near me, I have many bedrooms."

He laughed. "Yes, *near*-near was the optimum destination I had in mind."

"So, while you're waiting for new leads, if you want, you could stay here...but only if you want," Melissa said, and then picked a pecan off her slice of bread and popped it in her mouth.

Sully tugged at her hand. "That is a most generous offer, and I would be honored."

"Oh no, it wasn't generous at all. It was pure selfishness," Melissa said.

Sully laughed. "I always did like a woman who spoke her mind. Is tonight too soon for my arrival?"

Melissa's heart skipped a beat. *Oh my God, oh my God, this is actually happening.* "Nope. I'd say it was perfect timing."

Barb Holland was also surrounded by desserts and casseroles, but with no appetite to sample them. However, her family was due in from Texas sometime before dark, and they'd take care of that in no time.

When she'd called them two days ago to let them know what had happened, their sincere dismay and the love she felt from their voices finally eased the pain she'd been feeling. Her daddy was nearly eighty years old, but he was on the way, riding with one of her brothers, while the other brother was bringing her aunt and another carful of cousins.

When it came time for the family to be seated at the funeral, she would be surrounded by people who loved her, not the snide, catty people who'd destroyed, beyond repair, what she thought was friendship.

They'd released Niles's body to the local funeral home at just one o'clock this morning. Barb had gone in after sunrise to take clothes to bury him in and to set the day and time of the service. She'd walked in with his favorite suit on a hanger and was leaving with the receipt for his service marked Paid in Full. What she wasn't going to do was bury him here. They would be giving her his ashes to take away with her. His funeral was scheduled for the day after tomorrow, 3:00 p.m. at Blessings Baptist Church, and tonight, her heart was breaking.

When Sully got back to the B and B, Bud was behind the front desk, dozing in his chair. He woke up as Sully approached.

"Oops, you caught me," Bud said as he got up.

"Can't fault a man for taking a rest," Sully said. "I'm going upstairs to pack, so would you have my bill ready when I come back?"

"Sure. Did you get another lead on your birth mother?"

"No. Right now I'm on hold. All the leads have run out. But in the meantime, I'm going to be a guest at Melissa's house."

Bud grinned. "That's great. She's a wonderful woman and deserves some happiness. I'll have your bill ready."

"Thanks," Sully said, and went upstairs to pack.

About an hour later, he was on his way back to Melissa.

Melissa chose the best guest bedroom in the house for Sully. It had a king-size bed, a jetted tub and a separate shower in the en suite, and a mirror that ran the length of a very ornate vanity. All of the needed toiletry items were in one of the drawers.

The fact that it was across from her bedroom was immaterial. Things would develop between them as they were meant to, or they wouldn't. But she wasn't going to turn her back on this twist of fate and was anxiously waiting for him to return.

When the doorbell rang, Melissa ran to answer.

"That was fast," she said as Sully walked in with a suitcase.

"I didn't want to give you too much time to change your mind."

She grinned. "Follow me, and I'll show you the bedroom I picked out for you. It has a king-size bed."

"Much appreciated," he said, and followed the sway of her backside as she led him up the stairs.

"This is my bedroom," she said, pointing to the door on the right. "And this is yours." She opened the door and walked in, turning on the light as she went.

"Wow, this is beautiful! Thank you," Sully said.

"Wait until you see the bathroom," she said, and pointed the way.

He walked in, then turned to her with a grin on his face.

"Two rain showerheads? A jetted tub? Man, would the

guys at the station ever love something like this to come back to after a long, hard call."

Melissa smiled, pleased that he was impressed with the comforts she was offering.

"I'll leave you to get settled. All kinds of toiletry items are in that first drawer, but if there's something missing that you need, just ask. I'll be in the kitchen."

"You aren't cooking anything just because I'm here, are you?"

"No, just reheating some of the food Ruby and Rachel brought. Take your time. There's no hurry as to when we eat."

"Thank you for this, and for letting me into your life. I won't betray your trust."

"Oh, I know you won't, Sully. I wouldn't have offered it if I thought that might happen," she said, then turned and walked out.

He heard her footsteps going back downstairs and then threw his suitcase on the bed to unpack.

Barb Holland's family arrived in four vehicles. She met them at the door with tears in her eyes, and the moment she saw the empathy on their faces, she was crying.

"Lord, lord, I am so grateful to see all of you. Come in, come in."

Her brother Bobby Austin hugged her. "So sorry this happened, Sis. We thought the world of Niles."

Then Barb saw her eighty-year-old daddy, Jake Austin, and fell apart. "It was the whiskey, wasn't it, baby?" Jake asked.

"Yes. I just couldn't get him to slow up on it. I worried about it all the time. He wouldn't listen, and he wouldn't stop driving when he was like that."

Bobby's wife, Wynona, came up and hugged her. "Barbara Ann, I want you to hear me good. It was not your responsibility to control your man. He made a choice every day to do what he damn well pleased, and you know it. All this is on him, and it breaks my heart for your grief."

"Thank you, Wy. I think I needed to hear that. All the people I thought were our friends have been awful. They've been talking about Niles like he was some drunk walking the streets, and my girlfriends have decided to set themselves up as judge and jury and point fingers at me. It was so hurtful. Something I never saw coming."

When her family heard that, they exploded.

Her aunt, Belle, was her daddy's sister, and she was livid. "Don't you worry, sugar. You just point them out to us at the family gathering tomorrow. We'll take care of the rest."

Cousins Frankie, Eddie, and Waymon Houston—who were all from the Houston branch of the family—were up in arms, too.

"We've got your back, honey," Eddie said. "Oh…and just so you know, there's about twelve more family members who are planning to overnight in Savannah tomorrow night and drive on in to Blessings the day of the service."

Barb felt like the weight of the world had been lifted from her shoulders.

"All I can say is thank you. I am moving home when I can get everything tied up here. I still have Granny Austin's home in Dallas. I've been leasing it out, but it's been empty for almost five months now. I'm sure it needs work, but renovating it will give me something to do, and I'll be close to family again."

"That's the spirit," Jake said. "Now where do you want us to go?"

"Daddy, I'm putting you and Aunt Belle in the two downstairs bedrooms. They are spacious and comfortable, and you won't have to negotiate the stairs. The rest of you will be upstairs. Now grab your bags and follow me."

CHAPTER 8

SUPPER WAS OVER. MELISSA AND SULLY WERE CLEANING up the kitchen and talking over their plans for the next day.

"I have to get payroll out tomorrow, so I'll be busy at least until noon," Melissa said.

Sully nodded, but he was preoccupied by something she'd told him earlier about Lovey Cooper's rescue.

"Remember you telling me about an old man here in Blessings who is a psychic?"

"Yes, Elliot Graham. He won't claim the title, but when he knows something, he makes sure to let people know."

"So, how do you think he'd react if I asked to talk to him about my birth mother?"

Melissa paused. "I don't know, but that's not a bad idea. I know who you can talk to, who will find out for you."

"That's great. Who is it?"

"Danner Amos and his family live directly across the street from Elliot. They weathered the hurricane together in Danner's home and have become very good friends. As soon as we're through here, I'll give Danner a call."

"Thank you, Missy. You're the best."

A few minutes later, they went to her office.

"I'm going to pull up my customer info, where I have a number for the Amos family, and then I'll give them a call."

Sully sat down on the corner of her desk, watching as her fingers danced across the keyboard until she reached the customer list, found the name she needed and easily found the number, then wrote it down.

"Okay, now to call." She still had a landline in the office and punched in the numbers, then leaned back in her chair as it began to ring. A few moments later, she got an answer.

"Hello, this is Alice."

"Hi, Alice, this is Melissa."

"Melissa! Oh my goodness! How are you feeling?"

"I'm feeling good. I'm calling for a friend. Is Danner there?"

"Yes. Hang on a sec," Alice said, and then Melissa heard her calling for Dan.

A few moments later, Dan was on the phone. "Hello, Melissa. Good to know you're up and about. Alice said you needed to speak to me?"

"Yes. Sully Raines, the man who saved my life, wants to talk to you, so I offered to call and make the introductions. I'm going to hand Sully the phone now, okay?"

"Absolutely," Dan said.

Melissa got up, handed Sully the phone, then motioned for him to sit in her chair as she waved and left the room.

"This is Sully Raines. I appreciate you taking the time to talk to me."

"Of course. What's up?" Dan asked.

"I've been looking for my birth mother, and the clues I'd been following led me here to Blessings. But since my arrival, I've hit one dead end after another. Today, Melissa mentioned something about your neighbor, Elliot Graham, being something of a psychic…that he alerted people to Lovey's need for rescue during the hurricane."

"Yes, he did that," Dan said.

"So, what I was wondering was if you could ask him if he

would be willing to talk to me about my search. If he isn't, then that's that. But if he would, I would so appreciate it."

Dan chuckled. "Oh... Yes, I could easily ask Elliot. What he says is a whole other thing. He's a bit of an eccentric, but he is a man of great compassion. What's your phone number? If he's willing to meet with you, I'll call you back."

Sully gave Dan his cell phone number and then added, "If he will talk to me, the sooner the better. I'm at a loss as to what to do next."

"Got it," Dan said. "I'll call you back in a few minutes, one way or the other."

"Thank you so much," Sully said.

"Not a problem, and by the way, you are a hero to all of us here in Blessings. We think the world of Melissa."

"Just in the right place at the right time," Sully said. "I'll await your call." Then he hung up and went to find Melissa.

She was in the living room watching TV and muted the show when he walked in.

"How did it go?" she asked.

Sully sat down beside her and gave her a hug.

"He's calling Mr. Graham for me now. I'll find out in a few minutes whether he'll see me or not, but either way, thank you for helping make this happen."

She shrugged it off. "I'm happy I could help."

"What are you watching?" he asked.

"*Expedition Unknown.* I'm a fan."

"Seriously? We always watched that at the station. Josh Gates is funny and something of a daredevil, which of course spoke to the chest-thumping males that we were."

Melissa laughed. "Chest-thumping. That's a good one. I'm going to get something cold to drink. Do you want anything? I have Coke or Mountain Dew, and of course sweet tea."

"I'll have sweet tea. Yours is really good."

"Thanks. I won't be long. Keep track of Josh for me. He's looking for the tomb of the Snake King. It's ancient Mayan stuff."

She got up and kissed his cheek.

Sully smiled. "What's that for?"

"You make me happy. That's all," she said, then left the room.

"You make me happy, too," Sully said softly. Then his cell phone rang. He dug it out of his pocket. "This is Sully Raines."

"Mr. Raines, this is Elliot Graham. I understand you'd like to talk with me."

"Yes, sir, very much so."

"Excellent. Do you know where I live?"

"No, sir, but Melissa Dean does. I'll ask her."

"Would tomorrow morning, say around ten, be a good time for you?"

"Yes, it would be perfect. Thank you."

"See you then," Elliot said, and disconnected.

Sully was still smiling when Melissa came back with their glasses.

"I heard your phone. Was it Elliot?"

Sully took the glass she handed him. "Yes. I see him tomorrow morning at ten. Can you tell me how to get there?"

She nodded as she sat down beside him. "I'll look up his address tomorrow, and then you can use the GPS in your phone."

"Perfect!" Sully lifted his glass. "A toast to psychics and all they know."

"And to finding your birth mother," Melissa added.

"I'll drink to that," Sully said. "And you haven't missed a thing on the show. Josh Gates is still traipsing through the jungle."

They watched for a while, until Sully noticed Melissa was nodding off.

"Honey, wake up. I think it's bedtime."

She blinked. "What?"

He smiled. "You were asleep. I think you've had enough of this day."

She yawned. "I think you're right," she said.

Sully turned off the television while Melissa set the security alarm, then gave him the code to disarm it. She gave him her extra door key that she kept in a basket on a table in the entry.

"We won't always be coming and going at the same time," she said as she laid the key in his hand.

His fingers curled around it. "Thank you for this...for making my search all the easier and for offering me a place to stay."

"I am blessed you came back in my life, whatever the capacity," she said.

"The capacity is creating an 'us' from the 'we' we used to be," he said, and took her hand. They went upstairs together, then paused in the hall. Sully kissed her forehead. "Rest well, love. I'll see you in the morning."

"You too. See you then," she said, and went into her bedroom and closed the door, then sighed. *You did it, girl. You kept your cool all evening, as if you invited men into your house all the time. If only Sully knew how much reluctance you had to let go to make this happen.*

And across the hall, Sully was already headed for the shower. Meeting Elliot Graham tomorrow might be just what he needed to learn where Janie went next or, God forbid, if she was no longer alive.

───────────────────

The next morning dawned with the new edition of the local paper and Niles Holland's obituary, which would become the talk of the day. Now that the date and time of the service was announced, along with the mention that a family visitation was being held this very evening from six to eight, people began making plans to go see how the grieving widow honored her alcoholic husband who'd gotten himself killed.

Very aware of what was ahead of her, Barb was focused on her appearance. She intended to stand beside Niles one last time with her head up and stare down his detractors. And part of her armor was appearance, which was why Barb, her aunt Belle, and her sister-in-law, Wynona, all had appointments at the Curl Up and Dye this morning. As Wy always said, "I dress to impress," and they had done that in spades.

They left Barb's house wearing every diamond they'd brought with them. Wy had the keys to their silver Lexus, and they were going in style. And to make the statement even starker, they were dressed in black.

Barb directed Wy to Main, and then they took a right down it, all the way to the Curl Up and Dye.

"Oh my lawd," Belle said, and then cackled with glee. "I can't believe this name! After we get our hair done, we need to get a picture of us in front of this salon. I can't wait to show my Bunco buddies back home."

They got out as a trio and walked to the door with Barb in the middle, and when they went in, Belle sailed through the door.

Ruby and the Conklin twins were waiting. Ruby came forward to meet them the moment they were inside. She hugged Barb close and then gently patted her cheek.

"You have my deepest sympathies, sugar. Now introduce me to your fabulous family."

Belle already liked the woman and took the introductions out of Barb's hands.

"I'm Belle Austin, Barb's aunt, and this is Wynona, Barb's sister-in-law."

"My sympathies to your families. Thank you for coming. We are ready and waiting," Ruby said, then led them back into the work area where Vesta and Vera were standing at attention, each holding a black cape over her arm.

"Ladies, this is Vesta, and her twin sister, Vera. They will be doing your hair, and since Barb is my regular client, I will be doing hers. We have a coffee station, and the little tea cookies are fresh from the bakery this morning."

"It's a pleasure to meet you both," the twins said. "I'm Vesta, and I'll be taking care of Miss Belle. Vera will be taking care of Miss Wynona. If you'll take a seat in the chairs for a moment, we'll cape you and then move to the shampoo station."

Belle caught Barb's eye and gave her an approving nod, and Wy was already in the chair and talking to Vera, marveling how twin sisters went into the same profession.

Barb sat long enough for Ruby to fasten the cape around her neck, and then she moved to the last shampoo station. When the warm water began flowing over her hair, then soaking into her scalp, she closed her eyes and relaxed. Ruby's place was always the sanctuary of Blessings. Here she was safe.

As the appointments progressed, the talk among the three chairs grew lighter in tone.

Ruby knew how Barb wore her auburn shoulder-length hair, but paused before she started to dry it.

"Did you have something special in mind today, honey? Anything in particular about the style?"

"Maybe, but I didn't quite know what to settle on."

Ruby began running her fingers through the length, then pulling it up on the top of Barb's head to make sure it was long enough for what she was thinking, and it was.

"You have such beautiful bone structure and this gorgeous widow's peak. What do you think about sleeking it all back away from your face into a topknot, then curling the length into a soft waterfall of curls?"

"Yes! Do it!" Belle said.

"I love the idea," Wy added.

"Then let's do it," Barb said. "It will show off my earrings perfectly tonight."

Ruby smiled. "Wonderful!"

Ruby and the twins were almost finished when the door opened, then closed.

Ruby felt Barb suddenly tense.

"That's my next appointment," Ruby said. "And she's early, so no worries."

Barb nodded, but without knowing who it was, she

dreaded the confrontation, however brief it would be. She didn't realize Wy and Belle had seen her smile disappear, but they had and immediately gave each other the eye.

The sudden silence in the shop was noted by Ruby and the twins, but they just kept working. A few moments later, they all heard footsteps coming into the workroom, and then Rachel Goodhope appeared.

"Ruby, I'm going to get a cup of—" She stopped, then shifted her direction from the coffee station to where Barb was sitting. "Barb, sweetheart, I didn't know you were here. I am so sorry for your loss. Bud and I send our deepest sympathies to all the family. We will be at the service, and we're praying for you."

"Thank you so much, Rachel."

Rachel patted Barb's hand and went back to the coffee station, got her coffee and a couple of tea cookies, and headed back to the waiting area.

"Rachel and Bud own the B and B at the far end of Blessings. They are very nice people," Barb said softly.

Belle and Wy relaxed.

A couple of minutes later, they were on their way out and stopped to pay.

"No," Ruby said. "The girls and I are gifting you with the appointments, and it was very nice meeting you."

"Well, that is just the sweetest thing," Wynona said. "I wonder if I could ask one of you to take a picture of us outside the salon? We just love the name of your place, Ruby, and want to show our friends back home."

"I'll be happy to," Vera said, and went out with the ladies. She took several pictures with all three of their phones, until they decided they had one they liked.

They were already talking about how nice the girls were in the salon as they drove away.

Vera waved and then walked back inside, quivering from excitement.

"They're driving a silver Lexus! Do you know what those cost? And did you see the diamonds on those girls' hands? Lord, lord, Vesta. Why didn't we grow up in Texas?"

Ruby grinned. "Not everybody in Texas is wealthy."

"Oh, I know," Vera said. "But I just waved goodbye to some who sure are."

"What's even more special is having family to lean on in the sad times and the bad times," Ruby said.

They all knew Ruby had no family left, which was why people often called Ruby *Sister* instead, because she was loved by the residents of Blessings as if she were one of their own.

In another part of Blessings, Melissa was in her office working on payroll, while Sully was on his way to Elliot Graham's house with the letter his adoptive mother had written to him, revealing their deceit in keeping the circumstances of his birth a secret.

The GPS directions were precise and easy to follow, and he was soon turning up into Elliot's drive. It was ten o'clock on the dot as he parked. He couldn't help but admire the stately elegance of the house, but it was obvious all through Blessings how the landscaping of the homes had suffered through the storm.

His stomach was in knots by the time he rang the

doorbell, but when Elliot appeared at the door, his anxiety disappeared.

The smile that dominated the little man's face was framed by the soft sweep of cotton-white hair, bright-blue eyes almost dancing with secrets, and the ascot he was wearing beneath a black velvet jacket.

"Mr. Raines, I presume?" Elliot said, and then chuckled. "Do come in."

"Thank you for seeing me," Sully said.

"Of course," Elliot said as he led Sully into his library. "We'll sit here," he said, indicating a leather sofa near a massive fireplace.

Sully sat at one end of the sofa, and Elliot sat at the other end, then turned to face him.

"Where are you from, Mr. Raines?"

"Please call me Sully, and I'm from Kansas City, Missouri."

"Missouri… It's a beautiful state," Elliot said. "Even though I already know the answer to this from Dan's phone call, would you please state your intentions for coming?"

"I'm looking for my birth mother and have been following leads through several states with help from a DNA researcher I hired. I didn't know I was adopted until after her passing, and she wrote an apology letter and left it for me."

He got up and handed the letter to Elliot, who put it in the palm of his hand and then closed his fingers over it.

"Please continue," Elliot said.

"The last lead I had was a letter from my birth mother with an address here in Blessings, but I have found no evidence of her being still here, despite searches in court records, land deeds, and back issues of the Blessings news-paper. Oh...I almost forgot. Her name was—"

"Yes, Janie Chapman, but you're looking for a Janie Carter, is that right?"

Sully nodded, assuming Elliot had heard this from locals who knew why he was in town.

"Do you have any leads on your birth father, Marc Adamos, yet?"

Sully nearly fell off the sofa.

"I didn't know his name! Is that his name? It wasn't on my original birth certificate."

"Oh. Sorry. I assumed you knew, or I would not have blurted it out so carelessly."

"Don't apologize," Sully said. "This is good news. It just startled me."

Elliot nodded. "Your adoptive parents were afraid your love and allegiance to them would be transferred to your birth mother, if you knew."

"Why would they think that? They were amazing par-ents. I loved them."

Elliot shrugged.

"Can you tell me if she's still alive?" Sully asked.

"I know she's not in the spirit world."

Even though Sully was puzzled by the roundabout way Elliot had of imparting information, hearing this was a relief.

"Okay, good," Sully said. "Can you tell me where she is? Do I need to search in a different area of the country?"

"Don't leave Blessings," Elliot said.

Sully's stomach was in knots. The suspense was killing him.

"So she's here?"

"Don't leave Blessings. That's what I'm supposed to tell

you. This and nothing more. I cannot tell more than what Spirit wants me to say."

When Elliot stood up, Sully was startled but followed suit. Obviously, the meeting was over. Elliot handed the letter back to Sully and smiled.

"It was a pleasure to meet you, and I am most impressed by how you saved our dear Melissa Dean. She is your soul mate, but of course you already knew that. I wish you both a long and happy life."

Sully was nodding and trying to absorb all this, so he completely missed the fact that Elliot had escorted him right to the front door and was holding it open.

"Thank you, Mr. Graham—for your time, for your help, and for your kindness," Sully said.

Elliot smiled. "We're going to be great friends."

Sully was so surprised that he laughed out loud. "That's an awesome thing to know, sir. Have a nice day."

Just as he walked across the threshold, the door behind him shut with a firm thump, followed by a click.

"He locked me out, too," Sully said, and smiled all the way back to his car. These were things to celebrate, and he knew how he wanted to do it.

Melissa was at the cleaners handing out paychecks and talking to the employees about the newly installed machine.

"How's it working for you guys?" she asked, and was inundated by the vocal appreciation for her getting it.

"It cuts down time tremendously and does a much better job," her manager said.

"Then that's what we wanted, right, Randolph?" She held up two envelopes. "These are Gus and Rhonda's paychecks. I know they'll be by sometime today to pick them up, so I'm leaving them in the office."

"Works for me," Randolph said. "Oh, we have Mr. Raines's laundry ready."

"I'll take it, and this is on me, so mark him paid," Melissa said. "I could do his wash forever for saving my life and still would not have repaid him enough."

"Yes, ma'am. Absolutely," the manager said, and got the laundry. "I'll carry it for you, ma'am."

"Thank you," Melissa said, and held the door open for him before going to unlock her car. "Just hang it all on the hooks," she said, and as soon as he was finished, she smiled. "Okay. Then I'm out of here. Have a great day, and you all know how to get in touch, should an emergency arise."

She waved goodbye, then noticed as she was getting in the car that the sky was clouding up.

She glanced at the time and thought of Sully, wondering if magic had occurred for him today, then started the car and headed for home so she could get his laundry inside before the rain started.

Sully drove straight to the flower shop. A bell rang as he walked in, and an older woman in a colorful floral smock appeared from the back.

"Hello. I'm Myra. How can I help you?"

"I want to get a bouquet of flowers. Do you have some made up?"

"Yes. Here in the cooler behind this stand of stuffed toys. But if you don't see what you want, I can easily make something else while you wait."

"Okay, thanks," Sully said. "Let me check these out first."

"Seeing as how fall is upon us, we have several different sizes of fall bouquets, and with different kinds of flowers. And, of course, the roses," Myra said.

He pointed to a bouquet of red roses in a crystal vase with a ruby-colored base.

"Those, in that vase with the ruby-colored base. How much are those?"

"Well, it's a dozen American Beauties, and the vase is crystal, which makes it a bit pricier than others. It's one hundred and ten dollars."

"I'll take it," Sully said.

Myra beamed. Her husband, Harold, had fussed at her nonstop because she'd used a vase that expensive, and now she could say "I told you so."

"Wonderful," she said, as she removed the bouquet from the cooler and carried it to the register. "Will this be cash or credit card?"

"Card," Sully said as he pulled it out of his wallet.

"If you want to sign a card to go with the flowers, you can pick from these," Myra said, pointing to the little rack on the counter.

"No card, I'm handing them to her in person."

Myra pulled up a new screen on the computer. "Your name, sir?"

"Sully Raines."

Myra gasped. "You're the man who saved Melissa Dean's life, aren't you?"

"Yes, ma'am."

"This is wonderful. I'm glad to meet you. Everybody loves Melissa."

Sully smiled. "I'm finding that out, but I'm not surprised. She was a sweetheart when we were kids, and she's only gotten better with age."

"You knew each other! Wow. Then you must have been really frantic when you were trying to get her out of the burning car."

"I'd only arrived in town about an hour before it happened. I didn't know anybody here, and I sure didn't know it was her until we were in the ER. The last time we'd seen each other, we were thirteen."

"Oh my! What an amazing story. If these are for her, please give her our best."

"Yes, ma'am," Sully said, and then they finished the purchase.

He made the drive back to Melissa's house slowly and carefully, and he was happy to see her car in the driveway when he arrived. He got out carrying the vase, and then instead of using the key she'd given him, he rang the doorbell.

When Melissa opened the door, her eyes widened in delight.

"Delivery for the prettiest woman in Blessings," he said.

She laughed. "I think you must have the wrong house."

"Nope. I know exactly where I am, and these are for you. Where do you want me to put them?" he asked.

"I think here on this table in the foyer. That way I'll see them all the time, coming and going."

He set them on the table, then turned around and hugged her.

"Does this mean Elliot gave you good news?" Melissa asked.

"He gave me news," Sully said, and felt the knowing of *meant to be* when he kissed her.

Melissa's heart fluttered from the gentleness of the kiss, but she was dying for information.

"But what news? Did he know where she was?"

"That man talks around a subject more than anyone I've ever met. He told me my birth father's name, thinking I already knew."

"Oh my gosh! What is it?"

"Marc Adamos. I never found the name on any papers, but now I know."

"And your mom? What did he say?"

"He told me not to leave Blessings."

Melissa frowned. "But what does that mean, exactly? That she's here? Then where?"

"He just kept repeating, 'Don't leave Blessings,' so I'm not leaving."

Melissa laughed and hugged him. "Don't expect me to be sad about that."

"He also said you were my soul mate and wished us a long and happy life together."

She gasped. "Did he really say that?"

Sully nodded.

Melissa sighed. "Well, it took us long enough to find each other again. Maybe that is why it was so easy to fall back into this."

"Works for me," Sully said, then kissed her again until he heard her moan. "The feeling is mutual."

Melissa felt like her whole body was humming—like someone had turned up the energy in the room.

Sully saw her shiver. "Are you afraid? Don't be afraid. This is not anything to act on until we're ready."

"Afraid? Of you? No, Sully. I just don't know what to do with what I feel."

"Then don't do anything. When the time is right, there won't be any confusion. That I can promise." He wrapped his arms around her. "It's all good, love. It's going to be all right."

"I feel like a forty-something idiot. This should not be so hard," she muttered.

He chuckled, and when he did, she started to push away, then felt his heartbeat. Without moving, she put her other hand on her own. Their heartbeats were in rhythm.

"What's wrong?" Sully said.

She reached for his hand and put it over his own heart, and then put his other hand on hers.

"Feel that?" she asked.

"Feel what... Oh, wow! We're in sync." Then he laughed. "I love this."

"I know," she said. "It's pretty amazing. I adore the roses, and I adore you, too, Sully Raines."

"Is this where I sweep you off your feet and take you to bed, or is this where we go eat pie?"

Melissa burst into laughter, and once the joy bubbled up, more kept coming, and she laughed until there were tears in her eyes.

Sully grinned and then put his arm around her and led her to the kitchen.

"I think it's pie."

"Just because you went to see a psychic doesn't mean you're turning into one."

He stopped in the middle of the kitchen floor. "Are you saying it's not pie?"

"Not pie. Cake!"

"You and your sass," Sully said, and kissed the laugh right off her face.

CHAPTER 9

Barb Holland and her family arrived at the funeral home ahead of the scheduled visitation. She had given specific orders that the casket would be opened only for the family to view and closed for the public, and she wanted to make sure that order was being carried out.

Their so-called friends had shown her what they thought of Niles, and the last thing she was going to do was put him on display. He was to be cremated after the service, and she was taking his ashes with her back to Dallas.

And per Barb's request, she and her family arrived at the funeral home in full array of their wealth and status, knowing the people who had betrayed Barb's friendship would be taken aback.

Her daddy, Jake Austin, was standing tall in a black western-style suit and gray alligator boots. And his turquoise bolo tie was starkly beautiful against his snow-white dress shirt. Aunt Belle's hair was as silver-white as her brother Jake's, but hers was coiled and coiffed and tastefully sprayed into an immovable helmet. She was in a black Vera Wang sheath, red Jimmy Choo heels, and dripping diamonds from her ears, around her neck, and on her fingers.

Brother Bobby was sporting clothing similar to his daddy, but instead of a turquoise setting in his bolo tie, his was black obsidian mounted in Navajo silver. His wife, Wynona, was also in black, wearing silver Jimmy Choos and a single diamond on her finger the size of a quarter. The dangle earrings were diamonds, as was the choker around her neck.

Barb's cousins Frank, Eddie, and Waylon were brothers from the Houston side of her family, and they, too, were wearing black western-style suits and boots. The family as a whole was striking. They were Barb's payback to the friends who'd broken her heart. Shame them into silence. Dare them to say one denigrating word about Niles. And if they did, Wy and Belle were waiting to step in with a razor-sharp comment and a smile.

But it was Barb the people knew, and it would be her they would remember best long after this ordeal was over. The updo Ruby had suggested had changed her entire appearance. From the smooth cap of dark hair pulled away from her face to the soft fall of curls topping her head like a crown, she was elegance personified.

Her black dress had a mandarin collar and three-quarter-length sleeves, with a hem that ended just at her knees. Her heels were Louboutins, and the dashing red soles for which they were known were obvious only when she walked.

She was wearing her mother's diamonds, as well as the ones Niles had given her over the years. With her hair up, her earrings, which were two-carat studs, caught the light every time she turned her head. She had six diamond tennis bracelets on her right wrist, along with the emerald-cut diamond in her wedding ring on her left hand and her mother's diamond rings on her right. Without shoes, Barb was just shy of six feet tall, but in her red Louboutins, she stood eye to eye with both her daddy and her brother.

"Mrs. Holland, visitors will be arriving in a few minutes,"

the director said. "Is there anything else you need, or anything I can do for you or your family?"

"No, but thank you for asking," Barb said.

"Of course," he said, pausing to straighten the floral casket piece and then slipping out of the room only moments before the first guests arrived.

"Sugar, when one of your so-called friends comes in, just point them out. Wy and I will handle anything that isn't proper," Belle said.

"Yes, I will," Barb said, and gave her aunt's hand a quick squeeze. "I don't know what I'd be doing right now without all of you with me."

She was dreading the first arrivals, and as fate would have it, the first couple to arrive was Don and Retta Durrett.

"Well, shit," Barb muttered. "Both of them bad-mouthed Niles, and Retta made me cry."

Belle's head went up. She caught Wy's eye and then patted her hair, just to make sure every strand was still in place.

The Durretts did a double take when they saw Barb and her family.

"Well, lordy," Retta whispered. "Barb said she came from money, but I didn't expect this."

"Just flashy Texans," Don muttered, but he was secretly envious. He didn't know anything about Retta's little visit to Barb the day Niles died, nor did he know his own wife had outed him for bad-mouthing Niles. He was just expecting to be received as the old friends they were. "Barb, we are so sorry. This is such a tragedy," Don said.

Barb looked at the both of them without responding, then began introducing them to her family.

"Daddy, this is Don and Retta Durrett. They were friends from the club. Niles golfed with Don."

Retta immediately caught the "were friends." It was the only warning she was going to get that this might not go as smoothly as planned.

Jake stared them down without comment.

Don offered his hand. "Nice to meet you, but unfortunate it's under these circumstances."

Jake didn't move and left it up to his sister to cut them down. Belle didn't disappoint.

"There are many unfortunate things in life, one of which is the betrayal of people you thought were your friends," Belle drawled.

Retta blinked. Had Barb told them about the words they'd traded? That comment sure felt like it, but she wasn't the kind to let a catty woman scare her off.

"I'm sure that's true," Retta said, and then pointed to Belle's necklace. "That is a beautiful necklace."

"Thank you," Belle said. "I got it on the Riviera."

"Oh, the Mexican Riviera! Don and I love it there," Retta said.

"The *French* Riviera," Belle said. "Bless your heart."

Retta's face turned red. She was Southern to the core, so she knew exactly what that meant, and that she could take it either of two ways. That diamond-studded bitch had either called her stupid or told her to go to hell. And all the while, Barb kept introducing her family as if that old biddy hadn't just insulted her.

Retta's chin went up, and her eyes were blazing. She just couldn't figure out who to be mad at, because they were standing beside a coffin with Niles's dead body in it, and his widow and family were looking holes through her and Don, and Barb just kept introducing family.

"This is my aunt Belle Austin, my brother Bobby Austin, and his wife, Wynona. And these are cousins from the Houston side of the family, Frank, Eddie, and Waylon."

"So, you live in Houston," Don said.

"No," Waylon said. "We're direct descendants of Sam Houston, the man for whom Houston is named. Our cousin Barb comes from the Austin side of the family...Stephen A. Austin, for whom the city of Austin was named. Where might you be from?"

"I, uh, I'm a native of Blessings."

Don knew when he said it that he'd just lowered himself to the status of hick, and the only semifamous people in the history of his family had been hanged for horse thieving. He knew when he'd been bested and put his hand under Retta's elbow.

"Barb, we'll be going now. I see more people are coming in, and we just wanted to pay our respects."

Barb lowered her voice, for the first time speaking directly to them.

"Don't pretend with me, Don Durrett. I know what you and all of Niles's friends were saying about him at the club...and on the day he died. Please feel free to leave."

When her brother Bobby shifted his stance, Don squeezed Retta's arm, and out the door they went.

After that, people began arriving in a steady stream, most showing surprise that the casket wasn't open as befitting tradition, but having the manners not to ask why.

They were alternately kind or curious, but all in awe of Barb Holland's family. The ones who didn't know her well were impressed, and the ones who thought they'd known her were in shock.

But there were many who were kind, sympathetic, and truly sorry for Niles's passing. When Peanut and Ruby Butterman came in behaving like the decent people they were, Barb introduced them to her family.

"Y'all, this is our local lawyer, Peanut Butterman, and his wife, Ruby. Aunt Belle and Wy already met her when we went to her salon. It's a wonderful place."

"Thank you, Barb," Ruby said. "We're just so sorry for your loss."

Jake Austin eyed Peanut and smiled. "I have to say, you have a most memorable name."

Peanut rolled his eyes. "The actual name on my birth certificate is a capital *P*, all by itself. Then my second name is Nutt, with two *t*'s. I had to beat up the school bully when I was in first grade for calling me Pee."

"Sweet baby Jesus," Wy said.

"Exactly, but not even the good Lord could help. After two black eyes and both of us getting a whipping for fighting at school, the kids wisely switched to Peanut and it took. Add Butterman, and my whole existence has been one of explanation. My parents were hippies. Mostly I just tell people my mama was stoned on weed when they named me. It used to really tick her off when I said it, but I told her it's no less than what she deserved for tacking that dang name to me."

The story was a great moment of levity in a hard evening, and Barb was grateful for it, because every time she glanced at the casket, she remembered Niles's body was in it. It was a continuing nightmare that seemed to have no end.

When the chief of police and his wife appeared at the door, it was Barb's family that stared in awe at her beauty.

"Who in the world are they?" Belle whispered.

"That's Lon Pittman and his wife, Mercy. He's the police chief here in Blessings, and Mercy is the baker for the local restaurant. Her baking is off the charts, and her biscuits are to die for," Barb said.

Wy gasped. "She's a cook? I have never seen anyone that stunning in my entire life. Is she classically trained?"

"The story goes she was raised in foster homes all her life," Barb said. "But they're very nice people. Chief Pittman is the one who came to the house to tell me what had happened to Niles. He was so very kind," she added, and took a deep, shaky breath, willing herself not to cry.

When one of Barb's girlfriends came to pay her respects, she was so impressed by the ostentatious show of wealth Barb's family exhibited that she completely forgot to offer her condolences, or even acknowledge Niles's casket, and started talking about Barb's hair.

"Girl, I love what you've done with your hair. You need to wear it like that at the Christmas ball at the club."

Barb stared at the woman as if she'd lost her mind.

"Shirley, see that casket you're leaning on?"

Shirley gasped. "Oh, I'm so—"

"No, you're not sorry Niles is dead. None of you are sorry, and Christmas balls are obviously the last thing on my mind today," Barb said.

Shirley's eyes narrowed angrily, but before she could voice what she was thinking, Wynona slipped her arm through Shirley's elbow and smiled.

"Your welcome just ran out, honey. Let me show you to

the door," Wynona said, then proceeded to walk the woman out as if they were old friends, talking as they went. Except Wy was the only one talking, and Shirley was too humiliated to make a scene.

And all through the visitation, if one of the people who'd betrayed Barb arrived, her family stepped up and stepped in.

Barb was numb, exhausted, and struggling hard not to cry as the evening was coming to an end. There was less than thirty minutes left, and fewer than ten people in the room.

But outside in the parking lot, Melissa and Sully were just getting out of the car.

"You sure you want to do this?" Sully asked.

"I have to, Sully. Just thank you for coming with me."

"I wouldn't have it any other way," he said, and reached for her hand.

They were still holding hands when they walked in. Melissa breathed a sigh of relief that the casket was closed as they headed straight for Barb.

A hush went through the room when everyone saw them walk in.

Barb gasped, her shock evident.

"Is this bad?" Wy whispered.

"Not like you mean. That's Melissa Dean, the woman Niles nearly killed."

At that point, her family turned to watch the tall, dark-haired woman coming toward them. The bruising on her face was obvious. They waited, not knowing what this meant.

But the moment Melissa walked up, she reached for Barb's hands with tears in her eyes.

"Barb, my deepest sympathies," Melissa said softly, then

addressed the family with her. "To all of you. I am so sorry for your loss." She put her hand on Sully's arm. "This is my friend, Sully Raines. He's the man who saved me. I asked him to come because I wanted him to meet you. Ever since this happened, I've been heartbroken. Up until I inherited Mr. Mathis's house, Niles was my landlord."

Barb frowned. "I don't think I knew that. He did all the business for the properties, and I didn't know who the renters were."

"One of them was me. I lived in the same little house for twenty years, and rain or shine, no matter what went wrong, one call to Niles and he was immediately on-site, making sure whatever had gone wrong was corrected. When I had hard times, he let me carry my rent over until I had enough money to catch up, and never a word from him of being late. I just wanted you to know how much he was appreciated. This is a tragedy. He will be missed."

Barb was shaking, but her daddy's hand was at her back.

"Miss Melissa, I'm Jake Austin, Barb's daddy. We are so sorry you were hurt, but thank the Lord Mr. Raines was there to save you. Sir, you have our sincere gratitude for that."

"Yes, sir," Sully said.

Barb sighed. "This must have been hard for you to come tonight, but the blessing you have given me is more than I could have ever expected. Thank you, Melissa. Thank you for this."

"Of course, and we waited on purpose, hoping most of your visitors would be gone. We want you to know we will purposefully not be at the service tomorrow. Tomorrow is to honor Niles. Not call attention to how he died, which is what would happen once we showed up. I just wanted you to know that my memories of Niles will always be good ones."

Then one by one, Barb's family stepped up to shake her hand and to thank both of them for coming.

Melissa was on the verge of tears as she and Sully left, and as soon as they exited the funeral home, she started crying.

"Oh, honey," Sully said, and took her in his arms.

"I didn't expect it would hit me like this. I just want to go home."

The moment they walked out the door, Barb's family began talking about the guts it must have taken for Melissa Dean to come, and the genuine kindness she'd shown the whole family.

When the visitation was finally over, Barb was numb. She didn't say a word all the way back to her house, or even argue when Belle and Wy took her up to bed. They were concerned. If the visitation had taken this much out of her, the funeral tomorrow could easily break her. She needed to rest, but all she could do was sit there and cry.

As soon as Sully and Melissa got home, they went upstairs to change. Melissa paused in the hallway and hugged Sully once again.

"That was hard. Thank you again for going with me."

"We go together like bread and jam," he said, then gave her hair a gentle tug. "How about a pajama party? Movies, popcorn?"

She sighed. "I think that sounds perfect."

"Your bed or mine?" he asked.

"Mine. That way if I fall asleep in the middle of the

movie, which I have been known to do, I'll already be in bed, and you can turn out the lights when you leave."

He grinned. "You have a practical side, too. I don't remember that."

She poked him on the arm. "As soon as I get in my pj's, I'll make popcorn."

"And I'll get the drinks. What floats your boat tonight? Coke or Mountain Dew?"

"Coke," Melissa said. They parted in the hall to go change, then came out into the hall almost at the same time.

Sully admired her pink pajamas with little white sheep on them. And she wore socks, not house shoes. Something new to note about her.

"Nice pj's," he said. "If you can't sleep, you can count sheep."

"So you go the sweatpants and old T-shirt route," she said.

"No, I don't sleep in anything, but I chose this fine ensemble just for you."

She laughed. "Good move. Let's go get our stuff."

Once they reached the kitchen, Melissa put a bag of popcorn in the microwave, while Sully took the cold drinks from the refrigerator.

"I don't know what movies are on," Melissa said.

"It won't matter to me what we watch, as long as we're watching it together," Sully said.

"You know what, Sully Raines? You're still fun to be with. That was always the best part of being your girl."

He grinned. "The best part of being your boyfriend was the kisses, but that's just me."

Melissa laughed out loud just as the timer on the microwave dinged.

"It's done," she said, then opened the bag and dumped the hot, buttery popcorn in a bowl.

Sully grabbed the two bottles of pop and a handful of napkins from the table, and followed her out of the kitchen.

Melissa had already propped multiple pillows against the headboard for them to lean against, and as soon as they were in her bedroom, she crawled into the middle of the king-size sleigh bed and put the popcorn between them.

Sully handed her a Coke and put his on the bedside table; then she handed him the remote.

"You pick the movie. I'll watch anything," she said as she put some popcorn in her mouth and started chewing.

She didn't comment on his choice, but after the steady sound of bar fights and gunfire for the first twenty minutes of the movie, Melissa finally glanced at Sully. He looked like he was in a trance. She could hardly believe they were sitting together in bed watching a really old, really loud movie.

"I can't believe we're watching this," Melissa said.

Sully looked surprised. "You don't like John Wayne?"

"This movie was made before we were born," she said.

"So we're watching a classic," he said, and threw a piece of popcorn at her. "I thought you said you'd watch anything."

She picked up the popcorn and put it in her mouth, then eyed him suspiciously.

"So, what is this? A test of my veracity?" she asked.

"Come on, Missy. It's John Wayne."

"You're cute when you whine," Melissa said.

Sully calmly removed the bowl of popcorn, and when he turned around, he grabbed her.

She was laughing as he pulled her down on top of him.

"I don't whine. Take that back," he said.

Still giggling, she shook her head.

"You're going to be sorry," Sully said as he slipped his hands beneath her pajama top, then ran the tips of his fingers against the soft skin at her waist. "I seem to remember you were ticklish. Am I right?"

Melissa gasped and started trying to get away from him. "Don't tickle, don't tickle. I give! You didn't whine. You never whine. You are a beast of a man and man-beasts never whine."

"Thank you for the vote of confidence," he said, and then rolled her over onto her back and kissed her senseless.

Just when she thought there was going to be more, he turned her loose, straightened up the covers, and put the popcorn bowl back between them. He'd just left her flat on her back, staring up at the ceiling. She raised up on both elbows.

"What the hell just happened?"

"John Wayne," he said, just as the sound of more gunfire filled the room.

She looked at him, then at the movie.

"He's my favorite," she said, then replaced her pillows, scooted back against them, and took a drink of Coke.

After that, the only sound in the room was more of John Wayne. Just as the movie was coming to an end, Sully glanced at her and then smiled. She was asleep, as predicted, and she looked so darn cute in her pink pajamas, all squished down into the pillows.

He turned off the TV and moved all of their stuff, then pulled back the covers and eased her down into bed.

When he leaned over to kiss her forehead, she murmured something he couldn't understand as he pulled up.

"I am so falling in love with you, girl. Please love me back," he whispered.

He turned off the lights as he went, leaving the nightlight on in the adjoining bath, and carried the remnants of their party back to the kitchen and cleaned it up.

The house was quiet as he walked through the rooms. He paused in the living room and pulled back the drapes to look out.

The streetlights illuminated.

The shadows hid what was within them.

He thought back to his meeting with Elliot Graham.

"Okay, Janie. I got the message. I'm supposed to stay in Blessings, so here I am. If I'm not supposed to search for you anymore, then come find me."

He let the drapes fall shut and went upstairs, pausing again outside Melissa's door.

"Sleep well, sweetheart. There won't always be a door between us."

Once in his own bedroom, he checked his phone before putting it on the charger. No calls. No texts. Nobody back home missed him, which made the decision to stay here even easier. He would have to go back to tie up the loose ends of his old life, but in his heart he was already gone.

The next day at noon, Granny's Country Kitchen was inundated with people in their Sunday best, all planning to attend Niles Holland's funeral but grabbing some food before the two o'clock service began.

The conversations were mostly focused on the

spectacular showing the widow's family had made last night, without noticing there were no comments on the passing of Niles. No one knew anything about his personal life. They'd only known the public side of him.

It was just after 1:30 p.m. when the dining room began to clear out. All of the waitresses were exhausted and sitting together at a back table eating lunch.

Lovey was too tired to eat as she went into the kitchen. Her hair was in a frazzled halo around her face, and she was dragging her feet.

There were beads of sweat across Mercy's brow, the fry cook's apron looked like he was wearing a little bit of everything he'd cooked, and there wasn't a dry thread on the dishwasher's clothes, but the commercial dishwasher was humming right along.

"Just look at us! Have you ever seen such a crowd?" Lovey said. She pointed at Mercy. "Child, get something cold to drink and step outside in the alley a minute and cool yourself off. Elvis, for the good Lord's sake, put on a clean apron." Then she eyed Chet and grinned. "What happened to you?"

"I fell. I don't wanna talk about it," he muttered.

Her expression was instantly replaced with concern. "Are you hurt anywhere?"

"Nothin' but my pride, Miss Lovey. I'm fine."

"Do you have any dry clothes here?" she asked.

"I have a T-shirt with a bad word on it, and some shorts, but—"

Lovey blinked. Mercy giggled, and Elvis snorted beneath his breath.

"Exactly what word is on that shirt?" Lovey asked.

Chet looked nervous. "You want me to actually say it? Like, aloud?"

Lovey glared. "Son, if you're gonna walk around wearing a socially unacceptable shirt, you gotta have the balls to pull it off. What's the damn word?"

Chet's face turned a very girlie shade of pink.

"It says *I GIVE A FUCK.*"

Lovey rolled her eyes. "Turn it wrong-side out, make sure you have one of your rubber aprons over it when you go bus tables in the dining room, and don't let this happen again."

"Yes, ma'am. I mean, no, ma'am," Chet said, and then took off to the employee lounge as if he was being chased.

Lovey looked at Mercy, and Mercy looked at Elvis.

Chet was stripping off his clothes when he heard them laugh. He groaned. They were never going to let him live this down.

While laughter ensued at Granny's, the people rapidly filling the pews at the Baptist church were respectfully quiet. From the first ones seated to those still coming in, it was impossible for them not to notice how many pews up front had been saved for the family.

Curiosity made tongues wag, and the room was fairly humming from the energy of the whispers among those gathered.

At straight-up 2:00 p.m., the pianist struck a chord.

"Please rise," the pastor said, and much rustling of clothes and scooting of feet ensued before a sudden silence blanketed the room.

Barb Holland entered wearing a stark-black dress without a single piece of jewelry save her wedding ring. She was escorted by her father, Jake Austin, and then the family behind her.

The people who'd been at the visitation the night before recognized the family who'd been with her then, but today there were more...so many more. All in black. In designer clothes. And more diamonds than you could shake a stick at. And they just kept coming.

By the time the last one was seated, ten whole pews on the left-hand side of the church were full. It was the largest gathering of any one family the town of Blessings had ever seen at a funeral. Their estimation of Niles and Barbara Holland was forever changed. And for the time it took to witness the service honoring the man in the casket, no one thought of how he'd gotten there. Just that there were so many people united in grief who'd come to honor the man they knew and loved.

CHAPTER 10

DURING THE ENSUING WEEK, MELISSA DEAN BOUGHT A new car—a blue Chevrolet Equinox—and the people of Blessings became more and more preoccupied with the fact that their supermarket no longer had a name.

For as long as anyone could remember, when they needed groceries they would say "going to the Piggly Wiggly." *But that store was gone now.* Now pig logo was missing, as was the big sign across the front. It didn't seem logical to them to just say "going to the store," because there were all kinds of stores in town.

They just wanted to know who owned it now. They needed a name on that store to replace that big ugly unpainted space where the Piggly Wiggly name used to be.

The clerks at the store didn't know, either. The first time a stranger showed up with their paychecks, they thought he must be the new owner, but he quickly assured them he was only the accountant delivering payroll.

Then a painting company showed up and spray-painted the entire exterior of the store a robin's-egg blue. The color alone caused a bit of a ruckus. They'd never seen a grocery store painted a color like that. Not that it mattered, they would add. But in a small town, people like familiarity. Change was a hard thing to accept, but after a couple of days, the color began to grow on them.

Since the season was going into late fall, the first employees showing up to work at the store were now arriving in the dark. Then one morning a few days later, they were driving to work and coming up Main when they saw an enormous image of a royal crown lit against the night in white and red neon. And when they realized it was at the store, they got excited.

As they drove up and began parking, they could now see the name CROWN GROCERS in giant orange 3-D letters on the front of the building. And the big yellow crown outlined in neon had been mounted between the two words.

The supermarket finally had a name.

The employees decided it had a nice ring to it, and they liked the logo. It would all look good during the day, and at night the neon lights illuminating the crown would make it impossible to miss.

Before the day was over, nearly everyone in Blessings had made a point to drive by and check out the new sign. But it was the notice posted on the entrance doors, announcing an official lighting of the crown tonight after dark, that caught their fancy. The fact that refreshments would also be furnished turned it into an event. The people in Blessings liked events, and this one sounded like fun.

As the day was coming to an end and the sun began sinking below the hills around them, people began to arrive. They brought their folding chairs and began gathering into little groups, already in the party spirit. It wasn't long afterward that employees from the store came out and set up three long tables end to end, then began carrying out tray after tray of crown-shaped sugar cookies with yellow icing. Then they added another couple of tables a short distance away with hot coffee and cold pop.

The closer it came to sundown, the more people arrived,

until the parking lot was full and people were walking in from the streets. Between the party-like atmosphere and the kids running about, the place was a minefield of energy.

Sully and Melissa were sitting on one of the exterior benches outside the supermarket, drinking coffee and eating cookies when Elliot Graham walked up with a cookie in his hand.

"May I join you?" he asked.

"We'd love it!" Melissa said, and scooted down a bit so Elliot had plenty of room to sit.

Pleased with his venture out into a public forum, Elliot sat down beside Sully and took a bite of the cookie.

"Mmmm," he said. "I taste a hint of citrus in the cookie. Lemon, I believe."

"I think I chewed and swallowed mine too fast to get anything but sweet," Sully said. "But they sure are good."

"Agreed," Elliot said, but his eyes were sparkling as he looked around at all the people. "I am amazed at such a crowd. I don't think I knew there were this many people in Blessings."

"Some of them are rural customers," Melissa said, then pointed to a couple near the cookie table. "There's Jake and Laurel Lorde. They don't live in Blessings. And that's their daughter, Bonnie, between them."

"Amazing," Elliot said. "My hesitation to mingle has only exacerbated the isolation I'd put myself in. I need to do better. I think I have been missing out."

"And I'm just learning what Blessings is all about," Sully said. "All I know is I like it."

"Of course you do," Elliot said. "It's where you're supposed to be now."

Then he dusted the cookie crumbs from his fingers and stood. "Thank you for the company," he said, and disappeared in the crowd.

"He seems like a really sweet little man," Melissa said.

Sully grinned. "According to him, he and I will be great friends."

Melissa smiled. "Really? I love that!"

Sully leaned over and kissed her. "And I love you."

She blinked. "We've never said that before."

Melissa's features were blurring in the growing dusk, but she was already imprinted on his heart.

"Don't you think it was about time?" he asked.

She nodded. "I think it's past time." She threaded her fingers through his. "Johnny Raines was my first love, and Sully Raines will be my last. I can't see my future without you in it. Love you forever."

He grinned. "My bed or yours?"

"What's wrong with both?" Melissa asked.

"Hot damn," Sully said. "They need to get this show on the road so we can go home."

"I'm good with now," Melissa said. "Good thing we parked on the street."

"Definitely a good thing," Sully said.

They walked out of the parking lot hand in hand.

On the other side of the crowd, Peanut and Ruby were visiting with Lovey. She'd closed Granny's up early so all her employees could attend.

"How are the repairs going on your house?" Ruby asked.

"I'd say they're more than two-thirds of the way finished. I love staying in your house, Sister, but it will be good to get home," Lovey said.

"Something to look forward to," Peanut added, and then sidestepped around two little boys who were running amok. "I'll bet their parents have no idea where they are."

Ruby pointed. "There comes a couple with worried looks on their faces."

"They went thataway!" Peanut yelled.

The man gave him a grateful glance and took off running.

A young woman passed between Peanut and his line of sight—a red-haired stranger in hiking gear, with a large backpack on her back. She was eating one cookie and carrying another, likely thinking how she'd lucked into some free food, and he didn't give her another thought.

Vesta and Vera Conklin were at the back of the parking lot, hanging out with Mabel Jean, who was the nail tech at the salon. The air was beginning to feel cooler, which spurred a discussion of the annual Fall Festival at the school gymnasium.

"Are you girls going in costume?" Mabel Jean asked.

"Of course. That's part of the fun," Vera said. "Are you?"

"If I can figure out how to make it, I want to go as a big bottle of red sparkle nail polish."

"How fun!" Vesta said.

"What are you two going to be this year?" Mabel Jean asked.

"Sherlock Holmes and Watson," Vesta said.

Mabel Jean laughed. "I can't wait to see."

And then on cue, someone inside the store turned on the lights, and both the store and the crown lit up.

The crowd oohed and ahhed in unison, not unlike the gasps of delight when the Fourth of July fireworks at the park began. Cell phones came out and began flashing all over the parking lot as people began taking pictures before beginning to disperse.

The checkers were getting overtime pay for staying past the normal closing time, and when the crowd began to disperse, quite a few turned into customers and went inside. It was almost 11:00 p.m. when the last customer left.

Wilson Turner, who'd been the manager for the Piggly Wiggly, was still the manager but with a raise in pay.

As soon as the last till was turned in for the night and the night deposit was ready to go, he turned off all but the night-lights inside the Crown and locked up on his way out.

On Chief Pittman's orders, the deputy on night duty was waiting for Wilson in the parking lot and escorted him to the night deposit drop-off at the bank.

Wilson waved his thanks and drove off. The grand opening of the Crown had been a huge success. But like everyone else in town, he was curious about the identity of the new owner.

The drive home was comfortably silent for Sully and Melissa. She was wondering if she even remembered how this went, and Sully was wondering how he would stack up beside the husband she'd lost.

Once inside the house, Sully set the security alarm while

Melissa went upstairs. She stepped into her darkened room to leave her purse and jacket, and was kicking off her shoes when there was a sound behind her.

Sully was standing in the doorway, silhouetted by the hall light behind him.

"The house is secure," he said.

Seeing him there and hearing his voice made her ache.

"You do realize I have no freaking idea how to be seductive," she said.

He walked to her, then took her in his arms.

"You still don't get it, do you? You turn me on with little more than a look. Your laugh makes my pulse kick, and your tears destroy me. I don't want a striptease. I just want you."

Melissa put her arms around his neck and leaned into him.

"I'm already yours," she said.

When Sully began unbuttoning her blouse, Melissa unfastened her jeans and let them fall to the floor. Her blouse landed on top of the jeans, followed by her bra. She stood before him wearing nothing but a lacy pair of black hipster briefs, and watched as he came out of his clothes until he stood naked before her.

For a few moments, neither moved. Then Sully pushed the briefs down her hips. She stepped out of them and walked straight into his arms.

"So damn beautiful," he whispered, and then took her to bed.

She stretched out beneath him, welcoming the warmth of his mouth on her lips. She locked her hands at the back of his neck and pulled him closer as their kisses grew longer, the intensity deepening by the moment.

When he shifted from her mouth to her body, she felt a sense of urgency in his touch. She'd forgotten the pleasure of that quickening in her belly and the growing ache for more.

She could feel the warmth of his breath upon her skin, and the pounding beat of his heart beneath her palms. When he gently pushed his knee between her legs, she moved to let him in.

The joining was so much more than she'd expected. Her eyes were awash in tears before she knew it. So long. It had been so long. And when he began to move, she wrapped her legs around his waist and fell into the rhythm of love.

Sully had lost all sense of time, but he could feel the urgency in her body as her muscles began to tense beneath his touch.

When her breathing shifted into a soft moan against his ear, he rocked harder, faster, until the moan turned into a cry of disbelief.

It was the sign he'd been waiting for.

He gave up all he was to the woman in his arms.

They made love twice more before morning. Once in a heated rush, and the last time just before daylight in the confines of his shower with her back against the wall and the water pouring down upon their heads.

On the same morning, Barb Holland was standing out on the back veranda of her home with a cup of coffee between her hands, her gaze on the horizon. There had been a faint glow of light in the east for a while now, but as she watched, the sky began to glow in shades of violet and gold, and then purple with shades of pink.

When the sun finally moved into sight, the colors from before were suddenly lit from within. Tears blurred Barb's vision. This was the last sunrise she would see from this place.

The furnishings she intended to keep were already in a PODS storage unit on the way to Dallas. She still had a house to strip down and remodel before she'd move in there, but it was a positive plan, and Barb desperately needed a plan.

Finally, she walked back into the house, turned off the old Keurig machine and cleaned it up to leave behind, then loaded two suitcases of clothes into her car.

There was a lump in her throat as she came back into the house to do a walk-through, making sure she wasn't leaving anything of value behind. What she hadn't expected to feel was the small niggling emotion of relief.

Yes, Niles was gone, and her heart was broken. She'd loved him for so long, she wasn't sure yet how much of herself was left. But there was one inescapable fact that couldn't be ignored.

Never again would she put a drunk to bed.

Never again would she worry when he left the house in a less-than-stable condition.

Never again would there be excuses to be made and signs of his addiction to be hidden.

Niles's death had shocked her. It had broken her heart. But it had also freed her. She just had to find a way out of the guilt she felt for being glad it was over.

She locked the door as she walked out, then left the key under the mat. The Realtor would be by later this morning to put up the For Sale sign.

What the town of Blessings had yet to discover was that Barb had given her lawyer, Peanut Butterman, one last job. She had deeded all fifteen of their rental houses to the present occupants. It was a gift to them in Niles's name, and she would never have thought of it if it hadn't been for Melissa Dean. It felt good, and it was the right thing to do.

She got in the car, then glanced at the box buckled up in the seat beside her. Her destination was Dallas, and Niles's ashes were riding shotgun.

Danner Amos was eating breakfast when his cell phone rang. He started to let it go to voicemail, then noticed it was the number to his rental properties and got up from the table to answer.

"Dan Amos speaking," he said, then heard a woman's voice.

"Mr. Amos, I understand you have rental properties."

"Yes, I do. What did you have in mind?" he asked.

"Do you have any furnished properties?"

"A couple, but both are only one-bedroom, one-bath properties."

"Perfect. Would it be possible to see them today?"

"Sure. I can give you both addresses and meet you there."

"I'm on foot. I've been backpacking across country, and with colder weather already an issue up north, I decided to stop for a while…maybe winter here. What are they renting for?"

He named the price, then added, "Where are you now? I could easily just come pick you up to show you the places."

"I would appreciate that," she said. "I'm actually sitting on a bench in front of Crown supermarket. You can't miss me. I'll be the only redheaded female with a backpack."

Dan chuckled. "Give me about fifteen minutes. I'll be the dark-haired guy driving a truck that says Amos Rental Properties."

"See you then," she said.

Dan went back into the kitchen to finish breakfast.

"We may have another renter soon," he said.

Alice looked up. "Really? Do we know them?"

"Not unless we know a redheaded woman backpacking cross-country," he said, and took his last bite of toast and jelly, then chewed and swallowed.

"How many empty houses do you have?" Alice asked.

"I only have two of what she's looking for. One-bedroom furnished."

"Oh...that makes sense... Backpackers wouldn't be traveling with furniture," she said, and laughed. "Do you want more coffee, honey?"

"No. I'd better grab those keys and get moving. I'm picking her up in front of the Crown. See you later," he said, and kissed her goodbye.

It didn't take him long to get to the Crown, and the woman was right where she said she'd be. He stopped in front of the bench and got out.

"I'm Dan," he said. "You can put your backpack in the truck bed if you want, and we can lock it in the truck when we're seeing the properties."

"I'm Cathy Terry. Thank you for the ride," she said, and took off her backpack and dropped it in as she passed, then got in the truck.

"One of these properties is closer to shopping than the other, so since you're afoot, it might be more convenient for you. I'll show it to you first, and then the other one."

She nodded without comment, sitting quietly as they drove. There were two blocks off Main when Dan turned to the left.

"It's the small blue house with the white shutters," he said.

"I like blue," Cathy said. When they parked, she got out, put her backpack into her seat, and followed Dan to the front door and then inside.

"The furniture is fairly new and in good condition. This TV works, but it's not hooked up to cable. You'd have to do that. All the properties have monthly pest control." He led the way into the kitchen. "Gas stove, and ice maker in the fridge. Garbage disposal in the sink." He kept walking through the house pointing out amenities, and Cathy followed without comment until they got back into the living room.

"So, this property doesn't have a security system?" she asked.

"No, but it's easy enough to have your own put in if you want. I have no problem with that."

She nodded. "I'll take it."

"Uh, you don't want to see the other one first?" Dan asked.

"No. This is good. Like you said, closer to stores. How do I get utilities turned on?"

"They're already on," Dan said. "I'll give you numbers to call to get them switched over into your name."

"Can I move in now?" she asked. "I have cash."

Dan blinked. He'd been a lawyer too long not to see some warning signs. Questions about security. Paying cash.

"I have the paperwork in my truck. I'll need to see some photo ID."

She pulled a wallet out of an inner pocket inside her jacket. "I have credit cards, too, but I don't use them," she said, and handed him her driver's license and a credit card with a platinum rating.

"I'm going to ask you two questions. And before you answer, I want you to know that in my other life, I was the most sought-after criminal attorney in Texas. So don't lie."

"Ask away," she said.

"Are you running from the law?"

"No. But I am running from an abusive ex-husband with as much power in his world as you had in yours. So if you don't want me here, just say so. I'd like to be somewhere else before dark."

Dan heard both truth and anger in her voice and nodded. "I'm going to get the paperwork, and I'll bring your backpack with me. Make yourself at home."

In another part of town, Sully and Melissa were moving his things into her bedroom, but it was taking a while. The random kisses, and brushing up against each other as they worked, reflected an unconscious need to touch the reality of where love had taken them.

"I think that's everything," Sully said. "There are only a few keepsakes I want from my apartment back in Kansas City. I'll donate the rest to Habitat."

"Are you sure?" Melissa asked. "This is a huge house. There is plenty of room to incorporate things you want to keep within it."

"You're the only thing from my past I want to keep. The furniture is stuff. I have no emotional connection to any of it. My lease will be up in a couple of months, so there's no real rush for me to go back and deal with it."

Melissa paused in the act of cleaning out another drawer. "You don't have to do stuff alone anymore, and neither do I. If you want a travel companion, you've got me."

You've got me. It was something he hadn't had in his personal life in a long, long time.

"Melissa…you have no idea what those words mean to me," he said, and put his arms around her.

They stood within their embrace, not talking, not moving. Just absorbing the fact that this was real.

Then Sully's phone rang and the moment ended. He picked it up from the bed, but when he saw the caller ID, he smiled.

"It's Elliot."

"I do believe you have charmed him right out of his hermit tendencies," Melissa said.

Sully sat down on the side of the bed to answer.

"Hello."

"Good morning, Sully. This is Elliot."

"Good morning to you, too," Sully said. "What's going on?"

"If you're not busy around ten or so this morning, would you mind stopping by the house? There's something I want to give you."

"Sure, I can do that," Sully said. "I'll see you then."

"Excellent," Elliot said, and hung up in Sully's ear.

Sully was getting used to the old man's eccentricities.

"So, I've been invited to his house at ten this morning. He has something he wants to give me."

"I can't wait to see what it might be," Melissa said. "And on another front…are you ready for breakfast? I haven't been hungry for food this early in the morning in years."

Sully grinned. "It's all that good sex."

"Maybe…but we need to get out of this room before it happens again because I need sustenance first."

"I'll make pancakes," Sully said as they walked out into the hall.

Melissa sighed. "I keep forgetting how multifaceted you are. Handsome, heroic, lover extraordinaire, and the man can cook. Thank you, Lord."

"Thank Station 12. I learned to cook under their tutelage. Mother wouldn't let me in her kitchen. She said I made a mess."

"I don't know about making one," Melissa said. "But I know from when we were kids that you *were* a mess."

He grinned. "Hey. I had a reputation to maintain."

Melissa went to the Crown to shop for groceries just before Sully left to go see Elliot. He could still smell the scent of her shampoo as he was putting on his shoes, then thought of that shower they'd shared and how gorgeous she was soaking wet.

One glance at the time hastened Sully's exit. He grabbed his keys from the dresser and hurried down to his car.

It was straight-up ten o'clock when he pulled into the driveway and got out. He was whistling beneath his breath as he walked up the steps and rang the doorbell. Before his finger was off the bell, the door swung inward.

"You're here!" Elliot said. "And on time! A timely man is a successful man," he added. "Come, come."

Sully grinned as he followed the little man through a maze of hallways until they were in a room at the back of the house. One whole wall was all windows and filled with so much natural light that it almost hurt his eyes.

"This is the most amazing room I've ever seen," Sully said.

"This is where I paint," Elliot said.

"You're an artist?" Sully asked.

Elliot smiled. "Back in my day, a most successful one. You might even say I was famous in certain circles."

Sully's eyes widened. "Wow. Apologies for my ignorance, sir. Now I'm going to have to do a little research to see what that's all about."

Elliot led him over to a painting on an easel in the center of the room.

"This is for you," he said.

It was a portrait of a young woman nursing the baby she was cradling. Her face was in partial profile, but the Madonna-like smile on her lips and the tender curve of her cheek as she watched the baby nurse were so lifelike Sully half expected the girl to look up.

"She's alive," Sully said softly, then he began to notice details. The baby's dark hair. The red and blue embroidery on the sleeves of her blouse.

And then he saw the necklace resting just above the

burgeoning curves of milk-filled breasts, and without thinking, he moved closer, his focus entirely on the silver pendant hanging from a fragile silver chain.

His head came up, his heart pounding from the shock of what he'd seen.

"Who is this? Why are you giving it to me?"

"Because it's you and your mother. I saw it the day when you put the letter in my hand."

"You saw it? What do you mean, you saw it?" Sully asked.

"In my head. I see lots of things in my head. Some have already happened. Some are yet to come. That's Janie Chapman with her baby boy, Johnny. Is that also your name?" Elliot asked.

Sully was in shock. "You painted this for me?"

"Yes, of course. Spirit wanted you to have it."

"Oh my God. Elliot...I don't know what to say. This is beautiful. She's beautiful. And that necklace around her neck... I have it."

"Your father gave it to her when they were still together. Do you know what it is?" Elliot asked.

"Other than it's some kind of cross, no."

"It's a Byzantine cross. That's a symbol of the ancient Greeks. And since your father's name is Adamos, which is also a Greek name, I would say it all fits! I love it when a thing comes together like that, don't you?"

Sully heard Elliot talking, but he could only nod. He wanted the girl to look up. He wanted to see her face-to-face. He wanted her to tell him what had happened. How did so much love become displaced?

When he noticed the baby's hand was fiercely clutching his mother's little finger as he nursed, tears welled.

Elliot took a step closer to Sully. "I think this is why your parents didn't tell you about her. There's a soul connection between mother and child, and I think it frightened them."

Sully tore his gaze away from the painting and looked straight into Elliot's eyes. They were sparkling—almost dancing—as if they'd seen the secrets of the universe but weren't ever going to tell.

"You know how much this means to me. *Thank you* will never be enough. How freaked out would you be if I hugged you?" Sully asked.

Elliot chuckled. "I believe I could bear it," he said, and when Sully wrapped his arms around him, Elliot returned the hug with a little pat on the back.

"Thank you, Elliot. Thank you from the bottom of my heart," Sully said.

Elliot beamed. "You are most welcome. You might want to get it insured one of these days. My pieces still bring enough money to make it worth a thief's while, and since this work is recent..."

"It's already invaluable to me. What would you suggest I insure it for?"

"Oh...since it's a new one, at least a hundred thousand."

Sully's eyebrows went up, but he managed to nod.

"Is it okay to take it like this? I can lay it down in the back seat."

"Yes, and it's ready to hang. I'd advise not in direct sunlight, although the painting does not need light to be displayed because I painted light into them." Elliot took it from the easel and put it into Sully's hands. "I'll escort you to the door," he said, and back they went through the maze of halls and into the foyer. Then he opened the front door. "Enjoy!" he said.

"That's an understatement," Sully said as he crossed the threshold and headed for his car.

The door shut behind him again, but not as abruptly, and he knew without looking that Elliot was at the window. Sully settled the painting safely in the back seat, then got in and drove home at a snail's pace, taking turns with great caution, as if the baby in the painting was behind him, alive and kicking.

CHAPTER 11

SULLY GOT HOME WITH THE PAINTING, PROPPED IT AGAINST a chair, and then ran upstairs to get his necklace. Not knowing where to hang the painting without asking Melissa first, he left it where he could see it and sat motionless on the sofa, trying to wrap his head around the journey he'd already been on with this young woman—a woman he didn't remember.

Melissa pulled up beneath the portico so she could go directly through the utility room and into the kitchen with her purchases. She was on her way inside with the first sack when Sully came loping through the kitchen, lifted the bag out of her arms, and gave her a peck on the cheek as he set it on the counter.

"How much more?" he asked.

"Just a couple," Melissa said.

"I'll get them. You get the door," he said, and brought the bags inside.

Melissa started taking things out to be put away, but Sully stopped her.

"What needs to go in the refrigerator?" he asked.

"Only the things in that sack," she said, pointing to the first one she'd brought in.

"Then let's empty that first before we do the rest. There's something I want to show you."

"Oh, that's right! Elliot gave you something? What was it?"

"I can't tell you. You have to see," he said, and began putting away milk, butter, and cheese, while she put up the fresh produce and meat.

As soon as they were finished, he led her into the living room.

"Stop here, and close your eyes."

She laughed but did as he asked. "What on earth?"

"You'll see," Sully said. He went to get the painting. "Okay, you can look now," he said, and held it up in front of him.

The smile was still on Melissa's face when she opened her eyes, and then she saw the portrait and gasped.

"Oh, Sully, that's beautiful. Who are they? Why did he give it to you?"

"He said it's my mother and me. He said he *saw it in his head* the day I showed him the letter she'd left for me. He said Spirit wanted me to have it. I don't know how that man's head works or what he hears and sees, but I will never doubt his word again as long as I live. See that necklace around the girl's neck?"

Melissa nodded.

Sully leaned the portrait against the wall and pulled the necklace out of his pocket and handed it to her.

"This was in the envelope with my birth certificate. According to the note I found, Janie left it by my crib with a note stating it was meant for me."

Melissa was stunned. "Oh, Sully! Oh, sweetheart! It's the same, right down to the unusual design on the edge of the cross!"

Sully nodded. "Elliot said my father gave it to her."

Melissa handed him the necklace. "Bring the painting, and let's find the best place to hang it."

Sully dropped the necklace into his shirt pocket, picked up the painting, and followed her into the living room.

"It needs to be in a prominent place," Melissa said. "Somewhere in plain sight that lends itself best to the story it's telling. It's beautiful on its own, but it's also such a personal thing for you." She cupped the side of his face, and when his gaze shifted to her, she had no words for what she saw. "I can't imagine how you're feeling. I have no concept of what it would be like to find out everything about my past was a lie."

"It was a shock at first. Now, I just want to find her."

"If Elliot told you to stay in Blessings, I'm taking that as a very positive sign," Melissa said.

"After this, I'll never question his veracity."

They began to circle the room with the painting, holding it up in first one place and then another, but they kept going back to the blank wall above an antique writing table. It wasn't in direct sunlight, and it would be visible both going into the room and walking out. And they could easily see it from the sofa, as well.

"I still like this best," Melissa said. "What do you think?"

"I think it's perfect," Sully said. "I'll get some picture hangers later and hang it up before supper."

"I think I have some, if they're large enough for the weight. Let's go see," she said.

He set the painting against the writing table and went with her to the utility room. She opened the doors to a cabinet full of little drawers, then pulled a couple of them open before she found the one she was looking for.

"Here are all of the ones Elmer had on hand. He kept a little bit of everything in this house."

Sully dug through an assortment of little packets until he found one of hangers with a twenty-pound weight limit and took it out. Then he saw a hammer on another shelf and took it, too.

"This should work," he said.

A few minutes later, the painting was on the wall. Sully stepped back to look at it again, then turned to Melissa and hugged her tight.

"You are the best woman I've ever known. Thank you for letting me into your life."

"Oh, Sully, sweetheart...I don't think I ever closed the door on our young love, because it was far too easy to welcome you home."

Her lips were slightly parted and warm as he kissed her, but when he pulled back, he got lost in the clear green gaze of her eyes.

"Are you thinking about sex?" he asked.

She nodded.

"Then hold that thought. Among other things, we have groceries to put up."

"Held and saved," she said. "After that pancake breakfast, we kind of skipped eating at noon. Are you hungry? I bought some sandwich stuff."

"Sounds good. I'll empty sacks. You do sandwiches."

"Deal," Melissa said.

Downtown, Peanut's secretary, Betty Purejoy, was getting the conference room ready for his 3:00 p.m. appointment with the people who lived in Niles Holland's rental houses.

She and Peanut had been working on the transfers of

ownership ever since Barb Holland contacted him and finally had the deeds and the paperwork ready. Peanut glanced up at the clock, then went to look for Betty. He found her in the hall, pushing a cart full of more folding chairs toward the conference room.

"Let me get those," he said, and pushed it the rest of the way down the hall and into the conference room.

By the time they were finished setting up, it was a quarter to three. Betty was back at her desk, and Peanut was in the conference room pacing, something he always did before going to court. It wasn't as though any of this would be bad news, but it was life-changing information for some very fortunate people.

Right on time, people began coming into the room. They looked nervous and anxious, and the solemn expressions on their faces told him they were braced for the worst.

"Come in and take a seat," Peanut said, motioning toward the chairs encircling the large oblong table. Eight people came in at once, and while they were seating themselves, seven more arrived.

Peanut stood up with the list of names in his hands.

"I'm going to read off names, and if you're here, just call out. I don't want to start this until everyone involved in this is represented."

One of the men held up his hand. "Uh, Mr. Butterman, I'm Delroy Sanders, and this is all of us from the fifteen houses Mr. Holland owns."

"Thank you, Delroy. Then I'll begin. This is all straightforward information. There are no decisions to be made. No deadlines to be met." He cleared his throat. "Barbara Holland, Mr. Holland's widow, has signed over the deeds to the properties you are living in as a way to honor her husband's passing. As soon as we sign the papers, you will be the owners of the homes you've been renting."

The collective gasp was loud, followed by cries of disbelief and joy as Peanut continued.

"Realizing this gift would come with costs you might not be prepared to pay, Mrs. Holland has also awarded each of you the sum of money needed to pay for one full year of property insurance, and the amount of money each of you will need for the property tax. That gives you a whole year to figure out how to adjust your budgets to meet the costs the following year."

Delroy held up his hand again, his voice shaking with emotion as he spoke.

"We all thought we were going to be told the houses would be sold. We didn't know if we'd have to move, or if the rent might go up. You don't know what a blessing this is for us. Having a home free and clear of rent or mortgage payments is nothing short of a dream come true for all of us. Thank you, sir."

Peanut smiled. "It's Mrs. Holland you have to thank. I only delivered the news. Stay seated, if you will, while Betty and I get situated. I'll call your names one at a time. You will go to Betty, sign the final papers, and get instructions on what to do next. And congratulations!"

The room erupted in more cries of delight as he went across the hall to get her. Two hours later, the last renter walked out the door. Betty stood.

"This has been a good day," Peanut said.

"The best," she said, and went back into the office.

It was just after 3:00 p.m. when a thunderstorm rolled in, warning all in its path by the grumbling sound of thunder and a sudden rush of wind that rattled the turning leaves off the trees all over town.

The cover of someone's trash can went rolling down the street in the neighborhood near the elementary school, rattling with every turn.

Two young boys on bicycles rode past it, pedaling hard and fast, trying to get home before it began to rain. When they turned the corner toward home, they saw their mama standing out on the porch and looking up at the sky. When she saw them coming, she waved at them to hurry.

Shoppers coming out of the Crown saw the sky and began to push their carts faster toward their cars, anxious to get home and unload their purchases before they got wet.

Granny's had a quick influx of customers who wanted a place to hang out until the storm passed, and the shop owners who had displays out in front of their stores began pulling them inside. School had just been dismissed, and teachers were trying to get the bus riders loaded and on their way. Bike riders were leaving school in all directions, while others who normally walked home were being picked up by parents or catching a ride with friends.

And Cathy Terry was suddenly grateful for the roof over her head.

Sully and Melissa had been working outside, cleaning up flower beds at the back of the house, when Sully felt the wind change. He looked up at the dark clouds boiling overhead and frowned.

"We need to get inside," he said.

Melissa looked up. "Oh wow."

She began grabbing the gardening tools as Sully gathered up the garbage bags of leaves and debris. The wind was whipping the limbs on the trees as they dumped everything inside the garden shed and ran for the house.

The first raindrops fell just as they made it to the back porch. They went into the utility room to kick off their shoes and then upstairs to clean up and change.

The wind that came with the deluge was blasting rain against the windows. Melissa shivered as she dug through a shelf in the walk-in closet for some sweats.

"Are you cold, baby?" Sully said, as he pulled a clean T-shirt over his head.

"More unnerved than anything," Melissa said. "This sounds too reminiscent of the hurricane. I may never be over the memories of those days or the weeks that ensued. It crippled Blessings."

"You just need a good cuddle," he said, and wrapped his arms around her.

Melissa could hear the steady thump of his heartbeat against her ear as she snuggled into his embrace. In this short time, Sully had completely ruined her for ever living alone again. She loved the sound of his laugh, hearing his footsteps in the house, and making love with him.

She loved him. So much.

Night came early because of the storm. Streetlights were already burning, and Melissa wasn't the only resident of Blessings who was remembering the onslaught of Hurricane Fanny.

Even though the central heat was on, the night called for comfort food—something of sustenance, something satisfying and warm.

So Melissa made potato soup and corn bread for their supper and introduced Sully to the Southern treat of pouring sorghum molasses onto a second piece of hot buttered corn bread for dessert.

"How do you like it?" she asked as the first bite went in his mouth.

His eyes widened. He nodded his head and gave her a thumbs-up as he chewed.

Pleased that he liked it, she buttered her own piece of corn bread, doused it in sorghum, too, and savored every sticky-sweet bite that she took. After they finished, Melissa was gathering up the dishes to carry them to the sink when Sully turned around and took them out of her hands.

"Honey, that was such a good meal. You cooked. I'll clean up and join you in the living room as soon as I've finished."

"Are you sure?" Melissa asked. "I could help—"

"I'm sure. Scat," Sully said.

"I'm scatting," she said, and took herself out of the room as Sully went to work.

Melissa sat down in the living room, kicked off her shoes and curled her feet up beneath her, and wondered what kind of damage this thunderstorm would leave behind.

It was almost 8:00 p.m. as she turned on the television and found a program to watch, then glanced up at the painting they'd hung earlier. The Madonna-and-child feel of it tugged at her heart. Elliot Graham's skill as an artist was evident in this portrait, but it was his skill as a psychic that floored her. She'd heard rumors about him, but never really believed them until now. This painting had changed her whole perception of his abilities. He was something special.

Then Sully walked up behind the sofa where she was sitting, kissed the back of her neck, then whispered in her ear.

"Hey, good looking, are you saving the seat beside you for anyone?"

"You know it's for you," she said, and patted the cushions.

When he climbed over the back and slid down into the seat beside her, she laughed.

"Shades of Johnny Raines. What made you pull that move out of your hat?" she said.

He grinned. "I didn't think you would remember."

Melissa shook her head. "I remember my mother nearly had a stroke when you did that at our house."

He put his arm around her shoulders and pulled her close.

"She got over it, though, before I left," Sully said.

Melissa sighed. "She liked you, that's why. I wish she was still alive to see this…to see us. She would love it."

"Do you ever think about what might have happened between us if you hadn't moved?" Sully asked.

"I think we would have had babies. Now I'm too old."

"The world is full of babies," Sully said. "Before I came here, there was only one me and one you. Now there's us. I can't ask for anything more."

Melissa turned in his arms, crawled into his lap, and started kissing him. One thing led to another, and by the time the clock struck the hour again, they were in the floor, making love behind the sofa.

Hours later, and long after the thunderstorm had moved

out of the area, they were upstairs in bed, wrapped in each other's arms. The house was at peace.

Then Sully woke abruptly, thinking he'd heard the sound of alarms and sirens. He glanced quickly at Melissa. She was still asleep, but something didn't feel right. He reached for her, pulling her close into his arms, waiting for the thunder of his heartbeat to calm, until he finally felt safe enough to close his eyes.

He woke again to the sound of sirens, but it was daylight, and they were still screaming even as he was getting up to look out the window. He couldn't see any sign of smoke in that direction and guessed it might be ambulance sirens instead.

"What's going on?" Melissa asked as she rolled over.

"I can't tell," he said, and then crawled back into bed and pulled her into his arms. "Good morning, sweetheart," he said, and kissed the hollow at the base of her throat.

Melissa sighed and wrapped her arms around his neck. "You make it a good morning."

Sully stilled, absorbing the love in her voice and the gentleness in her touch. He knew, as well as he knew his own name, that nothing about them finding each other again was by chance. That soul-to-soul recognition of belonging was there between them. No matter how far apart, or how long the time, love finds a way home.

He lifted his head, kissed his way up to her lips, then after a time moved over her. Poised above her, hovering like a moth about to die in the flame, he took her. The joining was a pleasure and an ache, with a longing for more.

And so it began—like a courtship on the cusp of true love, the motion tentative, testing the rhythm, feeling the tension of muscles within, then giving up all hesitation to the need within them.

All sense of time faded into the need to burn, and then it happened. In the onrush of the climax washing through them, they forgot to breathe, and for the space of that little death, they were one.

The warning of an escaped convict came in an early-morning alert on Chief Pittman's cell phone from the Georgia State Police. An escapee by the name of Hoover Slade, who'd been incarcerated in the Coastal State Prison outside Savannah, was believed to be headed their way. He was to be considered armed and dangerous.

Lon immediately called the office. Travis Witty, the night dispatcher, would still be on duty.

"Blessings PD," Travis said.

"Travis, it's me. I need you to call in all of the deputies. We have an escapee presumed to be heading our way. I'm about to leave for the office now. I'll fill them in on what's happening when I get there."

"Yes, Chief," Travis said, and disconnected.

Lon pinned on his badge, dropped his weapon in the holster, and headed for the office, calling Mercy as he drove.

She answered, laughing. "You know this early in the morning my hands are sticky with dough and flour, so this better be important."

"It is, baby. We have an escapee from Coastal State

Prison who might be headed this way. His name is Hoover Slade. He grew up in the area, and he's considered armed and dangerous."

"Oh no! Are we in any danger?" Mercy asked.

"It's hard to say, but to be on the safe side, we're going to operate on the theory that we are. Better safe than sorry, which is why I called. Keep that back door in the kitchen locked until we get an all clear."

"Yes, yes, we will, and can we warn customers as they come in?" Mercy asked.

"Yes. Tell them to keep their doors locked today, whether they're home or not."

"Okay, and Lon, please be careful."

"I will, baby. Just take care. Love you."

"Love you, too," Mercy said. As soon as she hung up, she pointed at Elvis, the fry cook. "Lon just called. An escapee from Coastal State Prison might be headed this way. He said keep the back door locked today."

"Who in the world would get out of the state pen and run to Blessings?" Elvis muttered.

"Hoover Slade. Do you know of him?" Mercy said.

Elvis's attitude quickly shifted. "Oh hell... Excuse my language... Yes, he's known. He and his brother, Truman, have both done time. They grew up in the hills outside of Blessings. They still have an aunt who lives on the family homestead. I wouldn't put anything past either one of them. I'll lock the door."

Mercy checked the timer on what she had in the oven, then went out into the dining room to find Lovey.

After that, news spread quickly, and the added presence of more police on the street made the danger real.

CHAPTER 12

HOOVER SLADE WAS A DESPERATE MAN. HE'D GOTTEN himself into a mess with one of the other inmates that had started over a simple pack of cigarettes. Over a period of days the disagreement had escalated to Hoover receiving a death threat.

Telling the warden at Coastal State wouldn't change the danger he was in because if he squealed, someone else would take him out for being a rat. Even though he had less than two years left on his sentence, he wouldn't live to release day unless he ran. He took advantage of his trustee status and hid in a refrigerated delivery truck behind two huge stacks of boxes containing frozen chicken parts. When it left the prison, he went out with it. It was a cold ride into town, and the timing had to be perfect for him to get out before the driver found him.

The moment the driver pulled up and braked at the next delivery on his route, Hoover came out of the truck and ducked into an alley while the man was still in the cab.

Once he was out of sight of the driver, he began trying all of the delivery entrances in the alley until he found one unlocked. He couldn't believe his luck when he discovered he was in the employee break room of a laundry and cleaners. He needed out of his prison orange, and he'd just walked into a gold mine of clean clothes.

From where he was standing, he could see one person up front at the counter waiting on customers, two people in the back at the steam-cleaning machines, and two others folding laundry. And only feet away, there was an automated rack full of clean clothing. The noise from the steam cleaners was loud, but the music blasting from a nearby radio was deafening.

It was dark in the back of the store, so when Hoover slipped in behind the racks of clean clothes and began looking for some that would fit him, no one saw or heard a thing.

He grabbed a pair of jeans, a shirt, and a jacket, and ducked back into the little entryway and stripped. As soon as he was dressed, he began trying to get into the employee lockers to look for money, but they were all locked.

Then he heard voices coming toward the back and ran out into the alley before he got caught, wearing blue jeans, a black pullover shirt, the tan jacket, and his prison-issue black canvas slip-ons.

He dumped the orange jumpsuit in the first trash dumpster he passed and walked out onto the street. His clothes were clean, but he was broke and needed a ride.

Hoover walked for what felt like miles on his way out of the city. He was on the outskirts of Savannah when he saw a parking lot full of cars at a bar and grill.

"Bingo," he said, and headed into the lot, looking for an unlocked car.

It didn't take long to find one. When he got inside and shut the door, the first thing he did was check to see if the keys had been left behind the visor, or in the console, but no luck. Then he thought to look beneath the floor mat.

"Yes!" he said as he grabbed the keys and started the car. He guessed they would have security cameras outside, but he'd be long gone before the theft was discovered.

He was a couple of miles outside Savannah when he thought to look at the gas gauge. It had less than a quarter of a tank, which wasn't enough to get to where he needed to go.

"Son of a bitch!"

He dug through the console as he drove, looking for cash, and found a couple of quarters and a dime. Not close enough for a single gallon of gas, and now the fuel light was on, and had been for some time.

"Oh well, what the hell," Hoover muttered. "I'll figure something else out when the need arises." He kept heading to Blessings, taking care to stay under the speed limit at all times so he wouldn't be stopped.

He was already congratulating himself about reaching the Blessings city limit when the car began to sputter and jerk.

"Shit," Hoover said. He guided the car to the shoulder of the road and got out.

He put the key back under the mat, then crossed the road and went up into the trees, still moving toward Blessings. He was going to have to steal another car to get where he needed to go, and he had to do it quickly. If he could just get to Aunt Sugar's place, he could get some food and blankets. And the woods were nearly impenetrable. A stranger could get lost up in there and never be found. But he'd grown up there and knew where he could lie low until the hunt for him ended. Then he could go down on the other side and disappear. With one last glance toward the highway, he started to run.

Deputies were just beginning to arrive at the police station as Lon got back to his office. He stuck his head in the break room and saw two of his deputies making fresh coffee.

"Give me a couple of minutes, and I'll fill you in on what's happening," he said, then went up front. "Travis, did we have any kind of paperwork come in on Hoover Slade?" he asked.

"Yes, sir, just a few minutes ago. It's a rap sheet with his mug shot. I ran off some copies for you," Travis said, and got up to get them.

"Thanks," Lon said. "As soon as Avery arrives and clocks in, fill him in on what's happening, okay?"

"Yes, sir," Travis said.

Lon paused in the hall to scan the fax. He noticed Hoover had been identified on security footage stealing a car, and the info for the stolen vehicle had been added to the rap sheet, then glanced in the break room. The other deputies had arrived.

"Guys, come on into my office," he said. As soon as they walked in, he gave each of them a hard copy of the escapee's mug shot and rap sheet.

"We have an escapee from Coastal State reported to be headed this way, possibly in a stolen gray Ford Focus. The model and tag number are on your handout. Some of you are too new to know who this is, but the ones who've been on the job here for years will recognize him. Hoover Slade grew up in the hills above Blessings, and he still has family up there. I want a man on the highway coming in from the north to keep an eye out for that car. Deputy Ralph, you take that position."

"Yes, sir," Ralph said.

Lon continued. "I'll notify the schools to be on alert,

and if he's spotted in the area, they'll go on lockdown. I want another deputy patrolling the area around the schools nonstop. If you see anything suspicious, don't try to be a hero on your own. Call for backup. The rest of you patrol the town. Is that understood?"

"Yes, sir," they said.

"Okay, then get out there, and let's keep it safe in Blessings."

Lon sat back down at his desk and buzzed his dispatcher.

"This is Avery. Travis caught me up on what's happening. What do you need, Chief?"

"See if you can find a phone number for Sugar Slade. I need to notify her that Hoover is on the run."

"Yes, sir," Avery said.

Lon hung up, then called the county sheriff and notified him of the call he'd received. He started to get some coffee, then realized he hadn't made any for himself this morning and went to the break room to get some water. He had just poured it into his coffee maker and turned it on when Avery walked in.

"Chief, this is the only number I could find. It was in one of our old phone books from back in the day when everybody still used landlines. It may not be any good anymore."

"Thanks, Avery. If it's no good, I'll have to get an officer from county to go up and notify her."

"Yes, sir," Avery said, and went back to the front desk.

Lon sat down again, then used his landline to make the call. It rang once, then three more times before someone picked up.

"Hello. Who is this?"

Lon grinned. Sugar Slade's attitude had not mellowed with age.

"Mrs. Slade, this is Chief Pittman from the Blessings

Police Department. I'm sorry to bother you, but we felt it imperative to let you know that your nephew Hoover has escaped from Coastal State Prison, and reports have him possibly heading this way."

He heard her gasp, and then what sounded like a snort of disgust.

"Oh good grief! I don't want anything to do with him. He was mean as a kid, and he turned into a downright nasty man when he grew up," Sugar said.

"Yes, ma'am. That's why I wanted to let you know. Just be aware. Lock up your car, and hide the keys somewhere in your house to be on the safe side. And if you even get a glimpse of him, lock yourself in the house and call me or the county sheriff's office immediately."

"Yes, I will, and thank you, Chief. Maybe we'll get lucky and the state police will catch him before he gets this far."

Before he could comment, she hung up in his ear. He shook his head, but at least the call was finished.

The next call he made was to the school superintendent. This was Richard Powers' first year here in Blessings. They hadn't been in school quite three months, so Powers had yet to prove himself to the parents. Lon was about to give him his first test.

He looked up the number to the superintendent's office and made the call.

"Superintendent's office. This is Merle."

"Good morning, Merle. This is Chief Pittman. Is Mr. Powers in?"

"Yes, sir, he is. One moment, please."

Lon heard two little beeps, and then Richard Powers picked up.

"This is Richard. How can I help you, Chief?"

"I need to give you a heads-up on an alert we received from the state police. A prison escapee is reported to be heading this way. I have patrols out, but as of yet he has not been spotted in the area. However, if he's spotted anywhere, you'll need to put everyone on lockdown until he's apprehended. And just for your reassurance, I have a car patrolling the schools as we speak."

"Oh! This is not good news. I'll notify staff both here and at the elementary school to be aware of the possibility. We appreciate the police presence, for sure. Thank you for the warning."

"Certainly," Lon said, and disconnected. Now that everyone had been notified, he called Avery again.

"Yes, sir?" Avery said.

"The number for Sugar Slade was good. Everyone has been notified. I will be in the cruiser."

"Yes, sir."

Lon hung up the phone, grabbed his hat and keys, and went out the back way to his car.

Laurel Lorde was on her way into Blessings. Her cleaning business had grown to the point that she had hired three women to help. She had two women to a crew, and her first crew was already on the job. Laurel was on her way in to meet the third employee, who worked with her. They were meeting at Peanut and Ruby Butterman's house, and she was already planning her day as she drove.

She was nearing the city limit when she saw a gray Ford

Focus parked on the side of the road. She slowed down to see if someone was inside and needing help, but when she saw it was abandoned, she kept driving.

As she took the last curve into town, she saw one of the police cruisers parked at the city limit sign and frowned. They never did this unless they were on the lookout for someone.

When she saw it was Deputy Ralph, she waved. He waved back, and she kept driving until she reached the gas station at the edge of town and stopped to fill up.

She got out with her credit card, swiped it, removed the gas cap, and started to fill the tank. While she was standing there, another patrol car drove past.

Johnny Pine was on the other side of the pumps filling up his work truck.

"Hey, Johnny, what's with all the police cars today?"

Johnny turned around. "Oh, good morning, Mrs. Lorde. There's supposed to be an escapee from Coastal State headed this way. The police are all over the place. Keep everything locked up today, okay?"

"Who escaped?"

"Hoover Slade."

"Oh no!" Laurel said, and immediately thought of that abandoned car.

Hoover's brother, Truman, had once caused a lot of trouble for her family. As soon as she finished fueling up, she got in the car and called her husband, Jake.

Jake answered. "Hey, babe."

"Hi. I got to town and see police cars patrolling all over town. An escapee from Coastal State is reportedly heading to this area. Make sure your truck is locked, and keep the doors locked at home. You know how you get when you're working. You zone out to everything else."

"Yes, I will. You do the same. You only clean the one house today, right?"

"Yes, Peanut and Ruby's house, but there's something else. The escapee is Hoover Slade. Truman's brother."

"Okay, I know where you're going with this, and I'll be careful. But after all this time, I seriously doubt that his escape has anything to do with us."

"Yes, maybe you're right. I just remember how much Truman wanted to get back at you."

"And I put the fear of God in him when I followed him all the way to the Georgia–Florida line. This has nothing to do with us, I promise. But thanks for the heads-up anyway, and call me when you're about to leave town."

"I will. I love you, Jake."

"I love you more," he said. "Now go make dust fly and stop worrying."

Laurel grinned. He always made her laugh. "Yes, I will."

She left the station and was on her way to the Butterman house when she saw Chief Pittman. He was out of his cruiser and talking to an older woman in her yard. Laurel thought of that abandoned car again and, on impulse, stopped.

Lon heard the car brake and turned around. Laurel had her window down.

"Did you want to talk to me?" Lon called out.

She nodded.

"Be right there," Lon said, then ended his conversation with the woman. "Just go about your business today, but keep your car doors locked and your house locked, whether you're there or not."

The woman nodded and hurried back inside as Lon walked out across the street to talk to Laurel.

"What's up?" he asked.

"I passed an abandoned car out on the highway. It was just before the city limit sign. I didn't think anything of it until I got into town and saw all the police and heard what it was about. That's when I wondered if the car might have anything to do with him."

"What kind of car was it?" Lon asked.

"It was a gray Ford Focus. I'm no good at guessing the year, but it was in really good shape."

Lon's heart skipped a beat. They'd just gotten their first break.

"Thank you, Laurel. We'll check it out right now. Are you heading to work?"

"Yes."

"Then keep your car locked and the doors locked to the house you're working in, okay?"

"Yes, I will," she said, and drove off.

Lon got in his cruiser and picked up the mic. "Chief to Deputy Ralph, come in."

"This is Ralph, over."

"Check abandoned car just north of your ten-twenty and advise."

"Ten-four, Chief. Over and out."

Lon started the car and was on his way back to Main when Ralph radioed back.

"Ralph to Chief, over."

"This is Pittman, go ahead."

"Positive ID on vehicle in question. Over."

"Call a tow. Log it in, then resume patrol within city limits. Over."

"Ten-four, Chief. Over and out."

Lon keyed up the mic again, knowing they would all have heard the conversation between him and Ralph.

"All units. Suspect likely on foot. Be aware. Over and out."

Finding the car so close to town upped the danger level. Slade would be looking for wheels, and there was a town full for the taking. But the word was already spreading in Blessings to lock the doors and stay inside.

When Lon made the call to Superintendent Powers that a lockdown was necessary, it set off a whole other level of tension. Then he notified the state police that Slade was in the area.

Hoover had snuck into Blessings from the park side of town and was working his way through the alleys, looking for a new ride, when he saw the first patrol car. He thought nothing of it until a couple of blocks down he saw another, then another. He was starting to panic. The need to get out of town was immediate. There was no more time for caution. He couldn't go back to prison.

Neither Sully nor Melissa was aware of the issue until Sully went down to Bloomer's Hardware to pick up some caulking for a loose windowpane. He and Melissa had been in last week to get some washers to fix a leaky faucet, so he'd already met the man who'd fired Melissa from a twenty-year job. But with only one hardware store in town, holding grudges made no sense.

Sully noticed the police presence on the way there, and after he was in the store, he asked, "Hey, Fred. What's going on with all the police?"

"Oh, you haven't heard? There's an escapee from a state prison in the area. I just heard on the scanner that they found the stolen car he was in on the outskirts of town, so everyone is supposed to keep their cars and doors locked and stay inside."

Sully frowned. "I need to call Melissa and let her know," he said. "This tube of caulking is all I need."

"Then let's get you checked out," Fred said, and headed to the register at the front of the store.

Trash day was tomorrow, and Melissa was going through the house emptying wastebaskets into the garbage bag she was carrying. She emptied the last one into the bag and then tied it shut and carried it to the utility room, where the garbage bag from the kitchen was sitting, and opened the back door. The kitchen bag was heaviest, and the trash cans were all the way at the other end of the house. She pulled both bags out onto the patio and then picked up the kitchen garbage and started walking. She reached the trash can, lifted the lid, and was about to put the bag inside when she saw a man trying to break into her car. He was pulling on every door in a frantic way.

Then he looked up, realized he'd been caught, and started running toward her to silence her before she could alert the authorities.

Melissa dropped the sack and ran screaming for the house. Her heart was pounding, her focus on the open door. All she had to do was get inside and lock him out.

She didn't know he was gaining on her until she leaped up on the porch and heard the thump of his footsteps right behind her. She crossed the threshold and was turning to lock the door when he hit it with both hands and knocked her flat on her back on the kitchen floor.

She hit with a thud, but was scrambling back to her feet when he caught her again. She grabbed the carafe of leftover coffee and swung it toward his head, but he put up an arm to block the blow, and it hit his elbow and shattered instead.

"You bitch!" he screamed, looking at the blood running down his arm. When he looked up, she was already running through the house toward the front door.

She made it into the foyer before he caught her again, and this time they were both on the floor. He wrestled her down until he was straddling her body, with her hands pinned above her head.

"Stop it! Stop fighting!" Hoover said. "All I want is your car."

Melissa was gasping for breath and praying Sully would get here in time to keep her from dying.

"Then take it!" she cried.

"Where are the keys? I need the keys!" he said.

"In that dish on the table behind you. Just take them and go."

He rose up just enough to see a ring of keys in the dish, and when he did, she got one hand loose and clawed the side of his face with her nails, trying to kick free.

"You're dead!" he screamed, and drew back his fist and knocked her out.

He staggered to his feet, dripping blood from his elbow and his face, and grabbed the keys. The dish they were in shattered as it fell to the floor. "Oops," he said, and started out the door, then looked back at her again. A hostage might come in handy. So he ran back to the kitchen and got some dish towels, then came back and tied her hands together, and then her feet. He hauled her limp body up off the floor, threw her over his shoulder, and carried her through the house to the door that opened onto the portico, then outside to the car.

He unlocked the car doors and pressed another button to open the trunk. When the trunk lid popped up, he dumped her inside, slammed it shut, and jumped in the car. Within minutes, he was out of the neighborhood, taking back roads to get out of town.

The moment Sully got in the car, he called Melissa to warn her, but she didn't answer. He started the car and headed home, calling her over and over while telling himself everything was fine. He believed that until he neared the house and saw that her car was gone. As he pulled up in the drive, he noticed the garbage on the ground near the trash can and then looked toward the house.

When he saw the door under the portico was ajar, he got out in a panic, running up the steps and into the house, calling her name.

He found broken glass and blood all over the hall and followed the trail of blood into the kitchen, shouting her name as he ran. But when he reached the kitchen and saw more evidence of a struggle, and the back door open as well, he called 911 and started praying. All he kept thinking was that he couldn't lose her, too.

Within three minutes, the yard was full of police cars, and Chief Pittman was getting the particulars on the make and model of car Melissa had.

"It's a blue 2019 Chevy Equinox. I just put the new tag on her car. The number is CYG 777," Sully said.

Chief Pittman used his cell phone to call dispatch and told Avery to broadcast the info out to all law enforcement in the area, including notifying the Georgia State Police of Slade's last location, then started organizing officers, leaving one behind on duty in town.

"What are you doing?" Sully asked.

"We have reason to believe he's on his way up to the family homestead where he was raised. He has one relative still living, and we think that's where he'll go for food and water."

"And then where?" Sully asked.

"Into the woods. It's hard to trail anyone in there, and almost impossible to see them from the air."

"But he can't take a hostage and try to outrun the law. What will he do with her?"

"It's hard to say. That's why we need to catch him," Lon said.

"I want to go with you," Sully said.

"You can't. Stay put. I'll keep you updated."

Sully watched them pulling out and then ran. Melissa's life was in danger, and he wasn't waiting. He jumped in his car and followed them.

CHAPTER 13

MELISSA REGAINED CONSCIOUSNESS IN THE DARK. HER head and jaw were throbbing as she reached for her face, then realized her hands were tied, and so were her feet.

I've been taken hostage!

The horror was real, and with no idea of the kidnapper's intent or destination, she had to get free. She lifted her wrists to her face and began trying to untie the knots, using her teeth to bite and pull. As she did, she smelled the same fabric softener that she used in her laundry and realized he'd tied her up with her own dish towels.

Ignoring the pain in her jaw, she kept biting and pulling on the knot as the wild ride continued. She was just beginning to make headway when he took a sharp turn to the right. It threw her against the inside of the trunk, bumping her head and shoulder. She groaned beneath her breath. She didn't want him to know she was awake for fear of what he'd do, but she could tell by the sound of the tires that he'd turned off the highway onto another kind of paved surface—likely blacktop.

The change in direction was frightening. She began pulling harder, tugging and tugging on the knots, afraid of what might happen to her when he reached his destination, afraid she'd never see Sully again. She couldn't die. Not now. It had taken her such a long time to find happiness again. She wouldn't let herself believe it was going to end like this.

Melissa had the first knot untied before she realized it,

and when she did, she began pulling harder, loosening the knots enough that she could finally yank the bindings away from her wrists.

Now her hands were free, but she still needed to untie her feet. Her knees were bent in a kneeling position, with her feet behind her. The ride was getting rougher, and she was constantly being bounced around as she pulled her knees up to her chin and began working on the knots in that fabric. The car was slipping and fishtailing, which made her remember last night's rain. He was driving in mud, which had slowed him down, but it was also a rougher ride.

One minute passed, and then another, and another, and sweat was running into her eyes and down the back of her neck. Then, like before, when she got the first knot untied around her ankles, it was easier to undo the other.

Once her hands and feet were free, she didn't feel so helpless. She began feeling around inside the trunk for anything she could use as a weapon and thought of the doughnut spare beneath the carpeting on which she was lying, and the funky little jack and lug wrench that went with it.

She was reaching for the edge of the carpeting when the car hit a pothole. She reached out to brace herself, desperate to grab onto anything to keep from being bounced up against the trunk lid again.

After that big bounce, the driver stomped the accelerator. She could hear mud flying up beneath the fenders and grimaced. The ride was getting so rough that it was making her feel nauseous. She was searching for something to hold onto when she felt some kind of lever. Without thinking what it might be, she grabbed onto it with all her strength, bracing for the next jolt.

One second the car was moving, and the next it hit a hole so deep that it momentarily stopped. The sudden stop threw Melissa forward. The lever she was holding onto popped the trunk lid. One second she was in darkness, and the next she was looking at trees and blue sky. She'd been holding onto the safety release, and now she was free!

She scrambled up onto her knees and had one leg out of the vehicle when he stomped the gas again, sending mud flying out into the air behind him. The lurch was nothing short of a launch that ejected Melissa out of the trunk. The trunk lid slammed shut as the driver kept going, and so did Melissa. She landed hard on the edge of the road. When she tried to get up, she lost her balance and fell backward onto a steep slope that led to the hollow below. Her descent was out of her control, and she picked up speed as she continued to slide. She began screaming and grabbing for bushes and trees, reaching for anything that would stop her fall, but the slope was as slick as the road above, and she couldn't get traction.

She saw a sapling just below her that had grown up between two larger trees. If she could just catch it, it might save her. She stiffened her leg, and when her left foot hit one of the big trees, it slowed her down enough to make a grab for the sapling.

She caught it with both hands, but the pain that shot through her shoulders as it yanked her to a halt made her feel as though her arms were being pulled out of their sockets. The good news was she wasn't sliding anymore.

Still clutching the sapling, Melissa lay there trying to catch her breath and, in the quiet, heard sirens in the distance. The police! Sully had come home. He knew she'd been taken, and somehow they knew where the man was going. She had to get back to the road or they'd never see her, and the only way to make that happen was to crawl.

"Help me, Lord," she whispered, and managed to roll over onto her belly without sliding farther down.

Gritting her teeth against the pain in her shoulders, Melissa pushed herself up onto her hands and knees and started making her way back up the slope, grabbing at anything she could to anchor her as she crawled.

She didn't know she was crying, or that her body was covered in countless bleeding scratches. She was alive, which was all that mattered.

Hoover had seen the trunk lid fly up, but thought it was from the impact of hitting the pothole. When he took off and it slammed back down, he just kept driving. He knew the cops weren't far behind because he was beginning to hear the faint sound of sirens, but he was almost to Aunt Sugar's house. When he saw the curve in the road, he breathed a sigh of relief. Home was just beyond it.

He saw the rooftop as he took the curve, but when he drove up into the yard and saw Aunt Sugar sitting out on her porch, he frowned. She looked fit to be tied, which meant they'd told her he was coming. So what! She could get glad in the same shoes she got mad in.

Hoover stomped the brakes and then killed the engine. He couldn't drive any farther, but he had another card to play. His hostage. Aunt Sugar would surely help him if he promised to let the woman go.

Sugar stood up as he got out of the car, and the swagger in his steps ended when he saw her aiming a shotgun at him.

"You don't come a step closer, Hoover Slade. You have brought shame once again to my name, and I'm done with you and your worthless brother. You git, or I swear to God, I'll shoot you where you stand and those cops I hear coming can have what's left of you."

Hoover aimed the remote at the car without looking behind him. When he heard the trunk lid pop up, he started backing up.

"You might think again," he said, but when he backed into the car and turned around and saw the trunk was empty, he let out a cry of disbelief. "What the f—"

Sugar fired a shot over his head. "Shut your filthy mouth and run, boy. Run like you never ran before, or sit down and wait for the cops. You choose."

Hoover shook a fist at her, cursing her and the ground she stood on, but when she aimed the shotgun straight at him, he turned and ran—straight toward the trees just beyond the barn and down to the creek, where he jumped into the swift flow of runoff and kept moving upward.

Sugar sat down and laid the shotgun back at her feet, then set her jaw, glaring down the road and waiting for her peaceful little home to be invaded by the law. She'd never be able to hold her head up in church again.

Melissa was crawling as fast as she could, but was still a good fifty feet from the top when she heard the first police car fly past, and then another, and now she was sobbing, trying to catch them before they were all gone.

Another flew past, and she was crying "stop, please stop," even though she knew it was futile. She couldn't even hear herself over the sound of the sirens.

Then she heard a fourth car coming. She was less than ten feet from the top when she slipped. She dug her toes into the hill and caught the slide, and then had to regain the ground she'd lost, but the car was already gone. When the fifth car sped past and the sirens began to fade, she didn't quit.

There'll be one more. There will be one more.

All of a sudden, she felt the flat surface of the road beneath her fingers and looked up. She'd made it! She toed her feet into the ground again and pushed herself up a few more inches, but then stopped. If she moved her feet again, she'd slide back. Without anything to hang onto to pull herself the rest of the way up, she put her head down and started praying three words over and over again.

"Help me, God. Help me, God."

A minute passed, and then another, and the sweat on her body was making the scratches sting and burn. When she heard another car coming up the slope without a siren, she started shouting and waving her hand. She knew they couldn't see her body, but maybe they'd hear her. Maybe they'd see her waving. It was all she could do to help herself.

Without knowing the twists and turns of the road like the locals, Sully had been forced to back off the eighty miles an hour he'd been running and was praying this road only went one way. If the police took a turn, he'd lose them. Leaving the blacktop and having to driving in the muddy ruts of the cars ahead of him slowed him down even more. He'd already hit one pothole, and now he knew to watch for them so he didn't blow a tire.

He had just started up another slope and was looking at the road ahead of him when he saw movement at the side of the road. He shifted his gaze and then couldn't believe what he was seeing. Just a hand and part of someone's arm up in the air, and they were waving for help! The thought went through his mind that maybe Slade had dumped her off the side of the hill. He hit the brakes, then killed the engine, and the minute he got out of the car, he heard her voice.

"Melissa!" he shouted and ran toward the edge of the road, where he saw the precarious position she was in, then dropped down on his belly and grabbed her by the wrist. "I've got you, baby. I've got you."

Melissa looked up, straight into the horrified look in his eyes.

"You came! I prayed for help, and God sent you! I can't climb any farther without sliding back down."

"You don't have to do anything more. I've got you. Give me your other hand," he said, and when she turned loose and reached up, he caught her other wrist.

Slowly, slowly, he began scooting backwards across the muddy ground and pulling her up until she was on the road. Then he stood and picked her up in his arms.

"Oh, honey…baby… What did he do to you? Let me get you in the car."

She locked her arms around his neck as he carried her back to the car. The moment the door was open, she crawled inside on her own, shaking so hard her teeth were chattering.

"How can I feel cold when I'm bathed in sweat?" she asked.

"You're going into shock," Sully said as he buckled her in, then got a blanket from the trunk of his car, reclined the seat a little, and covered her up. "Did he throw you out of the car?"

"No. I was in the trunk. I got myself untied, but he was going so fast I didn't know what to do. Then he hit a big hole and the trunk lid popped up. I was about to climb out when he gunned the engine to get out of the hole. It threw me out of the trunk, and I rolled off the road and then fell over the edge. I'm caked with mud. Your car is going to be a mess."

"To hell with messes, and you're sitting on leather seats. Everything will wash, including us," Sully said.

He reached for the pocket on the back of her seat and grabbed a bottle of water and opened it, then remembered how raw and scratched her hands were.

"I'll hold it, you drink," he said, and when he put it to her lips, she drank thirstily.

"Thank you," she said, and then started to cry again. "I can't seem to stop."

"You cry all you want. I need to let the Chief know I have you, and then we're going to the ER."

Melissa laid her head back and closed her eyes as Sully got in the car and made the call.

Chief Pittman saw the caller ID and groaned. They'd just arrived at Sugar Slade's house and discovered the stolen car empty and no sign of Melissa. Sugar told them Hoover had arrived here without her, and that's all she knew. Now Lon and his men were waiting for the county sheriff and the Georgia State Police to show. He'd come after Melissa. The search for Slade was theirs. He didn't know what the hell he was going to say to Sully when he answered.

"Hello."

"Chief, I've got Melissa. It's a bit of a story, but she's somewhat mobile. I'm taking her to the ER."

"Thank God," Lon said. "When we got here and found an empty trunk, we were sick. Take care. We'll catch up with you later."

And while Sully was turning around to head back down the road, the chief was giving everyone the good news.

———————————

The news was spreading around Blessings that Slade had taken Melissa Dean's car, and her with it. It was Ruby's kidnapping all over again, except that Ruby had been missing for hours. Before the people could work themselves up into organizing a prayer vigil for Melissa, Sully carried her into the ER.

Their arrival caused something of a stir because everyone knew what had happened. The nurses had her in an examining room within moments, and Dr. Quick was right behind them. They began questioning her regarding injuries and the locations of pain, and when they started to cut her clothes away, they asked Sully to leave.

Melissa stopped them.

"He stays. It's nothing he hasn't already seen, and this

is the second time he's saved my life. I need to see his face."
Then she choked on the words, looking at him with tears in
her eyes. "I didn't think I would see him again."

Sully didn't budge, nor did he break his gaze. He could
tell by the changing expressions on her face when they
touched something that hurt. When they wheeled in a portable X-ray unit and focused on her head, ribs, and shoulders, he held his breath.

Once the nurses had cleaned up all her scratches and
treated them with antiseptic wash, they put her in a hospital gown, then covered her with blankets straight out of the
warmer.

"As soon as we get pictures back from X-ray, Dr. Quick
will be back in to talk to you."

Melissa watched them leave, and the moment they were
out of sight, Sully took off his T-shirt and turned it wrong-
side out and then put it on backwards. At least the front of
his shirt was presentable. His jeans, not so much.

He hurried to her side, leaned over and kissed her forehead, and then brushed a soft kiss across her lips.

"Giving you something better to think about," he said.

Melissa took a shuddering breath as he started talking.

"Fred told me about the escapee when I went to the
hardware store. I left immediately, trying to call you from
the car, but there was no answer. I kept calling you all the
way home. And then your car was gone, and the door was
open. I've never been so scared. I walked in to broken glass
and a trail of blood from the hall to the kitchen. I didn't
know what I would find. I knew he'd taken your car, and
then the blood… Lord. Thank God you're alive."

"That was his blood," Melissa said. "I was taking out the

garbage when I caught him trying to break into my car. He saw me and started chasing me. I ran for the back door, but I wasn't fast enough to lock him out. He tackled me in the kitchen. We fought. I broke the coffeepot on his elbow. I was aiming for his head. He caught me again in the foyer. I scratched my fingernails down the side of his face. That's when he knocked me out." Her chin quivered as she took a breath. "I thought I was going to die. I didn't think I would ever see you again."

"Ah, baby, I'm so sorry. I'm so, so sorry. I love you so much. Just know that you're safe now. That man is on the run up in the hills, likely with the state police and a bunch of dogs on his trail."

"I love you, too. I'm so tired," she mumbled, and then closed her eyes.

Sully sat on the edge of her bed with her hand in his, and when she began crying in her sleep, he knew she was remembering the pain and the fear.

About an hour later, Dr. Quick returned. Melissa woke to good news. Nothing was broken, and the strain to her shoulders could be eased by alternating hot and cold packs.

"Is she free to go home?" Sully asked.

"Yes. Just rest for the next few days. No lifting, either. Let those strained muscles heal."

"I'll make sure of it," Sully said.

"You cut up my clothes," Melissa said.

Dr. Quick patted her knee. "We'll get you a pair of scrubs to wear home. You can bring them back at your leisure."

As soon as she was dressed, Sully went to pull the car up to the entrance while an orderly wheeled her out.

Someone sitting in the waiting room called out Melissa's name, then waved and gave her a thumbs-up.

Sully was standing beside the passenger side, and when she came out, he opened the door. They loaded her up and buckled her in, and then together they headed for home.

He was thinking about the mess in the house as they drove, but as he approached the house, he saw several cars parked along the street.

Melissa noticed them, too. "That's Laurel's car," she said.

"Laurel who cleans the house? It's not her day to come," Sully said.

She sighed. "Blessings being Blessings, I'm going to assume someone sent her and her crew here to clean up. I remember making something of a mess."

"Really? The people in this town continue to amaze me," Sully said.

And sure enough, as he helped Melissa out of the car and walked her to the house, they walked in to the scent of lemon and shining floors. Laurel came out of the kitchen with a dish cloth in her hand.

"I thought I heard the door open," she said, and then looked at Melissa. "Oh honey, bless your heart. You've had more than enough of trouble. How are you?"

"Sore, but alive and grateful," Melissa said. "How did you know to come today?"

"Oh, we had just finished up at Ruby's house when she told us what happened. I called the other girls, and we came here. This is our gift to you. Now go get comfortable somewhere. We are so happy you're okay."

"Do you want to go to bed?" Sully asked.

"Yes, at least for a while. I want to get clean and put on my own clothes and lie down."

"I can make that happen," he said. "Just lean on me."

While calm was being restored in Blessings, the hills above Aunt Sugar's little house were swarming with Georgia State Police and officers from the county sheriff's office, looking for Hoover Slade. Search dogs had been called in and were tracking Hoover's scent from the blood he'd left in the stolen car, and a police chopper was flying recon for the police in the sky above.

With no legal authority outside the Blessings city limits, Chief Pittman and his men left the scene as soon as the state police arrived, with one of the deputies driving Melissa's car home.

Sugar was so rattled and upset about what had happened that looking out at the police vehicles parked all about her property brought her to tears.

She couldn't settle down to do anything she'd planned to do, so she made herself a cup of tea, added a bit of honey to sweeten it, and went outside to her swing on the back porch.

She could hear the hounds up in the woods, as well as the chopper circling the area. A couple of officers had been left behind at the house to coordinate the search areas and were standing at the hatch of one of their SUVs with a map spread out. She could faintly hear the radio chatter between them and the searchers.

There was a lump in her throat just remembering how Hoover had cursed her, saying ugly, hurtful things she would never forget. He and his brother had always been worthless, but never dangerous. Seeing him in this light made her fearful and ashamed.

"A disgrace. That's what this is, a disgrace," Sugar said, and took a sip of her tea.

Hoover hadn't planned on the ensuing chase, but in his mind, he had practiced the run in this creek every day since they'd slammed the door on his cell, and again every night in his sleep.

He'd been running now for over an hour, and the longer he ran, the wearier he became. He never tired in his dreams, but the reality of this run was real. His face burned like hell where Melissa had scratched him, and his side ached. The muscles in his legs were burning, and his lungs felt as if they were about to burst.

He didn't think the chopper overhead could see him in this creek from above, but he wasn't sure. What he did know was if he got on solid ground, the dogs and the cops would eventually find the trail, so he put his head down and kept running until he ran out of creek. He'd come to the source and stared at the water bubbling out of cracks in some rocks on the side of a hill. He no longer had a choice. From here, he would be moving on solid ground.

When they were boys, he and Truman used to prowl through the abandoned shacks left up here from the old days of their grandpa's moonshining, so he started that way, taking care to stay beneath the thickest trees and bushes.

About a half mile up, he paused to catch his breath. When he looked up, a tall, skinny woman of indeterminate age was standing in front of him with a squirrel rifle aimed straight for his head. Her long, messy hair was closer to gray than what bit of blond there was left. It had been braided into one big plait hanging over her shoulder, and she was wearing a raggedy red-plaid shirt and a pair of torn and baggy overalls.

"Don't shoot! Don't shoot!" he cried, and held up his hands.

"Are you the one responsible for that chopper flyin' over my 'sang?" she asked.

Hoover groaned. People killed to keep their ginseng patches secret. All he could do was nod.

"What did you do?"

"Escaped from the state prison."

"Did you kill anybody to get there?" she asked.

"No, no! I swear. I got caught with stolen property."

She frowned. "The state police are after you?"

Hoover nodded.

"I don't take to the state always bein' in people's business. See that path?"

Hoover peered into the brush and finally saw a faint trail. "Yeah."

"So you go ahead of me. I'll be right behind you."

Hoover started forward, then turned around to see what she was doing, and saw her shaking a few droplets on the path behind her as they went.

"What's that?" he asked.

"Deer urine. If the hounds are trailing your scent, this will confuse them. Now shut up and run."

Hoover leaped forward, slashing through brush, pushing tree limbs aside to keep from getting hit in the face, and didn't once look back until he ran out of tree cover and stopped.

"Stay in the trees as you circle the clearing. There's a root cellar on the side of the house about ten feet from the brush. Open the door and go down. I'll meet you from inside," the woman said.

Hoover breathed a quick sigh of relief.

"Yes, ma'am. Thank you, ma'am. I sure appreciate this," he said and kept moving.

The moment he saw the cellar door, he darted out of the trees and raised the door, only to walk down into the darkest hole he'd ever seen. When he let the door back down, he began to freak.

"Oh shit. Something smells dead in here. What have I just gotten myself into?" he muttered.

He was at the point of going back up the stairs and running like hell, when a door opened. It was then he saw the stairs below it that led up into the house. He could see light and then the woman's silhouette as she came downstairs with a flashlight and a glass of water.

"It smells a little rank down here, but I'm curing pelts and got a fresh one I'm still scraping on. Thought you might be thirsty," she said.

"Oh, thanks," Hoover said, and drank until the glass was empty.

She took the glass, then pointed the flashlight toward a dusty cot against the wall piled high with furs.

"Right there's your sleeping quarters. Just move my pelts onto that old table. You might want to shake the covers off a bit before you rest. I'll leave this here flashlight with you so you can see to move around. If you gotta go, don't be doing your business in my cellar. You go back out into the bushes for that."

And with that, she started up the stairs.

"Hey, lady! I don't even know your name."

"And I don't know yours, so let's keep it that way," she said, and shut the door between them.

Hoover heard her turn a lock and then shuddered. He didn't want to go back to prison, but this place was as close to a hellhole as he'd ever been in.

He clutched the flashlight in one hand and began moving the piles of pelts with the other, then set the cot on end to shake out the rags on the bed. When he glanced up to where the light was shining, he saw a huge snake curled up on a shelf.

"Oh, hell no," he cried. He dropped the flashlight and ran up the steps and out into the woods without looking back.

CHAPTER 14

THE SEARCH WAS IN FULL SWING UP IN THE HILLS. Despite the run Hoover had made through the water and the random application of deer urine the old woman had left on the trail, the dogs eventually tracked the scent straight up to her house.

The sun was setting, the air already turning cooler as the searchers came out of the tree line into the clearing surrounding the house. There was a light shining through one window.

Someone was home.

And someone was in the cellar, because the dogs were at the outer door, baying and scratching. Their handlers were holding them back, waiting for orders from the police, when the old woman came out onto her porch with a shotgun.

"What the hell is going on?" she asked. "Somebody shut up them dogs. I can't hear myself think."

The dogs were called off as a trio of officers approached.

"That's far enough until you tell me what you're doing on my property," she said.

They quickly produced badges as one of them took the lead.

"Detective Inman, Georgia State Police. Ma'am, what's your name?"

"Tansy Runyan. Now I'm going to ask you again. What are you doing on my property?"

"We're chasing an escaped prisoner, and our dogs tracked his scent to your cellar," Inman said.

Tansy gasped. "Oh laws! You mean that man is down there?"

"I don't know, but we need to search your house and the cellar," he said.

"Yes, yes, come right this way," she said, and started back into the house, while several of the officers started to go into the cellar from the outside.

"Wait!" Tansy yelled. "Wait! Larry's down there, and I don't want nobody scaring or hurting him in any way."

"Who's Larry?"

"Just a big old black snake. Best mouser I ever had. Let me go down from inside to make sure y'all don't hurt him."

"I hate snakes," someone muttered.

"Ma'am, if our prisoner is in there, he and your snake may have already met," Inman warned.

Tansy moaned. "I don't want anything to happen to Larry. Hurry up," she said, and darted into the house with a bevy of searchers behind her, as the others stood guard outside the cellar door.

The house was tiny and didn't take long to clear.

"No one here, sir," they said.

"This here door goes down to my cellar, but I always keep it locked from this side," Tansy said as she turned the lock, but when she started to go first, Inman stopped her.

"No, ma'am. If he's there, it won't be safe," he said.

"Oh my lord, I can't believe all this is happening," she said. "Yes, well...just don't hurt Larry."

"Yes, ma'am. We'll be careful."

"You'll need this," she said, and handed them her flashlight. The same one she'd retrieved from the cellar after she'd heard the prisoner running off. She guessed it was

Larry that had sent him running, and as it turned out for her, his absence was a good thing.

"There's no light down there?" someone asked.

"I don't have lights anywhere here except lamps," Tansy said.

They began breaking out flashlights. Nobody wanted to meet Larry in the dark. They filed down the stairs with Tansy right behind them.

"Oh hell! There's Larry," someone said, and someone else stumbled over an old three-legged milking stool in a panic to put some distance between him and the snake.

Tansy went straight to the snake coiled up on a shelf. "Now, Larry, no fussing at all the racket, okay? You're safe," she cooed, stroking his shiny skin.

"What the hell is that smell?" Detective Inman asked.

"Green pelts. I trap and sell. They aren't all cured up yet."

"Green as in fresh skinned?" he asked.

"Yep. Wanna see?"

"No, ma'am."

Then Tansy started looking around her cellar, playing the part that would keep her out of trouble for harboring a criminal.

"Oh my stars! You were right! Someone was in my cellar. All my pelts are on this table, and they used to be on that cot over there."

"You didn't hear anything?" they asked.

"No. Maybe he was already gone before I got back from my patch."

"Your patch of what?" the officer asked, picturing marijuana in his mind.

"'Sang. I got me a ginseng patch. It's another way I keep

myself fed. I trade pelts and 'sang for supplies. Don't have no use for money up here."

One of the officers radioed to the men above. "All clear down here. See if you can pick up a trail from the cellar back into the woods."

"Ten-four."

Inman walked out of the cellar into the yard just as the trackers were getting ready to move.

"Officer, when you followed the tracks up to here, whose tracks were laid down first? Hoover's or the woman's?" he asked.

"Oh, his for sure, Sarge. Her smaller footprint was on top of his."

Inman nodded. This confirmed her claim that she could have come home after Slade was gone.

"Listen, it's getting dark. Let's find a place to stop for the night. We're too far away to go back and resume in the morning. We'll have to cold camp."

"Yes, sir," the men said. "We'll let the dogs search to see if they can pick up his trail again, and then we'll follow it until we have to stop."

"Agreed," Inman said. "We'll be behind you."

The trackers took off with their dogs as the rest of the officers came out of the cellar. Again, Tansy was behind them.

"Ma'am, we're sorry to have disturbed you. We'll be leaving the area as soon as we pick up another trail."

He gave Tansy back her flashlight.

She took it, then held it against her chest.

"Good hunting," she said. "I sure don't want no more strangers messing around down in my cellar."

Then she shut the cellar door and went back into her house from the front. She stood there a moment, listening to the silence and nodded her head. Just the way she liked it.

She went to her wood cookstove and took the lid off a pan sitting at the back, stirred up the cold squirrel stew inside, then carried it to the table and sat down to eat.

———————————

Detective Inman saw the storm coming in and knew being up in the hills in a thunderstorm wasn't safe. When the first raindrops fell, he also knew they were going to lose the trail.

He grabbed his radio and called in the searchers.

"Inman here," he said. "A storm is coming. Get the dogs back to camp. We can't get off these hills and back to our cars before the storm hits. We'll have to take shelter somewhere safer than under these damn trees."

"Ten-four" came the answer, and minutes later, the trackers and their dogs began showing up in camp.

As soon as everyone was back and accounted for, Inman pointed downhill. "We're less than a mile from that abandoned cabin we just searched. Grab your gear and start running. We do not want to be up here dodging lightning strikes."

———————————

While they were running for cover, Hoover had already made it over the crest of the hill and was all the way back down into the hollow below, walking as fast as he could, looking for a place to hole up for the night. He was cursing himself for leaving that flashlight behind. It would be dark soon, and he could use it.

Then he heard thunder and looked up just as a shaft of lightning came down out of the clouds and hit something on the top of the hill.

"Hot damn, it's gonna rain out my tracks and my scent," he crowed, and headed right back to the same creek he'd come up in. That was something they wouldn't expect.

It was pitch-dark and pouring rain by the time he found the creek, but as long as he stayed in the water, he didn't need light to know where he was going. This was the same creek that ran right past Aunt Sugar's place, and it also ran through Big Tom Rankin's place a few miles down, then through the woods and under the bridge at the north end of Blessings before emptying out into a river.

Hoover wasn't sure where he would get out of the creek, but he wasn't messing with Aunt Sugar again.

It didn't occur to him that running in water with all the lightning strikes in the area was dangerous. But danger came to light when a shaft of lightning struck a tree on the bank just ahead of him. Even in the rain, the lightning lit a fire from the strike that blew up the tree, splintering it in all directions.

Hoover staggered back in shock, and then screamed as a hot, searing pain pierced his thigh. He fell backwards into the shallow water, momentarily blinded by the heavy rainfall in his face.

"What the hell just happened?" he moaned as he crawled out of the water and up onto the creek bank, then rolled over onto his back and sat up.

The pain was sharpest above his right knee, but without

light, he was left to guessing exactly what had happened. When he felt a sizable shaft of wood sticking out of his leg, he groaned. A piece of that tree was in his leg!

He couldn't tell how badly it was bleeding because of the rain, but he was scared. He had no idea where he was, and the thunderstorm was making too much noise to call out for help. He had outrun the only people who might have saved him, and now if he didn't get help, he could be in danger of bleeding to death.

Without hesitation, Hoover began ripping up the leg of his pants until he had a strip long enough to make a tourniquet. Afraid to try to pull the wood out of his leg, he felt around on the bank until he found a piece of deadfall. He broke a piece off from that limb and used it to make a splint.

After a good deal of groaning and cursing, Hoover managed to stand up. It occurred to him that he didn't need the creek anymore to hide his tracks. But he did need it so he wouldn't get lost. He knew where the creek went, but the woods were so thick and the night was so dark that he would easily get directions confused.

Reluctantly, he got back in the ankle-high water and, holding onto the tourniquet to keep it tight, he started walking. The rain was a deluge. The only light came from brief lightning flashes that illuminated his surroundings.

He'd lost all sense of time, but it felt as if he'd been walking for hours, and he knew as well as he knew his own name that he was about to lose consciousness. Afraid he'd drown if he passed out facedown, he crawled back onto the bank and sat down.

He thought about praying, but he and God hadn't been on good terms for a very long time. When he checked his leg again and realized he could no longer feel his toes, he reluctantly faced his destiny.

"I'm dying," he said, and passed out.

The storm ended. Day dawned, and Albert Rankin was up early doing chores alone because his daddy, Big Tom, was suffering a bad case of gout and was off his feet, unable to help.

Tom hadn't slept a wink all night and knew he couldn't take another day and night of this pain. As soon as Albert got done with chores, he was driving Tom into Blessings. They were both still dealing with the loss of Tom's older son, Junior, who died in the flood caused by the hurricane, and had acquired a hunting dog to add some life back in the house. They'd named him Red, and while Big Tom enjoyed the dog's company, Red was Albert's shadow, both in the house and out.

But today, as soon as Albert stepped into the barn, Red took off out the far end of the breezeway like someone had just set him on a trail.

"Red! Red! Come back here, dammit!" Albert yelled, but Red didn't stop and quickly disappeared below the hill. "Well, hell," Albert muttered, and took off after him at a jog.

He'd just topped the hill and was starting down the slope when he saw Red. It took a few moments to realize his dog was standing over a body. The fact that this was where his brother, Junior, had fallen into the floodwaters gave Albert the creeps. He took off running, hoping he didn't know who it was, and when he got there, dropped to his knees beside the body to check for a pulse. Almost immediately, he recognized the face and the scratches on his cheek.

"Aw, man! It's Hoover Slade."

Albert didn't expect to feel life beneath his fingertips, but once he did, his focus shifted to speed. He grabbed his phone and called 911.

Back at the Blessings Police Department, Avery had just come on duty when a call came in. "Blessings 911. What is your emergency?"

"Avery! This is Albert Rankin. My dog just found Hoover Slade. He's unconscious and with a pretty nasty-looking wound on his leg. Just have the ambulance come straight down below the barn. They can't miss us."

"Stay with him," Avery said. "I'm dispatching help."

"Yes, yes, I will," Albert said, and as soon as Avery disconnected, Albert called his daddy's cell phone.

Big Tom reached for his phone, and then frowned when he saw it was his own son.

"It's me. What's wrong?" Tom said.

"Daddy, Red just found Hoover Slade on the creek bank below the barn. I've called 911 already. Didn't want you to freak out when you hear them coming."

"Slade? Are you serious? Last night they said on the news he was up in the hills somewhere. Is he dead?"

"No, he still has a pulse, but he has a really bad leg wound. He's probably lost a lot of blood."

"It'll take me a bit, but I'll head that way," Big Tom said.

"Don't hurt yourself, Daddy. Just stay there. There's nothing either one of us can do."

"No, I hurt whether I'm sitting or walking. I'll be right there," and he disconnected.

About five minutes later, Albert heard their old lawn mower start up. He grinned. Daddy just got himself a ride. He watched Tom come over the rise and then down toward the creek.

They were both there waiting when they heard sirens in the distance. Albert ran up the hill, and when the first police cars and an ambulance drove into view, he waved to indicate where they were, then ran back down.

It didn't take long before they had Slade stabilized enough to transport, and then they were gone.

Albert cleaned up and then took his daddy to the doctor, and Red got a chew bone and a pat on the head for his find.

––––––––––––––––

Back at the station, chaos reigned. Once the chief was notified of the call, he contacted Detective Inman.

Inman was on his way back down through the heavily wooded hills with his men when his phone rang.

"This is Inman."

"Detective, this is Chief Pittman. We just got a 911 call that some locals found Hoover Slade on the creek bank below their house."

Inman held up his fist, and all the men behind him stopped.

"Is he dead?"

"No, sir, but he's unconscious and has a serious injury to his leg. The ambulance is transporting him from here to the hospital."

"Boy, did we catch a break," Inman said. "We lost his trail when the storm hit. We'll meet up in the ER, okay?"

"Yes, sir. We'll provide a police presence until you arrive."

"Thanks for the call," Inman said, then dropped the phone in his pocket. "We just got lucky. Some farmer found Hoover on a creek bank. He's unconscious and injured, and as soon as we get back to Blessings, we've got our man."

A small cheer went up as they increased their pace.

The sheriff's office was officially relieved of further duty, and when they reached their vehicles, they left to return to their regular duties.

Inman and his men left for Blessings.

––––––––––––––

Dr. Quick was on duty when the ambulance arrived, but he'd been given a heads-up as to who they were bringing in. Two officers from the Blessings PD were already on hand to stand guard outside Slade's treatment room.

The EMTs unloaded the gurney and wheeled Slade inside, updating the doctor on his condition when found, the fact that he'd had a tourniquet on the upper portion of his leg above the wound, and what his stats were upon arrival.

Dr. Quick grimaced when he saw the piece of wood in Hoover's leg and the mark left by the tourniquet they'd removed. A nurse began cutting away the convict's clothes, and the team went to work.

A short while later, Detective Inman and his men showed up at the hospital. They thanked the Blessings officers for their help and sent them on their way. Then Inman put two of his men on guard and went into the room without an invitation.

Dr. Quick looked up and frowned. "Who are you?"

Inman flashed his badge. "Detective Inman, Georgia State Police. This man is our prisoner. Can you tell me his prognosis?"

"Not yet. Just wait outside, and if we need you, we'll call you in."

Inman eyed the man on the exam table. He didn't look good, the detective thought as he went back into the hall.

But as Dr. Quick continued his examination, it became apparent that Hoover had a bigger problem.

"Somebody get Detective Inman in here, please," Dr. Quick said.

A nurse turned and darted out of the room. Moments later, she was back with Detective Inman.

"What's wrong?" Inman asked.

"We have a problem. We can remove the wood from his leg, but the leg is no longer viable below the wound. The tourniquet was left on too long. It cut off the blood supply."

Inman glanced over at Slade's body. "Has he regained consciousness yet?"

"No, sir," Dr. Quick said.

"What are his chances of getting through surgery?"

"It's hard to say. Maybe fifty-fifty. Maybe a little more."

"Can he be transported to a bigger hospital in Savannah?" Inman asked.

"Delay would lessen his chances, and we have a good surgeon on staff."

"Then do what you need to do to try to save him," Inman said.

And with that, they wheeled Hoover into surgery.

CHAPTER 15

SULLY TOOK MELISSA INTO THE BIG SHOWER IN THE room across the hall, started the water running to get it hot, then stripped both of them. She sat on the lid of the toilet without moving, almost in a daze. The emotional exhaustion of what she'd gone through was overwhelming. All she wanted was to get clean and lie down.

Sully reached for her. "Okay, baby, the water is just right. All you have to do is stand there. I'll wash the mud out of your hair, and then we'll deal with what's left on you. Can you handle that?"

"Yes," she said, and let him lead her into the shower.

The warm water felt like heaven as it sluiced down her sore, achy body, but the relief also triggered more tears.

"I'm sick of being hurt," she said. "I can't believe this has happened again."

"Neither can I, sweetheart, but it did. Right now, we're going to get you clean. First job is to get some shampoo in your hair."

And so she stood with her eyes shut as Sully washed her from head to toe and then quickly soaped himself before getting them out.

He wrapped one towel around her hair and then dried her back and legs.

"Want to dry the rest of yourself?" he asked.

Melissa managed a wry smile. "You're doing such a good job, you might as well finish," she said, and so he did, then wrapped a towel around his waist and walked her back across the hall.

"You didn't dry yourself," she said.

"Oh, I drip dry," he said. "Do you want your nightgown?"

"No. Just sweats. My hair's too wet to lie on the pillows, so I'll stretch out on top of the bed for now."

He got out the clothes she wanted, and then dressed himself and went to get her hair dryer.

"You don't have to do that," she said.

"It won't take but a few minutes," he said, then plugged it in and dried her hair enough so she could lie down.

He went to put up the dryer, and when he came back, she was already on the bed, curled up on her side. He got a blanket from the foot of the bed and covered her, then lay down beside her. When he finally heard her breathing soften and slow down, he knew she'd fallen asleep.

Satisfied she was resting comfortably, Sully got up, leaving the door open so he'd hear her if she called out, and went downstairs to make some coffee. The doorbell rang while he was still in the kitchen, and he went to answer it.

It was Elliot, holding a small jar of jelly.

"Elliot. Come in," Sully said. "Come look at where we've hung your painting."

"Well, just for a minute," he said, and then beamed when he saw it. "It looks fine there, but that's not why I came. This is a jar of quince jelly. I have a tree in the backyard. The fruit is terrible eaten raw, but it makes the most delightful jams and marmalades. This is marmalade and is quite good with meats. Give Melissa my best. She will recover just fine."

"Thank you," Sully said. "I will do that, and thank you for the marmalade as well."

Elliot nodded, let himself out, and was gone.

Sully smiled and held the jar up to the light, marveling at the rich red color and the fact that the old man was a jelly maker, too.

He took it into the kitchen and set it on the table where Melissa would be sure to see it, then took his coffee to the living room and sat within the silence of the house, thinking of the woman he loved upstairs and looking at the painting of Janie. A stranger, and yet she was the reason he was here.

Melissa woke up with a headache and went into the bathroom to find some over-the-counter pain pills. She took two, then finger combed her clean hair and went to look for Sully.

As she neared the kitchen, she could hear the washing machine on spin cycle. Sully was doing laundry, and something was cooking. The normalcy of it all was the best thing for her. At this moment, she would not have been able to ask for one more thing. She was home, and she was alive.

She walked in, saw him stirring something in a pot on the stove, then wrapped her arms around his waist and laid her cheek against his back. She felt the rumble of his laughter against her ear as he patted her hands and turned around.

"Hey, baby, did you sleep good?"

She nodded. "I missed you."

He brushed a kiss across her lips. "I didn't go far," he said, and then kissed the top of her head and tucked her under his arm as he went back to stirring.

"Whatever that is, it smells heavenly," she said.

"It's meat sauce for spaghetti, and all it needs to do now is cook down a bit." He turned the fire down to simmer. "I have coffee, but there are also the cold drinks. Would you like something?"

"Yes, something cold. I put Cokes in the fridge the other day."

"Then Coke it is. On ice?"

She nodded.

"I'll get it for you, honey. Sit down. Oh…one of the Blessings officers drove your car back. We'll have to take it to be checked out, but it's here."

She eased down onto one of the chairs and leaned back. The sight of him standing in her kitchen stirring pasta sauce was unforgettable. He put the lid back on the pot and fixed her Coke.

Melissa took a sip of the cold, fizzy drink, watching as he brought his coffee and a couple of cookies with him. He handed one to her and joined her.

She sat quietly, eating the cookie and sipping Coke, but still thinking about today.

"Sully?"

"What, baby?"

"A whole lot of your work life has been life-or-death situations, hasn't it?"

He nodded, wondering what was on her mind.

"And there must have been times when your life was on the line," she added.

"Yes, there were days like that."

Melissa leaned forward. "So how did you cope? I mean…how did you rationalize waking up on a normal day, having a life-altering event and living through it, and then coming home to being normal again?"

"First thing to consider is that risk was often my normal. I accepted it when I became a firefighter. And the other thing was simple gratitude for living to fight another day."

She let that soak in for a minute, then finally admitted what was bothering her.

"I'm struggling with that concept right now. Two really awful things have happened to me in less than a month. I wasn't responsible for either one of them, but they happened anyway…regardless of how normal my life was just before it happened."

Sully pushed his chair back from the table. "Come sit," he said and patted his leg.

Melissa got up and plopped back down on his lap. When he put his arms around her, she leaned against him and sighed.

"Here's the deal, honey. I learned a long time ago not to question what happens because most of the time it's out of our control. What I had to come to terms with was how to get through it. What lesson was I supposed to take away from coming out on the other side? I think you're looking at your life right now, trying to make sense of it from the viewpoint of the incidents. You're missing the fact that you continue to get up afterward. You heal with faith. You persevere with the strength of a warrior, my love. When I looked over the edge of that road today and saw you clinging to that slope and how far down it was…and how far up you had to climb…I couldn't believe you'd done it. And yet there you were."

"I never thought of it like that," Melissa said.

"That's because you were busy saving yourself," Sully

said. "I didn't save your life today. I just found you. You saved yourself. The end."

Melissa grinned. "The end, huh?"

"Yes. No more worrying about what's over. Just concentrate on healing your poor little body again."

"I'll get right on that," she said. Sully laughed.

Hoover woke, confused and in pain.

The recovery nurse put a hand on his shoulder. "Mr. Slade, you're okay. You had surgery, and you're in recovery."

He groaned. "Hurt."

"We're going to move you to your room."

He drifted back off to sleep, and when he did, the nurse began talking to him, trying to wake him up.

"Hoover, Hoover! Wake up. You need to wake up now."

He opened his eyes again. It was the same nurse, still pestering him.

"That's good. Okay, an orderly is here. He's going to be taking you to your room now."

"Hurt," Hoover mumbled.

"Once they get you situated in your room, they'll give you something for the pain."

He closed his eyes again as the orderly wheeled him out of recovery and then down the hall to an elevator. He slept through the ride up and woke up again surrounded by people.

"Hoover, we're going to transfer you to your bed. Just relax and let us do it for you."

Pain rocketed through him so fast he passed out again.

"Let's get him moved before he comes to," the nurse said.

Hoover woke up again surrounded by machines registering his blood pressure and his heart rate, and the pole with the IV drip.

"Mr. Slade, I'm Hope. I'll be your nurse for the rest of the day."

"Hurt," he said again.

"I just gave you some medicine. You should be able to feel it soon."

He blinked. "Water…thirsty."

"I have some ice chips," Hope said. "Let me raise the head of your bed just a little."

Hoover groaned at the movement, but once it stopped, the room stopped spinning, too.

"Open your mouth," she said.

Hoover opened his eyes and lifted his head slightly as she spooned a couple of ice chips into his mouth. As he did, he looked down toward the foot of the bed and then froze, the ice chips slowly melting on his tongue.

Something was wrong. He didn't look right, but what—

"My leg! Where's the rest of my leg!"

And right on cue, his surgeon walked in.

"Mr. Slade, I'm Dr. Hastings. I did your surgery. How are you feeling?"

"Like hell," Hoover said. "What did you do to me?"

Dr. Hastings gently put his hand on Hoover's arm.

"I'm sorry, but by the time you were found and brought to the hospital, the tourniquet you had on your leg was on there so long that the lack of blood supply had destroyed your leg. We had to remove everything below the tourniquet line. But you'll heal, and prosthetics have come a long way in the past few years."

"Oh my God," Hoover whispered, thinking about going back to prison a cripple.

"I'll be back to check on you this evening when I make my rounds. Just let the nurse know if your pain level is too severe. I left instructions," Dr. Hastings said.

Hoover watched the doctor walk out of the room—on two good legs—and wanted to cry. This was God's punishment for the way he'd lived. Every time the going got tough, he ran away, just like the incident in prison. Maybe when they took him back to lockup they'd take him to a different prison, but wherever he went, one thing was for certain. He wouldn't be running away from anything again.

––––––––––––––––

The tension of the morning lockdowns in Blessings was mostly gone by evening. With Melissa's return so soon after she'd been taken hostage, there was much discussion and rejoicing about the outcome.

Peanut and Ruby both came home from work exhausted and mutually agreed to dinner at Granny's. They walked into a place of laughter and friends and the best food in town, and slowly their exhaustion gave way to a sense of relief, and then gratitude for the place where they lived.

Lovey sat with them a bit as they waited to order, just in case there was any new gossip via the Curl Up and Dye.

"So, anything new to share?" she asked, then winked and grinned.

When Ruby rolled her eyes, Peanut laughed.

"What?" Lovey asked.

Ruby leaned forward and lowered her voice.

"Girl, you have no idea! One of the bankers' wives, and I will not say who, brought her two girls in with head lice. The girls were eight and ten, and I don't know who was more mortified when I found them, her or the girls. She said it had been going around school, and then she said…'I just never expected this to happen to us! We're not in the lower socioeconomic spectrum.'"

Lovey grinned. "She did not say all that mouthful?"

"Oh, yes she did."

"What did you do?"

"I told her bugs did not recognize social status, and I wasn't in the business of treating head lice. Then I sent them to the pharmacy and told them to ask Mr. Phillips how to get rid of the lice—and not to come back here until they were gone."

"Did it make her mad?" Lovey asked.

Ruby rolled her eyes again. "If she'd been on fire, she couldn't have been any hotter."

Peanut patted Ruby's hand in commiseration. "She's had a long, rough day, Lovey, and that's why we're here. What's good tonight?"

Lovey laughed. "Everything! Now I've got to get back to work before the boss fires me," she said, and went back to the register.

Ruby grinned. "She's said that for as long as I've known her. Funny thing about that is when I first heard her say it, I was new here in town, and I wondered for almost six months who owned the place. When I found out it was her,

I finally got the joke. Oh...here comes our waitress. What are you going to have?"

"You know me. When in doubt, I'm a burger man."

———————————————

Sugar Slade's evening was turning out less jovial, but relieved just the same. After finding out Hoover had been captured, and what condition he'd been in, she couldn't help thinking about what cute little boys he and Truman had been when she married into the family. She wanted to remember them the way they were, not what they'd become.

So she took her Bible outside as twilight was approaching and read aloud her favorite passages to the owl sitting in the tree by her porch, and to the rabbit hopping across her yard on its way home, and to the birds flying in to roost for the night. And when she was through, she closed the Bible and looked up, just in time to see the sun fall below the horizon.

The sky lit up in a vivid wash of purples and pinks, and then as it grew darker, it faded into black. Sugar sat as the night grew colder, waiting for the first star, and when she saw it, she nodded.

Her day was complete.

———————————————

By the time Lovey closed up for the night, she'd heard so many stories about what had happened to Melissa, and how she got away, and when Sully found her, that she made up her mind to go talk to her in person right after the breakfast rush tomorrow. Sometimes she felt like the world passed her by because she was always in Granny's. And then she reminded herself that Blessings and Granny's were the life-savers she needed. The town and the business were her family, and she loved what she did. There wasn't a lot to complain about.

_____

Night had come to Blessings, and Sully was asleep, curled up on his side and spooned against Melissa with his arm over her waist when he heard a car door slam, and then a dog begin to bark. A few moments later, the dog was quiet.

Someone came home, Sully thought.

Melissa was his home, and he'd come so close to losing her today. She stirred in her sleep and began to mumble. When he felt the tension in her body, he pulled her closer.

"You're safe, baby. You're safe, and you're home."

She sighed, and then she was still.

He closed his eyes, and the next time he woke, it was morning. He blew her a kiss and then eased out of bed and went across the hall to shower so he wouldn't wake her. As soon as he was dressed, he went downstairs to start the day. Coffee was first on the to-do list.

By the time Melissa came down, he had pancake batter made and was frying bacon. She stood in the doorway watching him, and then he looked up and saw her standing there.

"Hey, sweetheart!" He left the bacon long enough for a quick wake-up kiss, then hurried back to the skillet. "How long have you been standing there?"

Melissa smiled. "Long enough to think 'What's wrong with this picture?'"

"What do you mean?"

"Usually, the woman is in the kitchen, and the man arrives for food."

He frowned, waving his tongs in the air. "How caveman do you think I am? I'm a renaissance man. I fight fires. I rescue the occasional damsel in distress, I have an A+ in sex, and I do laundry and cook. This is what you get from a man who's lived alone forever."

Melissa laughed out loud. "Oh my lord, Sully. You had me at 'caveman.'"

Sully took the last piece of bacon from the skillet, then switched off the fire and turned and took her in his arms.

"It feels like I've loved you forever, and yesterday scared the hell out of me. I don't have a ring. I don't have a job. But will you marry me anyway and trust me for the rest?"

"In a heartbeat," she said, and shivered when his mouth brushed across her lips.

Pancakes and bacon became the engagement breakfast, with sorghum molasses instead of syrup.

"Georgia will make a Southern boy out of you yet," she said, eyeing the liberal pour of molasses on his second stack.

Sully shook his head. "All these years, I didn't know what I was missing. I was on a search when I came here, but I didn't know it was for you, too. You and sorghum might be the best things that have ever happened to me."

He winked when she grinned, then forked another bite into his mouth, rolling his eyes in delight at the tangy, sweet taste.

Melissa got up to refill their cups and was sitting back down when her cell phone rang.

"What did I do with my phone?" she asked. She could hear it ringing, but she didn't see it.

"It's on the sideboard," Sully said.

Melissa grabbed it, glancing at the caller ID.

"Hello?"

"Hi, sugar, it's me, Lovey. How are you feeling today?"

"Still sore and kinda beat-up looking, but I'm feeling great," Melissa said.

"Are you up for a little company this morning? It will be after the breakfast rush."

"Yes! Wonderful. We'll be happy to see you."

"I'll see you then," Lovey said, and disconnected.

"That was Lovey. She's coming over after the breakfast rush."

"Good. I really like her. You can tell what a good heart she has, and she doesn't mince words."

"She and Granny's are fixtures in Blessings. When she nearly died in the hurricane, everyone pitched in to clean up the restaurant and make needed repairs, and the staff ran it for her until she was well enough to come back. We love her to pieces."

It was a little after ten when Lovey arrived. Melissa was in the living room, reading the paper and watching for Lovey's arrival, when she heard her knock.

"I'll get it," Sully said, and went to the door.

"I'm here," Lovey said, handing him a bakery box. "It's coconut cream pie, one of Mercy's best."

"Sounds delicious," Sully said. "Come in. Melissa is in

the living room and anxious to see you. I'll go put this in the refrigerator and be right back."

Lovey caught the sparkle in Sully's eyes and smiled to herself as she went into the living room.

Melissa was getting up when Lovey stopped her.

"Hey, sugar! Don't get up. I'll come to you," she said, and gave Melissa a quick kiss on the cheek.

"It's good to see you," Melissa said.

Lovey plopped down on the sofa next to Melissa's chair.

"I think that man is gone on you," she whispered.

Melissa laughed. "It's mutual."

Lovey grinned. "I love it when a good thing comes together. I came just to satisfy myself you were still in one piece. The whole escaped prisoner thing and him taking you hostage when he stole your car unnerved all of us yesterday. I see your car is back under your portico."

"Yes. Lon had one of his officers drive it back."

"So tell me, did you really untie yourself inside the trunk and then get thrown out of the trunk and roll off the road into the holler below?"

"It sounds like an action-adventure movie, doesn't it? But yes, I did get myself free of the ties around my wrists and feet, and yes, I did get thrown out of the trunk when he hit a big pothole on a muddy road. The trunk lid popped up, and I was trying to get out when he gunned the engine. I went flying out of the trunk, but I didn't have my balance as I tried to stand and rolled straight down one of those slopes leading down into a hollow. I was sliding and rolling, trying to grab onto all those trees and bushes I kept sliding past. Then I caught myself about two-thirds of the way down.

"The problem became trying to get back up the hill. It

was slick from the rain the night before. I heard the police coming, but I couldn't get up fast enough. Then I got within a couple of feet of the top and could not climb another inch. There was nothing to hang on to. I'd been sliding backwards more than gaining ground, so I was just hanging there, waiting for a miracle. All Sully could see from the road was my hand waving. I can't tell you how relieved I was when he looked over the edge and then grabbed my hand and pulled me up. You know the rest."

Lovey shook her head, staring in awe. "You are amazing, honey. Thank God Sully found you, but you absolutely saved yourself!"

At that point, Sully walked in, smiling. "See, baby? That's exactly what I told you."

"Yes, and thank you for helping me see it from that angle. Come sit beside me."

Lovey saw the look in his eyes when he started toward Melissa, and sighed, remembering that kind of love. And then her gaze shifted from him to a painting he'd just walked past. She stared for a few moments, then got up without speaking and walked toward it.

Sully paused midstep and followed her, delighted that she'd noticed it.

"Isn't it beautiful? Elliot Graham painted it for me."

Lovey was standing in front of it now, still staring. Her voice was shaking when she finally spoke. "What is this?"

"It's a painting of my birth mother and me. I didn't know I was adopted until my mother passed a few months back, and I've been looking for my birth mother ever since. That's why I wound up here. The last known address that was found for her was Blessings, Georgia. I bugged everybody

I met, asking if they knew her, but it wound up a dead end. Someone told me Elliot Graham was something of a psychic, and I wasn't going to miss a chance that he might help. So I went to see him."

Lovey shook her head. "I didn't know that's why you were here. I don't hear so good anymore."

"Yes, I've gone to every possible place here in Blessings looking for records that would say she'd been here."

Lovey was beginning to shake. "But this painting? If you don't know who she is, how did you get this?"

Sully pointed at the painting. "See that necklace? I have it. It was in with the adoption papers I found, along with a letter my birth mother left. So I took the letter with me to Elliot's house. He held it, and then all he would say was to stay in Blessings. So I stayed. He only gave the painting to me a couple of days ago. He said he saw this in a vision when he held the letter and painted it for me. Isn't she beautiful? Her name is Janie."

Lovey swayed and would have fallen had Sully not caught her.

Melissa came running. "Honey, what's wrong? Are you sick? Come sit down."

Lovey curled her fingers around Sully's wrist.

"Your name...all of it," she asked.

Sully frowned. "John Sullivan Raines, but she called—"

Lovey's voice was shaking, and she couldn't look away from his face.

"Oh my God!" she cried, and then grabbed his arm. "She called you Johnny. You were born in Columbus, Missouri, on June 4, 1974, to a sixteen-year-old girl named Loretta Jane Chapman."

Sully's heart began to pound. "How do you know that?"

"Because I'm that girl. My last husband called me Lovey, and that's all anyone in Blessings ever knew. The girl in the painting... I had that blouse, and your father gave me that necklace."

Sully looked down at the woman in his arms. His eyes were full of tears, but he couldn't stop smiling.

"Oh my God, indeed. Hello, Janie Chapman. I've been looking for you," he said, and wrapped his arms around her.

Lovey was laughing and crying, and Melissa was ecstatic for both of them.

"Both of you, come sit," she said.

And so they did, still holding hands, still staring at each other in total shock.

"You have no idea what just happened to me," Sully said. "All my life, I questioned my parents about why I didn't look like either of them. Why my hair was black and they both had light hair. Why my eyes were dark. Why they were so fair and freckled in the summers and why I tanned so easily. They laughed it off. All of it, telling me it was recessive genes, or that I looked like their long-dead relatives...and I bought it. Right up to the moment I found that birth certificate. Finding you gave credence to my existence."

He lifted Lovey's hands and kissed the back of each of them with such tenderness that it brought tears to Melissa's eyes. She was dumbstruck by the revelation and so overjoyed for both of them and grateful she was here when it happened.

"Thank you for coming to look for me," Lovey said. "I'd made peace with not being able to raise you, but I never gave you up in my heart. I loved every tiny inch of your perfect little self for the time I got to be with you. The grief of giving you up so suddenly after all that time was heart-wrenching. I'm so glad you found me. And you deserve answers." She took a deep breath. "Lord, help me get through this," she said softly, then began to talk.

"I grew up with a boy named Marc Adamos, and the year we turned fifteen, we suddenly saw each other in a different light. We fell in love…so much love. And even though we knew the consequences, we made love, too. I want you to know you were conceived in love. I didn't know I was pregnant until Marc and his family had moved away. I told my parents, and they were horrified. They were very religious and so angry with me. I wanted to keep you… I begged to keep you, and they refused. I was only fifteen. Then I told them it didn't matter what they thought because I was going to find Marc and we'd get married. They said if I did, they'd file charges against him for rape, and I was young and scared and I believed them."

Lovey shook her head, trying to gather her thoughts.

"I'm so sorry," Sully said. "I can't imagine how afraid you were, and how confused."

Lovey sighed. "I think I was in a daze after the initial confrontation. I'd go to sleep and wake up hoping it was all a bad dream. You didn't become real to me until the day I felt you kick."

Melissa handed Lovey some tissues and then quietly moved away.

Lovey wiped her eyes and took another deep breath.

"I was still living in our house, but my parents basically shunned me. I was reaping the consequences of my free will. When I began showing and everyone found out, I was banished from school on the grounds that I might contaminate the innocence of the kids in my class."

"Oh my lord! That was the mid-seventies. Hippies and free love all over the place," Melissa muttered.

"Exactly," Lovey said. "I was praying to God nonstop for answers, and they came. Painfully, but they *were* answers to a hopeless situation, which is where Joe and Dolly Raines came in."

Sully was nervous. He didn't know whether they were going to turn out to be kind and helpful to her, or part of the problem.

"They approached my parents," Lovey said. "They'd been trying to have a baby for years and couldn't, and Joe had a heart murmur which kept eliminating them from adoption lists.

"Basically, they came to my parents stating they wanted my baby. *My* baby. And my parents were so relieved to have the dirty business done with that they said yes without even telling me. Joe and Dolly came into my bedroom and told me they were going to take the baby the day it was born."

Lovey wiped her eyes again, and the tears started anew.

"They walked into my life like I had something to sell and they wanted it for free. That night I seriously thought about running away, but then asked myself…run where? Run to who? I couldn't take care of myself. How was I going to take care of a baby? So I quit fighting it. I never once said the word *yes* to my parents or the Raineses. I just signed the paper the day you were born and waited to die."

Sully was too choked up to speak, and he needed to hear the rest of the story. He'd come all this way to find out what happened that made her leave.

"Then the weirdest thing happened," Lovey said, and reached out and stroked the side of Sully's face. "About an hour later, Joe and Dolly returned, but my parents were with them. My mother informed me that I would be going home with the Raines family as the baby's wet nurse. While the Raineses were at work, I was to consider myself a kind of nanny, and they would give me room and board until you were weaned."

Sully stopped her. "Before you continue, I'm going to say this now. During my search, I'd already figured out Janie Chapman was one hell of a survivor. And now I'm learning how truly tough and special you are. I know you were there with me for six months, and then you just disappeared. I came looking for you to ask you one question."

Lovey lifted her chin. "Ask away."

"I need to know what happened. Why did you leave so abruptly?"

Lovey sighed. "There's a little backstory to this, so let me begin there. Ironically, my parents died of carbon-monoxide poisoning when you were about two months old, so technically, I would be dead, too, if I hadn't been living with Joe and Dolly. With the help of the family lawyer, I buried them, sold the family house, and banked a little money that turned out to be my saving grace. But the break between the Raineses and me happened when you were six months old. You'd been babbling for some time, and Joe and Dolly thought it was adorable. They'd made a bet between them as to whether you would say 'mama' or 'dada' first. Only when you finally said it, you said 'mama,' and you said it to me."

"Oh no," Sully said. He knew immediately what that would mean to adoptive parents.

Lovey shuddered. "It was a rude awakening for the both of them. They'd left all of your care to me and in doing so left you and me wide open to the unbreakable bond of a child to his mother. That night after I put you to bed, Dolly walked into my bedroom, told me to pack my bags and get out, and said she didn't want to ever see my face again."

Sully groaned.

"This breaks my heart for you. It was cruel and heartless, and I don't know what to say. But it answers the question I had of why they'd never told me. And why I didn't know about my father's necklace until they'd both passed." And then it hit him. "The necklace! Wait a minute. I'll be right back."

He ran out of the room and up the stairs, and when he did, Melissa went to sit beside Lovey.

"I am so happy for the both of you," she said.

Lovey shivered. "I'm still in shock. I never thought I would see my baby again, and then look what he became. This big, wonderful man!"

Sully came hurrying back into the room and walked up behind her.

"Close your eyes, and don't open them until I say to." He put the necklace around her neck and fastened it, then circled the sofa and took her by the hand. "Now, come with me, please," he said, and led her to the mirror in the hall. When he was standing behind her with his hands on her shoulders, he spoke. "You can look now."

Lovey looked, straight into the mirror, staring in disbelief at her reflection. Marc's Byzantine cross was back around her neck.

"Oh, Sully," Lovey said, and leaned back against him.

"Thank you for this. It was a special gift when he gave it to me, and after I learned you were on the way, in my heart it became the 'wedding ring' I never had."

Sully turned her just a little toward the painting visible from the living room.

"There we were, and here we are," he said, looking at their reflections in the mirror, in the same amazement as he had when he'd seen the painting.

Lovey put her hand over the cross, but she was looking at Sully as he spoke.

"I made a promise to myself that if I ever found you, I was giving it back. My father gave it to you, and that's who it still belongs to."

Lovey sighed. "I haven't seen Marc since he moved away, so I don't know what he grew up to look like, but you have his coloring…the same dark eyes and black hair, and you have his nose. But you have my smile, Johnny Raines."

Sully smiled back at her reflection, then wrapped his arms around her neck and kissed the top of her head.

"Thank you for making such a life-altering sacrifice, Janie Chapman. Thank you for my life."

CHAPTER 16

SULLY AND LOVEY WERE LOOKING AT THE PAINTING again and Melissa was out of the room when Lovey's phone rang. Lovey looked at the time and gasped.

"Oh lord, they probably think I went off somewhere and died," she muttered as she answered without the usual greeting. "Yes, I'm fine. I'm on my way." She disconnected without letting anyone talk.

"This has been a most remarkable day," Sully said. "There's just one last thing. Mother insisted on being called 'Mother,' and I always wanted to be one of those kids who came in the door from school yelling, 'Hey, Mom.' It sounds silly now, but since I have a second chance to ask, how do you feel about me calling you 'Mom'?"

Lovey threw her arms up in the air and hugged him again.

"I'd feel blessed beyond belief."

He grinned. "Then, thanks, Mom."

Lovey beamed. "You're very welcome, my son."

Melissa walked back into the foyer and caught the last bit of their conversation, which made her think of how this news would spread.

"How are you guys going to reveal this?" Melissa asked.

Lovey and Sully stared at each other.

"I don't know," Sully said.

Lovey patted his arm. "I do, and it will save having to repeat the story over and over as the news spreads. People nowadays are having big baby reveals to announce the sex of

THE WAY BACK TO YOU 245

their babies. How about we have a Reveal the Birth Mother party? Everyone knows why you came. Let's let them in on it together!"

Sully grinned. "I'm in!"

"Then we'd better do it fast because I'm bursting with joy for the both of you and horrible at keeping secrets," Melissa said.

"I need a cell phone number so I can text the date and time to you after I figure it out." Lovey said, and opened Contacts on her cell phone. Sully gave her his number. "Got it saved," Lovey said. "We host parties all the time in the banquet room, but we can open the whole restaurant up at the dinner hour and have ourselves a ball. Now, I've got to get back to work before the boss fires me," she said, and out the door she went.

Sully turned, his eyes alight with a joy Melissa had never seen before.

"It happened, baby! It happened," he cried, and then took her in his arms. "Can you hear the music?"

Melissa's eyes widened. "The Winter Ball! Yes, I hear it. It's the 'Blue Danube' waltz! The band director's favorite!"

Sully waited a moment, as if he was counting through the melody to a point where they could start, and when he took the first step, Melissa was right there with him, dancing to the music only they could hear.

Lovey sailed back into Granny's at 11:15 a.m., shooed Wendy back to waiting tables, and walked around the rest of the day with a smile on her face.

Mercy noticed the necklace a few hours later when Lovey went into the kitchen to grab a bite to eat before the supper crowd.

"Lovey, I've never seen you wear that necklace before. It's beautiful."

Lovey touched it lightly and shrugged it off. "Oh, I've had it since I was fifteen. I just decided to start wearing it again. It holds good memories. Do we have any bacon left? I'm kinda hungry for a BLT."

"Yep! Got some right here, Miss Lovey," Elvis said. "I'll fix you right up."

"Thanks, Elvis. Just send it out when you get to it."

"Yes, ma'am," he said.

Lovey made herself a drink and sashayed back into the dining room.

Mercy caught the feisty little walk, then grinned and shook her head. God threw away the mold after he was done with that woman.

Lovey had the booking ledger at the table with her when they brought out her sandwich.

"Thanks," she said, and took a bite before returning to the pages for the rest of the month, checking the reservations already in place and, as usual, talking to herself when she did the books.

"Okay, today is Monday, so Lions Club is tomorrow at noon, but they always eat whatever the special is for the day so no special cooking. There's the baby shower Friday night, but all they want is cake and drinks. The Preston family's sweet sixteen party for their daughter is Saturday night. Tuesday is too soon. Not enough time to get that much food together. Wednesday night is church for about half the town, so Thursday it is."

She wrote down the new entry—Party, 6:00 p.m.—and grinned. This news was going to blow the roof off every house in town. The only thing left to do for now was notify Sully and Melissa. She scrolled through her Contact list for the new number she entered earlier and then sent a text.

Ruby was in the act of closing the Curl Up and Dye for the day when she got a text from Lovey.

> Sister, I need to talk to you. Won't be done until 9:30 or so. Is that too late to come by?

Ruby's heart skipped a beat. Lovey was the sister she'd never had, and this kind of text was a first. Something must be wrong. She quickly replied.

> It's never too late for you, honey. See you later.

Worried now, she locked up and headed home.

The time flew by for Lovey in a way like never before, but then she'd never had such a wonderful story to tell. She locked the doors at straight-up nine. Her cleaning crew was already at work in the back, and when she gave them the thumbs-up, part of them started in the dining room as well. By the time they left, Granny's would be shining and ready for another day.

Lovey picked up her night-deposit bag, turned off the lights, and headed out. She drove straight to the bank to drop off the night deposit, tossed a piece of biscuit at the ratty tomcat, then drove to Peanut and Ruby's.

All of the outside lights were on at their place as she pulled up into the drive. Ruby appeared on the porch to greet Lovey before she was halfway up the path.

"Thank you for waiting for me," Lovey said as they hugged on the porch and then went inside.

"Of course," Ruby said, and then asked, "Is Peanut part of this?"

"Yes. Wives don't keep secrets from husbands," Lovey said. "Where is that handsome dude?"

"I'm right here," Peanut said as he walked up behind her in the hall. "Ruby said this felt like an 'across the kitchen table' kind of night. Was she right?"

Lovey grinned. "That's where all the news is shared. Lead the way, and I need a drink."

"Sweet tea?" Ruby asked.

"I'll take a shot of Peanut's fine Kentucky bourbon, if you don't mind."

Ruby gasped. "I knew it was bad. Oh lord, Lovey. Please tell me you're okay."

Lovey laughed. "I am beyond okay. But this is also a 'knock your socks off' kind of story."

"I'll bring the bottle," Peanut said.

"I'll get the glasses," Ruby added.

Lovey took a seat. Ruby put a glass at each place, and Peanut poured the shots.

"Do we do this now?" Ruby asked.

"We do this now, because I don't think I can get it said

without it." She lifted her glass. "To the lost. May they always find their way home."

The glasses clinked. The whiskey went down. Three empty shot glasses hit the table at the same time.

Lovey took a breath. "Sister, I've been keeping a secret. A secret that nobody in this town ever knew about me, and you're my dearest friend ever. You and Peanut are the family I didn't have…until today. A little over forty-five years ago, I gave a baby up for adoption, and he found me today!"

Ruby's mouth dropped open.

Peanut slapped the table with the flat of his hand.

"Sully? Sully Raines is your son?"

"Yes! Yes!" Lovey said, and started to cry. "It's so stupid that I didn't ever hear anyone say his last name. But you know me. I can't hear enough to cause trouble anymore. And then something happened today when I went over to visit Melissa, and everything clicked."

"But wait! I thought he was looking for a woman named Janie," Ruby said.

Lovey sighed. "I was born Loretta Jane Chapman in Kansas City, Missouri, sixty-two years ago. When I was fifteen, I fell in love with a boy named Marc Adamos, and he loved me, too. We made a baby, but he moved away before I knew." And then Lovey began telling the story, much like she'd told Sully hours earlier. When she was finished, Ruby was in tears, and Peanut was pouring himself a second drink.

"Sweet lord," Ruby said. "This is the saddest, most loving thing I've ever heard a birth mother do."

Lovey touched the necklace she was wearing. "I left this behind for my Johnny. Marc gave it to me before he left, and I left it behind for my baby. Today, he gave it back to me."

Ruby reached for her best friend's hand and squeezed it. "What a journey you've had to get to this day."

"Yes, and now Sully and I are going to do the big reveal at a party and let Blessings in on the news. This coming Thursday, Granny's last meal served will be at noon. Then we're closing up to prepare for a reopening party at 6:00 p.m. Everyone will be invited. We're sharing our story together so there's no mistaking the truth. I'm sure it won't stop the gossip, but none of it will compare to what I went through back then. I'm asking you two to keep it to yourselves until afterward."

"Consider it done," Peanut said.

"What can I do to help?" Ruby asked.

"I want flowers. Can you organize that for me? Some small arrangements to sit on a few of the tables we'll push against the walls, and a showy arrangement or two. You have better taste than I do, and just have the bills sent to me."

"I would be honored," Ruby said.

"Is there anything I can do to help?" Peanut asked.

"Not that I can think of right now," Lovey said.

"As long as you don't ask me to cook anything, we're safe," Peanut said.

They laughed, but when the cuckoo clock in the kitchen began chiming the hour, Lovey stood.

"It's ten o'clock. Time for all working people to be in bed. Thank you for being here for me."

"Always," Ruby said, and then walked her out. "Sleep well, my friend."

Lovey just shook her head. "I'm so wound up, I don't know if I'll get a wink of sleep tonight."

But after the quiet drive through Blessings on her way home, as soon as Lovey walked in the door and closed it behind her, the adrenaline crash hit. It was all she could do to get cleaned up and in bed. She set the alarm and then closed her eyes and dreamed the dream…the one that made the baby conceived in love.

The bedroom was in shadows. The television was off.

Melissa was waiting for him.

She heard the shower go off and closed her eyes, imagining his body covered in glistening droplets, seeing them drop from the ends of his hair, from his dark lashes, then tracking down his spine to the long, strong length of his legs.

She shivered.

He turned her on with his laugh and his loving heart.

The body was just icing on the cake.

A few moments later, the door opened and he was standing on the threshold. The lights behind him illuminated the dark beauty of the silhouette, and then they went out, leaving him bathed in the pale-blue glow of the night-light.

"I waited for you," Melissa said.

He paused. "You just climbed a small mountain on your belly."

"I can handle one more mountain if I start at the top and go down."

Sully threw back the covers and eased onto the mattress. The shape of him crawling toward her on his hands and knees made her ache, and she waited. Then he was over her, hovering. She closed her eyes and felt his mouth on her lips, soft at first, and then harder, more insistent.

One kiss became a thousand, became a pain, became a

fire, and then he slid his hands behind her back and rolled, taking her with him.

Like the phoenix rising out of the fire, she went up on her knees, then eased down until he filled her. His hands spanned the width of her waist, then slid down to the sides of her hips and started rocking her against him until the ride turned wild, became an all-engulfing fire, and it burned and burned until the flames went out.

Sully awoke the next morning, and the first thing he saw was his reflection in the clear-green color of Melissa's eyes.

She was watching him sleep.

Last night had been magic between them, and today he needed to keep a promise he'd made to her.

"My lady…my love…can you leave town today? Nothing that needs to be done regarding the shop?"

"Yes."

"You are due one slightly late engagement ring, and today's the day I put a ring on your finger."

She sighed. "You're already in my heart so deep that all the sad and broken parts of me are gone."

"That's what love is supposed to do. It took us a long time to find our way back to where we began, but I don't want to wait any longer to make it official."

They hurried through getting dressed and settled for coffee and cereal before leaving town.

A little over an hour later, they were at a jewelry store, standing in front of a display case and getting ready to try on rings.

Melissa had done her best to cover up the scratches on her face and had on a long-sleeved top to hide the scratches on her arms, but there wasn't a thing she could do about her hands.

Sully knew she was embarrassed and quickly put her at ease with a brief explanation to the jeweler that she was recovering from an accident.

Melissa gave him a grateful glance, and when the jeweler began to size her finger, she happily obliged.

"We always start with your proper size, but if you find something you like that isn't in your size, we can size it for you. Do you know the style you want?" he asked.

"Not really. I'll know it when I see it," she said, and then for the next thirty minutes tried on three-stone sets, then the settings he called halos, and then the channel sets, none of which she cared for.

"If you don't care for the ones with multiple stones, maybe these would be more to your liking," the jeweler said, and took out a display of solitaires.

Melissa smiled. "Yes," she said, pointing to one with a white gold band and a small stone.

"No," Sully said. "That one. Let her try that one on."

Melissa's eyes widened. "But, Sully, it's big."

He grinned. "Honey, I've been single for a long time and didn't plan on ever doing this again, until you happened. Try it on for me, please."

"These are all in your size." The jeweler smiled as he handed the ring to Sully. "Maybe you'd like to put it on her finger."

Sully took the ring.

Melissa held out her hand, then looked up.

He winked, slipped it on her finger, then kissed her.

The emotions that swept through Melissa were a mixture of the past and the present. Andy was before, and sometimes it was hard for her to remember what he looked like. Sully was here and now, and they loved—oh, how they loved.

"It's beautiful," she whispered.

"You make everything beautiful, my love," Sully said, then glanced up at the jeweler. "Does she have to take it off?"

The jeweler smiled. "I think we can work around that. Do you want to look at a band to go with it?"

Sully nodded, and a short while later the final decision had been made. A simple band to complement the solitaire, and one swipe of a credit card, and they were out the door and back in the car.

Melissa kept looking at the ring and smiling.

"It's so beautiful, Sully. You were my first love. You were the first boy I ever kissed, and it's so special that fate put us back together again. I love you so much."

"Then we commemorate the first kiss with another to celebrate the engagement," he said, and leaned across the console.

She met him halfway, and it was sweeter the second time around.

"There's one more thing I need to do before we leave," Sully said. "I don't have any real dress clothes here. Do you know if there's a Big and Tall shop in Savannah?"

"We'll go to Oglethorpe Plaza. There's a Men's Wearhouse, and they have a big and tall section."

"Will you help me pick out something proper for the party?" She beamed. "I'd love to."

"We can get something new for you, too," he added.

"I don't need anything, honey. I already have several outfits I could wear," Melissa said.

"Wow, I may be the luckiest man in the world. I have fallen in love with a woman who turned down an opportunity to shop."

"Oh, just hush and drive," she said.

Sully laughed, and was still laughing when they drove away from the jewelry store.

They reached the plaza, parked on the side closest to Men's Wearhouse, and walked in hand in hand. Once they found the store, then went back to the section for big and tall, Sully went straight to black dress slacks and picked out a couple of styles.

Melissa was looking through them on her own and picked out one more style.

"Sully, I think you might like these, too."

"Okay. I'll try them on, and you choose."

"What about shirts? Do you want one to tuck in, or—"

"I brought my good belt, so a tuck-in, but with an open collar," he said.

"What about color?" Melissa asked.

"White…for the occasion," Sully said, and went into the dressing room while Melissa gathered up a couple of white dress shirts. One was made of a thick, crisp cotton, and the other was a polyester blend.

She was sitting in a chair outside the dressing room when he walked out in the first pair of black slacks, and she sighed.

"You are such a hunk," she whispered.

He grinned. "I'll go try the next ones."

He came back out a couple of minutes later. "What about these?"

256 SHARON SALA

"They both make your legs look even longer. They're a perfect fit on your cute little butt. You're still a hunk."

Sully laughed. "You're not helping. I have one more."

Melissa waited.

When he walked out in the last pair, Melissa sighed.

"Pick out the ones that feel the most comfortable, because you rock them all."

"Then the first ones it is," Sully said. "Are those the shirts?"

"Yes...the main difference is fabric. Cotton or polyester blend?"

"The one that doesn't wrinkle," he said.

"Polyester it is," Melissa said, and went to put the other one back while Sully went to get dressed.

He paid for the purchases, and as they were leaving the store, he lifted her hand to his lips and kissed the spot right below her ring.

"Thanks for all the help," he said.

Melissa paused. "Are you being sarcastic?"

"Maybe," he said. "When your eyes glazed over, I knew you were thinking about sex. I lost you after that."

She laughed. "You are such a smart-ass. It's not my fault you look so gorgeous naked."

An elderly woman walked past them grinning, winked at Sully, gave Melissa a thumbs-up, and kept walking.

He laughed. "Now look what you did. I have been scandalized."

"We just need to get to the car before I embarrass myself any more," Melissa said.

"Lunch here, or back in Blessings?" Sully asked.

"Lunch at Granny's. I can't wait for Lovey to see my ring."

CHAPTER 17

THEY DROVE INTO BLESSINGS A LITTLE BEFORE NOON, still locked in the joy of what they'd done. A pledge to marry was as serious to both of them as the act itself.

Melissa had smiled all the way from Savannah and was still smiling to herself as they drove up Main toward Granny's.

"What are you smiling about?" Sully asked.

"Oh, you…me…and life from this point. I don't know how to explain it, but life feels new to me. I quit participating in it for such a long time, but now I'm different, and life is different, too. We're going to be happy for a very long time, aren't we, Sully?"

"We're already being happy, baby. No doubts. Nothing but joy."

"Nothing but joy," she repeated as he pulled into the lot at Granny's and parked.

"Let's go start some new gossip," Sully said.

Melissa laughed. "You already have your finger on the pulse of small-town living, don't you?"

"I love it here," Sully said.

They got out of the car and walked into Granny's hand in hand.

Lovey grinned when she saw them, then slipped out from behind the counter and gave both of them a quick hug.

Melissa held out her hand.

Lovey saw the ring and squealed.

"Congratulations! My cup runneth over. Just good news after good news."

Sully was nothing but smiles, watching the two women in his life with their heads together, when three more people walked in, and Lovey shifted back into work mode.

"I'll be right with you," she said. She grabbed a couple of menus and led Sully and Melissa into the dining room and seated them at a table, then winked as she hurried back to seat the others.

"What are you hungry for?" Sully asked.

"I think today is the meat loaf special. If it is, that's what I want."

Sully closed his menu and set it aside. "Sounds good to me. Two specials coming up."

They were halfway through the meal when Lovey came sailing by, flashed the poster-board sign she was carrying, and kept walking.

Melissa giggled. "She's already putting up the Thursday afternoon Closed sign."

A couple of minutes later, Lovey went back into the kitchen and came out with another sign, which she also flashed at them.

Sully grinned. "She's really getting into this."

"Surprise reveal party Thursday night in Granny's. 6:00 p.m. Everyone's invited," Melissa said. "Lord. The last time the whole city was invited to something was Peanut and Ruby's wedding, and they had to hold it at the city park."

Sully eyed the size of the dining room. "How big is the banquet room?" he asked.

"It's bigger than this room," Melissa said, then pointed to the folding doors on the back wall.

Sully was thinking about how many people the state fire marshal would allow in one place, but then decided Lovey had been at this job for years. She knew what she was doing.

"One way or another, we're all going to be surprised how this turns out," he said.

———————————

Following Lovey's request, Ruby ordered small arrangements and two large floral arrangements—one for the dining room and one for the banquet area. Then she ordered another small arrangement to sit on the front desk, with delivery by 4:00 p.m. on Thursday.

Determined not to make the employees at Granny's cook and cater on such a grand scale, Lovey told them what was happening and that they were invited to the party as guests, not employees.

She had already contacted a married couple she knew who owned a big catering company in Savannah, asking them if they could do her event on short notice.

Once the caterers found out how casual it would be, and that while the number of people expected was large, all Lovey requested was simple finger foods and one giant four-tiered cake, they readily agreed.

Lovey didn't blink at the cost and described the cake decor she wanted—small silver Byzantine crosses made from fondant, winding around the cake like a staircase, with a gray-haired woman holding the sign HERE I AM as the cake topper. The caterers would arrive by four and have it all set up by party time.

All the employees knew was that something big was

happening, and when Lovey took off work again right after breakfast service on Wednesday to go buy a new outfit at the Unique Boutique, they were in shock. In all the years they'd known her, she'd never done this. Suppositions were flying.

But it was Mercy who finally put an end to the kitchen gossip when she banged a wooden spoon on her metal baking table and yelled, "Hey!"

Elvis, the fry cook, stopped talking. The waitresses all froze. Chet, the dishwasher, jumped and dropped a plate.

"It didn't break!" he yelled.

Mercy rolled her eyes. "You guys! Why does it matter what's going on? We adore Lovey. She's the best boss I've ever had, and I've had plenty. If she's happy, we should be happy with her and for her, right?"

They all nodded.

"Then calm down and go do your jobs. Wendy, get back to the register. The rest of you know what you're supposed to be doing."

They'd become so accustomed to Mercy being in charge when Lovey was recuperating from her injuries that they thought nothing of her calling them out and quickly went back to work.

Lovey was like a fish out of water in the dress department and finally settled on some dressy black slacks. The boutique already had outfits for the upcoming holiday season, and when she spotted a black-and-silver sequin top with long sleeves and a V-neck, she was sold before she even tried it on. When it fit, she quit looking.

"This is the one," she said as she came out of the dressing room.

Satisfied she was ready, all she had left was the Thursday hair appointment. She went back to work, and Wednesday came to an end.

It was the next morning before Lovey began to get nervous. There were parts of their story that Lovey would never share in a public forum, but the simple act of admitting she'd given away her baby still broke her heart. She'd buried the pain long ago, and the only time the memories came back was at night when her emotional defenses were down and she dreamed. The bottom line was she didn't want to bawl like a baby in front of everyone.

She got through the first half of the day, getting the PA system set up in the banquet hall, and as soon as she locked the doors, her staff began cleaning, getting the place ready for the party and the catering crew. Once they finished, Lovey walked out with them.

"See you this evening," she said, and locked the door.

"What time do you need to be back to open up for deliveries?" Mercy asked.

"The flowers will be delivered around four. The caterers will be here at four to set up," Lovey said.

"How about you go home and do whatever you need to do, and I'll come back to let in deliveries. You can come back whenever you want to, but you won't have to be in a panic. We don't know what's going on, but we know it's a big deal to you, so let me help."

Lovey hugged her.

"You stood in for me when I was hurt, and I can't tell you what it meant for me to be able to heal without worrying about what was happening to my place. You all saved it for me, and you're the sweetest thing for offering this. I will take you up on all of that, if you're sure."

"I'm sure," Mercy said. "I'll come back already dressed for the party. Go get prettied up."

And so Lovey did. She ran home to shower, then hurried to the Curl Up and Dye. Once her hair was fixed, she went back home to get dressed.

She got all the way into her bedroom and then collapsed in a state of nerves and called Ruby.

"Hey, Lovey," Ruby said when she answered.

"Oh, Sister, I am a nervous wreck. I'm so proud to introduce Sully as my son, but I don't know if I can do it without crying, and you know how I look when I cry. My eyes swell, my nose gets red, and I ugly-cry."

Ruby laughed. "You're gonna be fine, Lovey. So what if you tear up? You aren't going to lose it. I know you. Just hold onto the thought of what a blessing all this is. You two have had your own little miracle happen right under our noses. You won't be the only one tearing up, I promise you."

"You think?" Lovey asked.

"I know," Ruby said. "And we'll be there cheering for you when you reveal the reason for the party."

Lovey sighed. "You're right. I can do this."

"Of course you can. Now, make yourself pretty and give Blessings something to talk about tonight."

"That's gonna happen anyway, no matter what I look like," Lovey said. "Thank you. I don't know what I'd do without you, girl."

"The feeling is mutual," Ruby said. "See you later."

Lovey hung up, then called Sully.

"Hello."

"It's me, Sully. I forgot to ask what time you two plan on arriving."

"We'll be there when you want us to be," he said. "Is there something you need? Something you want us to bring?"

"If you can be there around five, that would be good. We haven't talked about whether you want to say anything, or—"

"We'll talk about it when I get there, Mom. Don't sweat it. I'm so happy this is happening. Nothing matters to me except finding you."

"It's a pretty big deal for me, too," Lovey said. "I'm so proud of the man you became. Oh...the parking lot will be roped off so that guests can spill out into that area as well. The caterers are setting up some chairs, and there will be bar tables so people will have a place to put their drinks as they visit. Parking is along the curbs."

Now Sully's worry concerning fire hazards had been put to rest. "We can handle that. See you soon."

Melissa came out of her walk-in closet carrying the outfit she planned to wear.

"Is Lovey okay?"

"I think she's nervous. She's known these people for years and years. Having to let go of her deepest secret is probably scary as hell. I can't imagine how that must feel," Sully said.

"Bless her heart. Should we get there earlier?"

Sully nodded. "She asked if we could be there by five. I said yes."

"Then I better quit dawdling," Melissa said, and they both began to get ready.

When Lovey walked back into Granny's a little after 4:30, Mercy gasped, then went to meet her.

"Oh, Lovey, you look beautiful! Your hair is gorgeous put up like that. The outfit is dynamite, and your silver cross sits perfect in the V-neck of your top. Don't do anything but watch. Whatever you want done, tell me. I don't want one thing about you messed up."

Lovey beamed. "I see the caterers are already here. Have they brought the cake in yet?"

"It's here. They weren't sure where you wanted them to put it."

"In the banquet room in front of the podium."

"I'll tell them right now," Mercy said.

Lovey took the time to look at how beautiful everything was. The dining room tables had been moved so that most of the space was left open for people to mingle, but they were all covered with white tablecloths, and each bud vase had a single rose. A large floral arrangement was on a round pedestal table in the middle of the floor. Lovey didn't know where that table came from, but she suspected Ruby was responsible. It looked dramatic, which was just what Lovey was going for.

She moved into the banquet room to check it out. One of her eight-foot banquet tables was in front of the podium, covered with a white tablecloth, awaiting the cake. The other large floral arrangement was on another pedestal table in the middle of this room as well. Some of the long banquet tables had been scooted against the walls, but most of them had been folded up and stored in the equipment room. It looked so grand, Lovey hardly recognized the place.

She was still standing there when Sully and Melissa walked up behind her and grasped her hands.

Sully whispered in her ear. "You look beautiful, Mom."

Melissa squeezed Lovey's hand. "You are radiant," Melissa said, "and the place is amazing."

"Thank you, Sully. Thank you, Melissa. I never dreamed this could happen. I can't wait to share our news, which brings me to the question of the announcement. How are we going to do this?"

"You need to be the one to say however much you want to say. They've all heard my story. Now you tell yours," he said.

Lovey nodded. "Okay, but will you stand beside me when I do it?"

"Of course, and proudly," Sully said.

"Then it's settled. Oh, look, they're bringing the cake. It goes in front of the podium."

They followed the people with the cake, watching as they transferred it from the cart to the table. Another cart followed with the serving setup. It was exactly the level of fuss that Lovey wanted, and as soon as they were gone, they got their first good look at the cake.

"It's huge!" Sully said, eyeing the size.

"I love this!" Melissa said. "The cross being stair steps! And the 'Here I am' flag on the cake topper is priceless."

Sully gave Lovey a quick hug. "This is awesome."

Lovey clasped her hands in delight. "It's exactly how I imagined it. It should be tasty, too. Two layers are vanilla with strawberry filling, and two are vanilla with Swiss meringue filling, and then it's all covered in white fondant. It's supposed to serve several hundred. I hope the turnout is good."

"Are you kidding?" Melissa said. "That's all people have talked about in town since you put up the signs. I heard all of the businesses along Main Street have volunteered their parking spaces, including the Crown which is closing early so their parking lot can be utilized as parking for this event."

Lovey looked up at Sully, briefly touching his cheek.

"So dear to my heart," she said softly, then blinked away tears. "After tonight, I can officially call you my son."

"It's getting close to time," Sully said. "We'll keep a little distance away from you until you're ready to make the announcement so it won't give away the surprise."

Lovey nodded. "Okay, guys. Let's do this," she said.

By the time she reached the front lobby, people were already coming in.

And so began the excitement of people seeing Lovey's appearance and how the interior of Granny's had been transformed. Almost immediately, the caterers began moving through the gathering crowd with finger foods and drinks.

Melissa's status as a newly engaged woman was noted, and the word quickly spread, with most of the crowd assuming this party was for her and Sully, until they mingled their way into the banquet room and saw the cake. Now they didn't know what to think.

It was 6:30 on the dot when Lovey gave Sully and Melissa a nod, then headed for the podium. Sully escorted her up the steps and then stood aside. Lovey turned on the microphone, then tapped it to make sure it was live.

The room had already quieted down and everyone was waiting, but they didn't know what for until Lovey began to speak.

"I know you all want to know what's going on, so I won't

keep you in suspense any longer. I have a story to tell about the saddest and happiest times of my life. When I was barely sixteen years old, I was forced, by my parents, to give my baby boy up for adoption. I never thought I'd see him again."

She paused and drew a deep, shaky breath. "So you know how I don't hear things so good anymore, and how most of my attention is always focused on Granny's…which is how I completely missed details that could have saved this delay. You all know Sully here has been looking for his birth mother, Janie Chapman."

Sully walked up beside her and winked.

Lovey blinked away tears as she reached for his hand.

"Although I've been Lovey to all of you for as long as I've lived here…I was born Loretta Jane Chapman, and tonight I want to introduce you to my son, John Sullivan Raines."

The room erupted in cries of shock, then surprise and delight. And when Sully wrapped his arms around her and hugged her, there wasn't a dry eye in the house.

"Way to go, Mom," he whispered.

"You say what you want now. I can't do any more," Lovey said.

When Sully moved to the podium, the room went silent again.

"You've all heard my story about not even knowing I was adopted until a few months ago. But you have no idea what finally finding my Janie has meant. I have answers to why I look the way I do. I now know the name of my father. I know why my hair is black and my eyes are dark, and that half of my heritage is Greek. I know that the bonds of parent to child are stronger than anything science could ever prove.

"The moment this happened for us was the moment my

lopsided world finally righted. Melissa and I were already in the process of getting ready to move all of my belongings here to Blessings, because I have fallen in love with her and this town. But after forty-five years without knowing I had another mother, little did I know I'd already found her. Finding out she is such an amazing person was a bonus. It's evident how much my mom is loved and admired here, so I feel like I just won the lottery."

The room erupted into cheers and clapping, and more tears, and then Lovey stepped up to the podium again.

"Thank you for coming so I could share this news with all of you. I think it's time we cut this cake and party."

After that, Lovey was engulfed. Hugs of congratulations, people wanting pictures of Sully and Lovey together, and more congratulations to Sully and Melissa.

Newcomer Cathy Terry had seen the sign on Granny's and came out of curiosity, and for something to do. Now she was glad that she had. It was a good feeling to know some people still had happy endings in their lives.

People moved in and out of the building and back again, talking among themselves about what a miracle this was, and talking about how strange it was to know and love someone for so many years without knowing anything about their past.

By the time the party was winding down and the caterers were packing up, more than a dozen men stayed behind to help Lovey put Granny's back together again.

Peanut showed up with a borrowed truck to pick up the pedestal tables the flowers had been on, and they put the flowers in the banquet room to be used tomorrow for the next event.

Finally, Granny's was in place and ready for morning

customers, and Lovey was going around checking locks and equipment in the kitchen to make sure everything had been turned off and cleaned.

As soon as she was satisfied all was well, she went through turning out the lights, and then found Sully and Melissa waiting for her in the lobby.

"I didn't know you two were still here," she said.

"I was helping the caterers load up the bar tables and folding chairs so we could take the chain off the parking lot," Sully said. "It's all ready to go for tomorrow now."

Lovey stared at him then. "I just realized something."

"What?" Sully said.

"Well, Granny's has been here for a long time, but I'm not getting any younger. I've wondered now and then if someone else would buy it when I'm gone, or if it would just go by the wayside. Now I don't have to worry about that anymore. This will all be yours one day...if you want it."

The smile that spread across Sully's face lit up the whole world.

"If I want it? Mom! I would be honored to carry on what you've built. I know how to put out a fire in the kitchen, but I don't know anything about running a place like this. I'll bus tables. I'll sweep floors. I'll even be your bouncer if the need ever arises, while you teach me what I'll need to know."

"Well, now I am gonna cry," Lovey said, and hugged him to her. "It would be my delight to do just that."

"Sully, I think you just found your job," Melissa said. "He's been trying to come up with something ever since he decided to move here. You are an answer to his prayer, in more ways than one."

"It's late, and you must be exhausted," Sully said. "So I'm

going to take this as my first lesson. Do you leave on night-lights, and if so, where do you turn them on?"

Lovey pointed them out, and as soon as Sully turned them on, she turned out the lights in the lobby and walked Sully and Melissa out.

"Usually, I have a night-deposit bag with me when I come out this door, and I go straight from here to the bank, but that's all for another day."

"Melissa and I are making a quick trip to Kansas City to close up my apartment and bring back my personal belongings. Once that trip is over, I will gladly show up anytime you want, any days that you want. Just let me know." Then he looked around. "Where did you park?"

Lovey pointed across the street at the Seed and Feed store. "That lone car in the parking lot is mine."

"As soon as I get Melissa in the car, I'll walk you across."

Once they reached his car, Melissa gave Lovey a big hug. "I am so happy we're going to be family."

"Oh, child, so am I," Lovey said.

After Melissa was safely inside, Sully walked Lovey across the street, gave her a good-night kiss and another hug, then waited until she was driving away before jogging back across the street to where Melissa was waiting.

He slid into the seat, then leaned across the console and kissed her.

"Love you, honey. Thank you for helping me make this time so special for Mom."

"It was the best, seeing how she blossomed when she realized her news had not caused people to feel disdain toward her. I think that was her biggest fear...how she would be received."

"Which says a lot about how she was treated when she found out she was pregnant," Sully said. "The ridicule and shaming for a teenager would have been devastating... and to be facing it alone. She said my dad was never told. I wonder what he'd think if he found out about me, kind of like I found out about them?"

"I don't know. Maybe you'll find him one day, like you did your mom."

"That would be the best. To know both of them."

He started the car, then made a U-turn in the empty street and headed home, holding her hand all the way.

"Hey, honey, I've been thinking about my stuff back in Kansas City. After all that's been happening, and what you've gone through, a road trip is not the best idea."

"If you need to go alone, that's fine. You won't hurt my feelings," Melissa said.

"Oh no, I'm not leaving you. I'm going to make a couple of calls tomorrow. I'll make a list of what I want packed up and sent here, and I'll donate the rest to Habitat for Humanity."

"What if they miss some stuff you want?" Melissa said.

"The only thing I'm leaving behind is furniture and the like. Everything else will come here, and I'll sort out what I want to keep then," he said. "Now no more worry. It's settled."

CHAPTER 18

Marc Adamos was finally back home in Springfield, Missouri, after his long flight from the Hawaiian Islands. He'd been on Hawaii, the Big Island, for a couple of months, getting live footage of the recent activity from the Kilauea volcano, as well as the extreme flooding that had happened on one of the other islands.

He was in his office going through still shots and video. Once he'd scanned in the stills, making notes as to which ones he might use for the documentary, he moved to different footage he'd gotten earlier in the year. The first set he picked up was what he'd gotten on the California fires. He'd moved on to the extensive fires that burned the Pacific Northwest. He'd been on-site during hurricanes for footage and video during and after the storms that had hit along the southern border of Texas, as well as a later hurricane that had impacted the East Coast along the Florida and Georgia coasts.

He loaded what he wanted onto his laptop and then took it with him into the kitchen to make himself some lunch. He'd been gone so long that ready food in his place was sparse, but he did have a couple of cans of soup and some crackers in the pantry and settled on that rather than ordering in.

After having worked for *National Geographic* most of his adult life, he was getting ready to retire. The story he was working on now would be his last and eventually would be aired on the National Geographic Channel on cable TV.

Since it was his swan song, he was determined to give it his full attention.

The topic of the program was natural disasters, marking the increase in earthquakes and volcanic eruptions and even the change in weather patterns.

His job as a photojournalist for Nat Geo had left little room for a personal life. He'd never married. It was hard to have a relationship when a job was as fluid and mobile as his. Life had not turned out the way he'd once expected, but he was satisfied with where it had taken him.

The soup was heating on the stove, and he'd put a fresh pot of coffee on to brew when his cell phone rang. He set the soup off the heat to answer it.

"Hello. Marc speaking."

"Marc, it's me, David."

Marc smiled. His younger brother, David, was his best friend.

"Hey, Bro, what's up?"

"I know you just got home, but I'm afraid I have bad news. Uncle Wayne passed away early this morning."

Marc frowned. "Oh man, the cancer?"

"Yes," David said. "He's been in the hospital for the past three weeks and on life support all of this past week. Aunt June and the girls finally agreed it was time, and they took him off this morning. He passed about three minutes afterward."

"I'm so sorry. I guess it's too soon to know when the service will be," Marc said.

"They've had three weeks to make decisions," David said. "They're at the funeral home as we speak, setting a date. As soon as I find out, I'll text you. Can you come?"

"Absolutely," Marc said. "You know how we are. Family is everything."

David sighed. "Yes. I'll get back to you later today. Glad you're home. It will be good to see you again. I suppose you are still rocking your silver-fox look. No hope you finally got fat, or that you finally shrunk so I'd be the taller son?"

Marc laughed. "What are you complaining about? You're the one with the beautiful wife and grandkids."

"True," David said and laughed, but he knew there was a sadness in Marc that he had neither. "When I know more, I'll text."

"Okay, and tell Aunt June I love her and I'll see her soon."

"Yeah, I will," David said.

The smile on Marc's face disappeared the moment the connection ended. Their uncle Wayne had been the father figure in their lives ever since he and David were in their early twenties. But the old man had suffered too long with inoperable cancer, and he had lived a long and fruitful life. In Marc's eyes, there was no greater blessing.

He poured the soup and took the bowl and a soup spoon to the table, tossed a handful of oyster crackers on the surface of the hot chowder, and then took a small bite. The time he'd been on the phone had been the perfect cooling period, and he ate the rest of the soup without issue.

He got a text from David about three hours later regarding the funeral and began making plans to head to Kansas City, Missouri, for the family gathering that would be the night before the funeral, then stay over the next day for the services before heading home.

Knowing he was going to be gone in a couple of days, Marc worked diligently all the next day at compiling stills and footage for the show and typing narrative to go with it. He was going through some stills from the East Coast hurricane when he ran across some he'd pulled from the AP news service. They'd been taken in a small town called Blessings, which was near Savannah, the city where Marc had been when the hurricane hit. Blessings was about an hour inland from Savannah, but the little town had suffered devastating flooding, and months later they were still in a healing and rebuilding mode.

He flipped through a handful of photos before pausing at one that was particularly startling. A huge tree limb had been driven into the side of a house by the wind, but it was the story that went with it that caught his attention.

The woman who lived in that house had been seriously injured when that happened. Not only had she been trapped, but she would have died from her injuries had it not been for a daring rescue by one of the townspeople.

There was another photo related to the same story that had been pulled from security footage at the local hospital when the woman was first brought in. The hospital had been operating at half-staff and running on backup generators when the rescuers arrived with the victim, and the photo illustrated the extreme danger they had put themselves in to get her inside.

One young man had used an enormous bulldozer to rescue her from the house where she'd been trapped and then driven it through floodwater to get her to the hospital.

The photo showed the driver being buffeted by the hurricane-force winds as he exited the cab with the woman in his arms. A few steps below him was an orderly from the hospital standing partway up the dozer, trying not to be blown off as he was reaching out to take the woman, and another waiting below him in bucket-brigade fashion to get the woman down from the dozer.

Marc saw their plan, and it was a gutsy one. That man who was holding her in the photo would have to maintain his stance against the wind, and the weight of the woman, as he turned to hand her down to the man below him, and the same danger would apply to him, and then the last man until she was safe. Even though the photo was a still shot, it captured the danger and the drama in the different expressions on the men's faces. Marc couldn't see much of the woman, but the info with the photo stated she was badly injured.

This would be a great piece to add to the hurricane section, Marc thought. *I need to talk to those men...to understand what kind of courage it takes to brave something like that, and find out what happened to her.*

He glanced at the text that had come with the picture and saw that it mentioned two names: Johnny Pine, who owned and drove the dozer to save her, and Lovey Cooper, the woman he'd saved. Marc clipped the photo to the information that had come with it and laid it aside.

He spent the next day packing and getting ready to drive to Kansas City. Even if he was going for a sad reason, he'd grown up there with a large extended family and considered it home.

Early the next morning, he loaded up and left Springfield, then connected later to northbound I-49. The day was clear, the traffic moderate. It was about a four-hour drive away, give or take, and he should be there around noon.

He was braced for the tears and stories that would be

flying at the family dinner tonight, but he would be glad to see his brother, David, again.

He already knew from David's phone call this morning that David's wife, Linda, would be at their aunt June's house helping get ready for the family gathering, and neither of his kids would be coming home to attend. David's daughter was in college in California, and his married son was in the Coast Guard and stationed along the Florida coast. Both children had opted not to come, so Marc and David would go to the gathering together.

David told him where the spare key to his house was hidden, and if Marc got there before he got off work to just go in and make himself at home. So when Marc arrived a little after eleven, he got his bag, let himself in the house, and went straight to the guest room where he'd stayed before.

David Adamos took off work at noon and would not be returning until the day after the funeral, so when he saw Marc's car already in the drive, he broke into a grin then came in the front door, calling out Marc's name.

"Marco."

Marc grinned as he came up the hall. "Polo," he answered, which was exactly what David was expecting.

David laughed out loud, then gave Marc a quick hug.

"Have you had lunch?" David asked.

"No."

"Then how do you feel about burgers and fries? You know the food tonight is going to be mostly traditional

Greek dishes and loads of them. Linda and one of the cousins are making dolmas right now. I wouldn't want to be anywhere near that kitchen today while they're making the rice and lamb stuffing. They'd have the both of us rolling it up in grape leaves."

"For sure," Marc said. "I remember dolmas were Uncle Wayne's favorites, and yes, burgers work for me," Marc said. "Let me wash up. It won't take long."

"Can I drive your Hummer?" David asked.

Marc grinned. "Sure, and you can buy me lunch, too."

David laughed. "Done."

They talked all the way to the restaurant, and all the way through their meal, catching up on family news, and as always David wanted to hear about Marc's latest adventures.

"So, was it as scary seeing that volcano on-site as it was for us seeing it on the news? When I found out you were there, I said a few prayers for you. Did you have any close calls?"

"A couple. I was a little too close once and had the soles of my shoes start to melt."

"Oh hell, Marco…please tell me you're serious about retiring," David said.

"Yes, I've already given notice. I just have to finish up this last piece."

"What else besides volcanic activity will be in the story?"

Marc popped a fry into his mouth and chewed before answering.

"Oh, fires and hurricanes, and some human-interest stuff

to go along with each one. I'm actually going to Georgia after this to do some follow-up there. I have a couple of really amazing stills of a life-and-death rescue during a hurricane, and I want personal interviews with the people to back it up. I don't know if one of the victims who was in a photo even survived."

"What are you going to do afterward?" David asked.

"Oh, that's easy. I have a life's worth of photos that have yet to see the light of day. If I want, I can do coffee-table books forever. But what I really want to do is find the little out-of-the-way places in this country and get human-interest stories there."

David reached across the table and took one of Marc's fries, dunked it in Marc's ketchup, and popped it in his mouth, then saw the irked look on his brother's face.

"What? Mine are gone. You were letting yours get cold. I didn't want that one to go to waste."

Marc laughed. "If you only knew how many cold leftover meals I've eaten in my life."

"Besides having to outrun fires and volcanoes, is that how you've stayed so thin?"

Marc shrugged. "Maybe. Getting the crap scared out of you *can* ruin an appetite."

They laughed and talked their way through the rest of the meal, then finally headed back to David's house.

"Rest for a while if you want," David said. "I'm going to check in with Linda and see if they need us to bring anything."

"I think I'll stretch out on the bed and watch a little television. Just let me know when it's time to get ready," Marc said.

A couple of hours later, Marc was up and shaving, his

mind on the family he knew he was going to see and wishing it wasn't for such a sad reason. Even though his uncle Wayne was no longer suffering, his presence would definitely be missed.

This time when they left David's house, Marc was driving, and as they wound their way through the city he couldn't help but remember when he'd lived here.

"Hey, David. Remember the day we came home from school and Mom and Dad sat us down and told us we were moving?"

"Oh yeah. I cried, and you hit the ceiling. I didn't want to leave my friends, and you didn't want to leave that girl... What was her name?"

"Janie Chapman," Marc said. "We'd spent the entire year together, and just as we were getting ready to go back to school, I had to tell her we were moving. Broke both our hearts."

"I was going to be a freshman. Officially a teenager... the most awkward age ever, and I had to be the new kid in school. I hated most of my freshman year," David said.

Marc remembered that time all too well.

"I became that angry, brooding teen. If it hadn't been for the photography classes I took at the community college on weekends, there's no telling how I would have wound up."

"Well, we both turned out okay in the long run, but it was a hard transition, for sure. And for me, the biggest loss was being torn away from all our extended family."

"I'm really looking forward to seeing some of them tonight," Marc said.

He braked for a light and then turned right on the green arrow. Ten minutes later, they were pulling up to the

Adamos home. The driveway was already full of cars, so he parked against the curb.

"It's sure going to be weird without Uncle Wayne here," David said.

Marc nodded, and then they both got out and headed to the house. The door was always unlocked during family gatherings, so they walked in without knocking.

Marc was immediately surrounded by family, all welcoming him home. He went into the kitchen to look for his aunt, and when he saw her at the sink, he walked up behind her and gave her a quick hug.

"Hey, Aunt June."

June turned in his arms. "Oh, Marco! You're home! I'm so glad you came," she said.

"I'm so sorry about Uncle Wayne," he said.

"So am I, but it was a blessing. He suffered so much this past month." Then she wiped away tears. "I hear you are retiring."

"Yes. Getting too old to chase rainbows, I think."

She smiled and patted both his cheeks. "You are such a handsome man. Still young enough to find a wife. Someone to grow old with."

Marc laughed. "I've been growing old just fine by myself. Is there anything David and I can do for you?"

"You can go answer the door, show people where to put their things, and play host for a bit until Leo gets here."

Marc thought of their oldest son and the good times they'd had as children.

"It will be good to see everyone again."

"And they will be glad to see you," she said.

Marc greeted his sister-in-law with a hug, and then two aunts and a cousin, before leaving the kitchen.

After that, he and David took turns answering the door and welcoming the family until Leo and his family arrived. Once he'd been relieved of his duties, Marc took it upon himself to work the room, making sure everyone had a drink of some kind and a place to sit.

It wasn't until later when the food was laid out buffet-style in the dining room and people started pairing up to get in line that he realized he was the only single male in the room, and the only Adamos with no children. It didn't actually leave him regretting his life choices, but not for the first time did he wonder what he was missing.

But he got in line with everyone else, then found an empty chair to sit in while he ate. He was sitting in a chair behind a sofa where Sophia, Marlee, Tina, and Rachel, four of his cousins, were visiting, waiting for another urn of coffee to brew before they tackled a piece of baklava.

He was paying little attention to their conversation until he realized they were talking about teenage girls back in their day getting pregnant, and how they had not been allowed to go to high school with others as if it was something contagious. He heard them mention that out of their class of eight hundred, they only knew of three.

He was thinking how times had changed since then, when he heard them mention Janie Chapman's name as one of those girls. At that point, his heart nearly stopped. He thought back to their lives together before he moved and knew they'd had unprotected sex more than once. But he'd moved away. Surely that must mean it happened after he was gone. He couldn't believe Janie would not have contacted him if it was theirs. She had known too many of his relatives for her to think she didn't know how to find him.

But now that his cousins had captured his attention, he was listening to everything they said.

"Did you ever hear what happened to her after she quit school?" Sophia asked.

"Yes, and it was sad," Marlee said.

"I know, too," Tina said. "Her parents wouldn't let her keep the baby. They said she was too young."

"So what did she do?" Sophia asked.

"They made her give the baby boy up for adoption, but here's what's strange about it. When the adoptive parents took the baby home, they took Janie with them. They were both working people, so she stayed with them and nursed her baby and was basically their live-in babysitter for months. While she was there, her mom and dad died of carbon monoxide poisoning in their home, so Janie would have died, too, if she hadn't gone home with the adoptive parents."

"Are you serious?" Sophia said. "Wow! I couldn't have done that. I mean, you're bonding even more with your own baby, and you still know you gave him away. I wonder what happened."

"I remember hearing my mom and dad talking about that," Marlee said. "She said the adoptive parents woke up one morning and Janie was gone. No note, no explanation, no nothing. She had a car and a driver's license and whatever money she'd gotten for the sale of her parents' house, and that's all anyone knew."

"Did anyone ever hear what happened to her?" Rachel asked.

"Not that I know of," Marlee said.

Marc stood abruptly, walking blindly through the crowd toward the front door, passing his brother as he went.

"Hey," David said as he grabbed Marc's arm. "Everything okay?"

"I just need some air," Marc said, and kept moving.

The evening air was cool. The stars were hidden by the clouds moving in, and the three-quarter moon was only intermittently visible. It smelled like it might rain.

Marc walked away from the light on the porch, then down the steps all the way to the sidewalk in front of the house. He looked up the street, then down the street at all of the houses along both sides of the block, seeing the lights within.

Once he'd known a lot of his uncle Wayne's neighbors, but these people were strangers. He inhaled slowly, trying to calm the sick feeling in the pit of his stomach. He knew, with every cell in his body, that the baby Janie had given away was his.

He turned around and stared at the house he'd just exited. He was nearing another birthday, and tonight he felt every day of those years weighing heavily on his heart. He had a forty-five-year-old son out there somewhere. Janie would be turning sixty-two before this year was over—if she was still alive.

All of a sudden, he had an overwhelming urge to find them both. He needed to apologize to Janie for the heartbreak she'd gone through on her own, and he needed to look into the face of his son before he died. The task was daunting. Janie surely had married during the ensuing years, and the baby would have been given his adopted parents' last name.

He turned around and went back in the house, looking for the four cousins. They were still sitting on the sofa.

"Hey," he said, as he walked up to where they were sitting. "Can we talk?"

They smiled. "Sure, Marco. Here, I'll scoot over," Tina said.

"No, in private," he said.

They didn't even blink, but got up and followed him back through the crowd and out onto the porch before they spoke.

"What's wrong?" Marlee asked.

"You were talking about Janie Chapman a few minutes ago."

They nodded.

"Do any of you happen to know the name of the people who adopted her baby?"

"Momma said it was people who lived across the street from her. Why?" Tina asked.

"Because I think that baby was mine, and I never knew about any of this. It must have been around the same time we moved."

The four women were shocked into silence, and then they all came to their senses and surrounded him in a group hug.

"Oh, Marc, we are so sorry. I didn't remember that you two dated," Sophia said.

"It doesn't matter," Marc said. "What matters is family. You know how we are. Adamos blood is thicker than water. I need to see my son's face. I need to tell Janie I'm sorry."

Now they were all teary and trying to remember, and then Tina gasped.

"I'll bet Mama would know. Do you care if I ask her?"

"If this night wasn't all about Uncle Wayne's passing, I'd be in that room right now, asking everyone present. Go ask her. I'll wait."

The quartet shot back into the house, on a mission.

Marc walked to the edge of the porch and glanced back up. The sky was completely dark now, and he thought he could hear thunder in the distance—or maybe it was just the pounding of his heart.

The front door opened, and Tina was the only one who came out.

"Raines. Their names were Joe and Dolly Raines."

Marc hugged her. "Thank you, cuz. I owe you big time."

Tina patted his arm. "The four of us have already talked. We're saying nothing about this to anyone. This will be your story to tell or not to tell. We just wanted you to know."

He was too emotional to answer and could only nod.

After family night was over, David and Linda drove back together in her car, and Marc followed. All he could think about was leaving for home as soon as the funeral was over. He needed to be back in his office with all the tools of research at his disposal. It should be easier to find his son than to find Janie. But life being what it was, easy wasn't often part of the answer.

He went to bed that night and dreamed of Janie calling his name. He could hear her, but she couldn't hear him answer. And then the dream morphed to a little boy growing up and wondering what was wrong with him, and why had he been given away.

It was all Marc could do to get through the funeral. When it was over, he said his goodbyes without attending the dinner afterward and drove straight home with a fire in his gut.

He'd taken pictures all over the world of children in the midst of war. And of women who'd survived brutal rape and capture in war-torn countries and had given birth to their rapists' children.

He'd done a whole series on children orphaned or sep-
arated from their parents by natural disasters. And now, to
learn he had a child in this world who did not know him
was the worst of sins.

It was nearing sundown by the time he reached
Springfield, and all he could think about was beginning his
search. But the project for Nat Geo wasn't finished.

He'd never failed to deliver a job. He'd never been late
with a project. But he'd failed terribly as a man, and that
was not to be borne. He wasn't backing off on his search.
Not even for one day. If he had to, he'd finish the project
on the move.

He kept thinking of Janie and what she must have
endured alone. And the son who did not know the blood-
line of his ancestors. In reality, they might have worked out
all their issues years ago and might be perfectly happy with
where they were now, but this was new to Marc, and the
horror of it was real.

He threw his luggage on the floor of his bedroom and
headed for the office. He'd acquired a few hacking skills over
the years. Nothing worth doing time for, but he was able to
find his way around the World Wide Web with alacrity.

The first thing he did was start a search for Joe and Dolly
Raines of Kansas City, Missouri. He found them and their
address through property records, and after further searching came up with their occupations and the mention of one
child named John Sullivan, age five.

So now he needed to find a John Sullivan Raines,
around forty-five or so years old, who was born in Kansas
City, Missouri.

Instead, he found a death notice for Joseph Frederick

Raines, listing survivors as his wife, Dolly, and one son, Sullivan Raines, also of Kansas City, Missouri.

Marc paused, staring at the name. It didn't seem real. He needed a face to go with it, so he kept digging.

Then he found a very recent death notice for Dolly Raines. The only surviving member of the family was a son, Sullivan Raines, with no wife or children listed. Marc frowned. His son's life was eerily similar to the life he had been living. He had not put down roots with a family, so what the hell had his son been doing with his life?

It wasn't until he ran a search on the name Sullivan Raines that he began to get hits on the same subject matter and finally came to the realization that his son was a fireman. That sent his search in a whole other direction, as he began looking through Kansas City newspapers for mention of him. He found one very poor photo showing a fireman in full gear carrying out a victim of an apartment fire. The photographer had attributed the rescue to a Fireman Raines and mentioned the station he was from, but Marc still didn't have a photo of his face.

And then he found a notice about Sully Raines retiring after twenty-six years of service, which surprised him. Sully must have joined the fire department straight out of high school.

But it wasn't until he found a photo of the retirement ceremony that he finally saw his son's face. It was a blow to the heart to see his face on a stranger. The thick, black hair like Marc's used to be. The dark eyes like his. The slight hook on the bridge of his nose. The classic shape of a very Mediterranean face. *An Adamos face.*

He stared at the picture until his vision blurred, and then he covered his face and wept.

CHAPTER 19

MARC'S DREAMS THAT NIGHT WERE NIGHTMARES. HE woke up the next morning with a heavy heart, but as he was making coffee, it dawned on him that he might be able to contact his son through the fire department where he used to work.

After a short search to find the phone number of the station, Marc made the call.

"Station Twelve, this is Rick."

"Rick, my name is Marc Adamos. I'm trying to locate Sully Raines."

"He doesn't work here anymore," Rick said.

Marc frowned. He wasn't giving up this easy. "I'm Sullivan Raines's birth father, and I'm trying to find him. By any chance do you have a contact number for him?"

"The Sully Raines I know wasn't adopted, or at least he never said anything about it."

Marc frowned. "Maybe he didn't know. I just found out that I had a son. Could you at least give him my phone number? Then if he chooses, he could call me."

"I guess I could do that," Rick said.

Marc gave him the number to his cell and his address.

"Okay, got it," Rick said. "I'll send him a text, but I don't know where he is right now. He's traveling."

At that moment, Marc heard the alarms going off inside the station.

"Sorry, mister. We've got a call. Gotta go," Rick said. He

disconnected, dropped the note pad with the number on the chief's desk, and ran.

"I appreciate anything you can do," Marc said, but the man had already hung up.

Marc disconnected and put some bread in to toast. Right now, he'd done all he could do, and in the meantime he had to finish this project for Nat Geo.

He pulled out the notes he'd made about follow-up trips and decided to revisit the Georgia locations first. That dramatic rescue using the bulldozer for transportation was nothing short of heroic. He wanted to interview this man, Johnny Pine, and he needed a picture of the woman Johnny had saved. Maybe he'd find something interesting about the story that played into how natural disasters changed the landscape of countries and the landscape of lives in the people who inhabited them.

When the toast popped up, Marc covered it with peanut butter and jelly and ate as he worked, looking for the exact location of Blessings, Georgia, and the kind of motels available for travelers.

Once he'd located Blessings on the map, he googled motels and got two hits. One was a small motel; the other was a very inviting bed-and-breakfast. He called the B and B and made a reservation, after estimating how long it would take him to get there, then finished his PB&J and went to pack.

He was going to overnight in Nashville and then drive on to Blessings the next day.

He made it to Nashville without incident. Exhausted from a drive of over eight hours, he stopped at a La Quinta Inn and got a room. He showered and crawled into bed, then for the first time in ages, forgot to set his alarm.

When he woke and saw that it was almost noon, he

groaned, got up and showered and shaved, ate a quick lunch in the motel café, and continued southeast.

He drove into rain just as he crossed the border into Georgia, then drove by a wreck that blocked traffic for almost two hours before motorists were allowed to proceed. At that point, he called the B and B to let them know his arrival was going to be delayed. The nice woman who answered assured him that it was no problem and told him to travel safe.

He stopped once after that to refuel and then drove through intermittent thunderstorms the rest of the way.

It was just after 11:00 p.m. when headlights flashed across the front windows of the Blessings Bed and Breakfast. It had been raining for hours, but the lights were on outside in the parking lot and along the walkway to the entrance, as well as inside the front lobby.

Bud and Rachel's late check-in had finally arrived. They saw him run up to the porch, then pause to shake the rain off his jacket and run his hands through his hair. When he came in carrying a bag, they were at the door to greet him.

"Mr. Adamos?" Bud asked.

"Yes, and call me Marc," he said. "Thank you for staying open for me. I apologize for the late arrival."

"Not a problem. We're glad to have you," Rachel said as she introduced herself and Bud, then began explaining the B and B's schedule as Marc registered.

"The kitchen is closed, but if you didn't get a chance to have dinner, I can bring up a tray of fruit and cheese, and some toasted baguettes—homemade, of course."

"I did not take time to stop and eat, and that offer is much appreciated."

"A bottle of wine perhaps, or would you prefer something else?" Bud asked.

"A glass of wine would suffice," Marc said.

"I'll get the tray, and Bud will show you to your room. We have other guests, and they may already be asleep," Rachel added.

"I will take care to be quiet," Marc said, then picked up his bag and followed Bud up the stairs.

Bud took him to the last room on the right at the end of the hall, and Rachel followed a few minutes later with his food. Ignoring the suitcase he had yet to unpack, Marc sat down at a little table with his tray of fruit and cheese, put a slice of smoked Gouda on a still warm, toasty baguette, and turned on the TV, making sure to keep the volume low.

He hadn't seen or heard much in the way of news since he left Springfield, so he turned the TV on to CNN. His feet were up. The tray of food was in his lap, and the glass of wine on the table at his elbow.

This was as relaxed as he'd been through the whole trip. Tomorrow he'd check at the police station for the whereabouts of Johnny Pine and find out about the lady Pine had rescued, along with the identities of the two orderlies who'd helped get the woman into the hospital. Just the thought of a new piece to add to his story was exciting.

It was nearing half past one in the morning when he finally crawled into bed. This time, he set his alarm so that he wouldn't miss breakfast and then fell into a deep and dreamless sleep.

When the alarm went off the next morning, Marc was up in a flash. He showered and shaved, then dressed casually for the day, choosing a pair of navy slacks and a long-sleeved light-blue polo shirt to go with a pair of black loafers.

He came down the stairs, sidestepping three elderly ladies at the desk who were settling their bill.

"Enjoy your breakfast. It's buffet-style," Bud said as Marc walked past.

"Thanks," Marc said, and walked into the dining room and picked up a plate.

This was a much more enticing menu than the honey bun and coffee he'd had yesterday. When he had what he wanted to eat, he carried his plate to an empty table and was sitting down as Rachel came in from the kitchen.

"Good morning, Mr. Adamos. Is there anything I can get you?" she asked.

Marc smiled. "No, ma'am. This looks and smells amazing."

Rachel beamed. "Enjoy," she said, and went back into the kitchen.

Marc was already planning the morning as he ate. First stop was the local police to find out how to contact Johnny Pine and Lovey Cooper. Marc was also thinking about the man at the fire station, and if he had given Sully his number. He didn't want to consider it, but there was always the chance that his son wouldn't be interested in meeting him. He let the thought go. No need worrying about something that might never happen, so he settled down to enjoy the food.

The best-laid plans are often sidetracked, and such was

Marc's morning. He had just finished breakfast when he got a call from his boss at Nat Geo. To answer the questions his boss wanted, Marc had to go back to his room and boot up his laptop, send the information in an email attachment, and then wait to make sure that was all the boss needed. By the time that message came, it was half past 10:00 a.m.

Marc left the B and B and drove back to Main Street, then all the way down to the PD where he parked and got out. After last night's downpour, the air smelled fresh and clean.

There was a man at the front desk with a panel of radio equipment behind him. Whatever else his job entailed, it appeared he was also the dispatcher. Marc walked up to the desk.

"My name is Marc Adamos. By any chance is your police chief here?"

Avery curiously eyed the tall, gray-haired stranger.

"He's on his way back now, if you care to wait."

"Yes, I'll wait, but maybe in the meantime you could answer a couple of questions," Marc said.

He pulled out his ID as well as one of his business cards and a copy of the photo that had brought him here. "I work for *National Geographic* as a photojournalist and a documentarian. This picture came off the AP wire service, along with a brief description of the story behind it. I know the young man's name is Johnny Pine. I was hoping to interview him and the woman he helped save and include the film in a documentary I'm working on."

Avery's eyes widened. "Yes, sir! Johnny pulled off quite a rescue there and saved Lovey Cooper's life. She runs Granny's Country Kitchen up at the other end of Main. She was hurt real bad, but she's back at work now."

"I would like to contact the both of them for an interview, but I understand about protecting people's privacy. Maybe you could contact Johnny Pine and tell him why I'm here, and see if he'd be interested in doing an interview."

Before Avery could answer, Lon Pittman walked into the lobby from the hall.

"Oh, Chief! I didn't know you were back," Avery said. "This gentleman was wanting to talk to you. Here's his info."

"I just got here," Lon said as he glanced at the ID and the business card, and then recognized a picture that had run in the first issue of the local paper after power was restored. "What can I do for you, sir?"

"I'm Marc Adamos," he said and reiterated his reason for being in Blessings.

"We're a fan of Nat Geo documentaries in my house. I can only imagine the things you've seen in this world," Lon said.

"Many things. Some beautiful and amazing. Some unbelievably horrifying. Man and nature are often at odds. That's the focus of the piece I'm working on now."

"I can find out where Johnny's working," Lon said. "Avery, what's the number to Pine Dozer Service?"

Avery pulled up Google Search. "I've got it, Chief. Want me to dial the number for you, or do you want to take it in your office?"

"Give me the number," Lon said. "I'll call him right here." He made the call and waited for an answer, knowing Johnny's wife, Dori, usually answered the phone for the business.

"Pine Dozer Service," Dori said.

"Dori, this is Chief Pittman. Nothing's wrong, but I have

a guy here wanting to talk to Johnny, and I wondered where he was working today."

"He's not at work today. Beep got sick in the night, and Johnny took him to the doctor this morning. They just got back. Hang on a minute, and I'll put him on the phone."

"Thanks," Lon said, then glanced at Marc. "He's coming to the phone."

Marc loved it when plans fell into place. He stood and listened to the chief explaining the reason for the call.

"He'd be happy to talk to you," Lon said as he disconnected. "He said he could meet you at Granny's in about ten minutes. That way you can meet him and Lovey at the same time."

"That's awesome," Marc said, then shook Lon's hand. "I really appreciate this."

"Sure," Lon said. "And here are your photo and ID. Glad we could help."

Marc left the station and headed to Granny's. He'd already seen it on the way to the PD, so no searching was involved. The parking lot was more than half empty as he pulled up and parked, then wasted no time going inside.

A young, muscular man was sitting on the bench in the lobby, and when Marc walked in, he stood.

"Mr. Adamos?"

"Yes," Marc said. "Are you Johnny Pine?"

"Yes, sir."

"Johnny, I need to shake your hand. I've seen a lot of things in my life, but nothing that exceeds the photo I saw of you perched on the side of that giant dozer in hurricane-force winds with that woman in your arms."

Johnny shrugged. "You do what you have to do in life.

Lovey matters to all of us, and Granny's is the heart of Blessings."

"You're still a hero in my book, which brings me to why I'm in Blessings. I want to include you and Lovey in my film. It's the last documentary I'll be doing for Nat Geo, and I will be retiring after it's turned in. I just wanted to meet you, get a feel for the story, and see if you and Lovey would be willing to participate. If so, we can set up another time when the two of you would be available to talk, and I could get some updated photos to prove you both survived. Also, maybe get a bit of info from the two hospital employees who helped you get her down from the dozer."

Johnny grinned. "Yes, sir. I'd be honored. I think Lovey will agree, but I can't speak for her." He handed Marc his card. "This has my cell number on it. Just let me know a day ahead of when you want to do this, so I'm not out on a job somewhere."

"Will do," Marc said. "I'll be in touch. Now how do I go about finding Lovey?"

"Just wait at the counter. She should be back any minute."

"Got it, and thank you for agreeing to do this," Marc said.

"Sure thing," Johnny said. "See you soon."

Marc walked up to the register and was leaning against the counter when he saw a pretty gray-haired woman in jeans and a red shirt hurrying toward the counter. Then he looked at her again and straightened up, staring at her face, at the smile—and felt like he'd been sucker punched.

"Janie? Janie Chapman?"

Lovey gasped. "Oh. My. God." She felt like she was dreaming. "Marc Adamos? Is that you?"

"Yes. What are you doing here?"

"I own the place," she said.

Marc frowned. "I was told a woman named Lovey Cooper owns it."

"That's me. No one in Blessings calls me Janie."

His eyes widened in disbelief, remembering that lifeless-looking woman in Johnny Pine's arms and looking at her now. He just shook his head and wrapped his arms around her.

"I came to interview the survivor of a hurricane, never imagining in a thousand years it would be you. And I just found out what happened to you less than a week ago. I went home for Uncle Wayne's funeral, and some of my cousins were talking about the old days, and when I heard them mention something about how sad it was what happened to you, I nearly lost it. I'm sorry. I'm so damn sorry," he said. "Is there somewhere we can talk? Can you come sit in the car with me a bit?"

"Give me a minute," Lovey said, and spun out of his arms and went into the dining room. He followed, curious as to what her life had become, and was surprised by the size of the place and her obvious expertise.

Within a couple of minutes, she came back with one of the waitresses.

"Marc, this is Wendy. Wendy, this is Marc Adamos. I'll be gone for a bit. I have my phone. Call if there's an emergency."

Wendy's eyes were big, and she was smiling. "It's so nice to meet you, sir."

"Um, it's nice to meet you, too," he said, but as soon as they were out in the parking lot, he took Lovey by the arm. "Why did she act like she knew who I was?"

"It's a long story," Lovey said. "Which one is your car?"

"Oh. Right. It's over here," he said as he aimed the remote and unlocked it. They got in together, then turned to face each other.

"Janie...I mean, Lovey...I had already planned to start searching for you as soon as I finished the story I'm working on. Talk about the hand of fate delivering you into my lap! I'm still in shock."

"What story?"

"I'm a photojournalist–documentarian. I've worked for *National Geographic* most of my adult life, and as soon as I finish this last documentary, I'm retiring." Then he reached for her hands. "Why didn't you tell me about the baby? You know I would have come for you!"

Lovey sighed. "Lord, help me get through this," she whispered, and then once again began to explain. "The first thing you need to know is that keeping it from you was not my decision. You'd been gone two months before I realized I was pregnant, and when I told my parents, they hit the ceiling. I told them I needed to find you, but they cut that dream off fast. They already didn't want the baby in their lives and told me if I contacted you, they'd have you arrested and charged with raping an underage girl because I was only fifteen."

"Oh my God," he said, and wiped a shaky hand over his face. The words of her story were like blows to the gut. "If only we hadn't moved."

Lovey stopped him short. "No! I gave up on all the what-ifs years ago, so don't do that."

Marc took her by the shoulders, his voice rough with pain and anger. "I don't care what your parents threatened. If I'd known, I would have found you both. My people don't abandon their own blood."

There were tears running down Lovey's face now. She'd been afraid to cry in front of the people of Blessings, and yet here she was crying with him.

"It was too late, Marc. I signed the paper. I gave our baby away. He was no longer legally mine."

"I heard you stayed with him for a while, and then one morning you were gone."

Lovey nodded. "It was bound to happen. I was nursing him and only going to stay until he was weaned. But he had started to babble, and when he finally said 'mama,' it was to me, not Dolly Raines. She came to me later that same night and told me to pack my things and get out, and she never wanted to see my face again. I left in the night. It nearly killed me, but I never looked back."

Marc lifted her hands to his lips and kissed them, over and over, as his eyes filled with tears. "This breaks my heart for you. How did you survive? I heard your parents died while you were with the Raineses."

Lovey nodded. "And that's how I *did* survive. I was sixteen by then, and I'd inherited the car, the house, and their little bank account. I'd already sold the house when my ultimatum came, so there was some money in the bank and it was the nest egg I needed to find a place to be. It took me several years of running and marrying two different men who weren't all that good to me, but I never felt safe enough to stop running until I came to Blessings. Within a month, I found a good man. I married him for a place to live, and he loved me enough to save me. He owned this place. We got married in Vegas and came back here. He always called me Lovey, not Janie, and that's how everyone here came to know me. I didn't care. In a way, I felt reborn. Finally leaving Janie behind gave me a reason to stop running."

Marc grabbed a handful of tissues and began wiping the tears from her cheeks.

"No matter what else happens, from this day forward, Lovey Cooper, you are part of the Adamos family and the beloved mother of my child. I never married. I never met anyone I couldn't live without. I didn't know what I'd missed until I found out what I'd lost. My apologies that you bore the brunt of your sacrifices alone, but never again. Do you hear me? Never again. Wherever I am, all you need to do is call and I'll be at your side. We've gotten a whole lot older, but in my eyes you will always be my girl."

"Thank you, Marc. This is where I belong, and I'm very happy here. But I still can't believe you just walked into the restaurant like that."

"Fate. Meant to be." Then he touched the cross hanging around her neck. "You still wear this?"

Lovey smiled. "I hadn't...not for a very long time."

Marc nodded. "I found out about our child's adult life because of my cousins...but I can't find him. He was a fireman and just retired. I called the station where he used to work and left my number, but he never called me back. I had to accept he probably wants nothing to do with me."

Lovey smiled. "Start the car."

"What? Why?"

"Trust me. Just start the car, and drive where I tell you to go."

Marc never said another word, and as they drove back onto Main, he began following her directions wordlessly, driving through a residential area until she pointed to a big redbrick two-story home.

"Pull into that drive and park."

So he did, and when she motioned for him to get out, he followed her all the way up to the door, watching as she rang the bell. But when she turned and looked up at him, her eyes were sparkling.

He grinned. "What are you up to?"

And then Sully opened the door.

"Oh my God! It's you!" Marc said.

Sully looked at his mom, then looked again at the man standing beside her. That's when it hit him. He was looking at an older version of himself. He began backing up as Lovey pushed the man in the door ahead of her.

"Are you my father?" Sully asked.

"Yes!" Marc said, and wrapped his arms around Sully and began thumping him on the back, and then looking at him, and then hugging him all over again. "I can't believe you're here! I just found out about all of this less than a week ago. I am still horrified at what your mother went through alone, and had no idea she was here. Because of my cousins who still lived in the area where you grew up, I knew enough about your adoptive parents to find you, only to learn you'd just retired. I called the station where you worked, told them who I was, and asked a man named Rick to give you my phone number. But when you didn't call, I just assumed you weren't interested in meeting me."

"I never got the message, but I'm so glad you found me, anyway," Sully said, and then Melissa walked into the foyer.

"Hi...what am I missing?" she asked, smiling.

"Honey, this is Marc Adamos," Sully said.

Melissa gasped. "Your father?"

Sully grinned. "What do you think?"

She started laughing. "Well, now I know what my future husband is going to look like at that age. I'm still going to be giving women the evil eye."

Marc grinned. "Please introduce me to my future daughter-in-law."

"Marc, this is—"

"Please... Dad, Pop, Father...anything," Marc said.

Sully sighed. Marc Adamos had just thrown out the anchor he needed to settle his world.

"Dad, this is Melissa Dean, my fiancée and soon-to-be bride."

"It is a true pleasure to meet you," Marc said.

"I don't know how all this happened, but I'm so happy you found us," Melissa said. "Come sit," she said, and led the way into the living room.

They'd barely cleared the doorway before Marc stopped, then turned and walked toward the painting of mother and child hanging on the wall. He touched the face of the girl, then the necklace around her neck, and then the baby. Then he saw the name of the artist who had signed it and turned abruptly.

"Elliot Graham? Is this an original?"

Sully nodded. "He just gave it to me last week."

"You *know* him? How? He disappeared from the art scene probably twenty years ago."

"He lives here," Sully said.

"But the scene... Did he paint it from a photo?" Marc asked.

"There were never any pictures taken of the baby and me," Lovey said.

"Then how? I don't understand," Marc said.

Sully patted his dad on the shoulder. "It's a long story. I'll have to introduce you before you'll understand, but it's the necklace you gave her that unlocked the mystery of where she'd gone. Mom left the necklace for me when she disappeared. I didn't know I was adopted until my adoptive mother died. Then I found the necklace with my adoption papers and a letter stating my mother wanted me to have it. I swore if I found her, I'd be the one to put it back around her neck, and there it is," Sully said, and winked at his mom.

After they settled in to visit, the two men began filling in the gaps of each other's lives, until all the questions had been asked and answered.

"As soon as I'm finished gathering up the info I need on Johnny and Janie…I mean, Lovey's, story, I'll be going back to Springfield to finish the piece and turn it in to Nat Geo. At that point, I am officially off the clock. Please say you'll all come to Kansas City to meet the family," Marc said.

"We'll all come to Kansas City to meet the family," Lovey said, and when they laughed, Lovey frowned. "What?"

Before she could say anything more, her cell phone rang. She glanced up at the clock.

"Work is likely calling me back." She got up and walked into the foyer to take the call.

The trio sat quietly, not wanting to talk over the conversation that took a sudden turn for the worse.

"What do you mean, it fell in the toilet?" Lovey shrieked.

Sully arched an eyebrow and looked at Melissa.

"No!" Lovey said. "If Chet dropped it in there, Chet can fish it out. Lord love a duck! I can't walk out of the place for five minutes without shit hitting the fan! And yes, I know that's a good pun because I meant to say that. If he can't get to it, call the plumber. I'll be there soon."

She stuffed the phone back into her pocket with a frustrated jab and came back into the living room.

"Chet, the dishwasher, dropped the only key we have to the extra freezer right into the toilet. It remains to be seen why they ever gave him the key in the first place, and why he went to the bathroom with it instead of straight to the freezer where he was sent. They're running out of hamburger patties, and the extra order is in that freezer. Sully, remember you saying you wanted to learn the job? Well, this is it. Are you sure you're still up for it?"

Sully grinned. "I was a fireman. I have pulled cats out of trees. Puppies out of storm drains. Freed a thief who got stuck in a chimney, and delivered three babies. I got a man's foot unstuck from a toilet bowl and have cut too many wedding rings off of swollen fingers to count, and the list goes on. Unless Chet already flushed the toilet, all I need is a coat hanger and a little luck."

Marc stared. "I am in awe of the both of you."

"Lord," Lovey muttered. "Well, get your keys, Son, and let's go."

Sully followed as Marc took Lovey back to Granny's.

It occurred to Marc as he drove how truly amazing Janie Chapman and her son had turned out to be with no help from him. He couldn't wait to become a part of their lives.

Once they got to Granny's and parked, Lovey took them in through the alley and straight into the kitchen. She frowned at Chet, who was frantically putting dishes into the washer.

"I'm sorry, Lovey," Chet said, and there were tears in his eyes.

"Can I talk to him a minute, Mom?" Sully asked.

"I'm leaving this in your hands and going to relieve Wendy so we won't be short a waitress during dinner," Lovey said.

Sully smiled at Chet. "I have a quick question, and tell me the truth, okay?"

Chet nodded.

"Did you see the key fall into the toilet?" Sully asked.

"No, sir."

"Then how do you know that's where it went?"

Chet sighed. "I told Mercy I didn't flush the toilet, but I did, because that's why I went in there. And when the key wasn't in my pocket anymore, I guessed that's where it went."

"So you guessed. Where is the bathroom back here?"

Chet pointed.

"And you're sure you put the key in your pocket, and you're sure you don't have a hole in your pocket?" Sully asked.

Chet paused, then jammed his wet hands down into both pockets and grimaced. "There is a small hole in this pocket, but I don't think it's—"

"Where is the key kept?" Sully asked.

Chet pointed. "Right there. The key hangs on that hook."

"Oh, so it's on some kind of key ring," Sully said.

Now Chet's eyes were getting bigger. "Yeah, with a yellow plastic tab."

"Okay, thanks. As you were," Sully said, and he walked off.

Chet looked at Marc and frowned. "What did he mean, as you were?"

Marc grinned. "It means carry on...go back to what you were doing."

"Oh!" Chet said, and went back to work.

Sully was moving along the path Chet would have taken—walking behind Elvis, who was at the griddle, dodging waitresses picking up orders—all the while looking for a place the key might have fallen unnoticed. When he reached the door to the bathroom, he started to go inside, then paused. He squatted just outside the bathroom door and began looking under the wall of shelving beside it.

"What are you doing?" Marc asked.

"If the key fell out of his pocket on the way to the bathroom, he could have kicked it and never known it. Instead of looking for a key, I'm looking for something—"

All of a sudden he got up and grabbed a broom from the corner, got down on his knees and ran the bristle end beneath the metal shelving, then swept it along the wall.

The key ring came flying out from beneath.

"—something yellow!" Sully crowed, as he grabbed the key, put up the broom, then took the key back to Chet.

"Here you go, son. Now go finish what they sent you to do, and bring me the key when you're done."

Chet was beaming. "Thanks!"

He dried his hands and took off in a lope. Within a few minutes, he was back with the large box of frozen hamburger patties that Elvis wanted and had put them into the walk-in near the griddle.

"Thanks, kid," Elvis said.

"Sure thing," Chet said, and went back to work.

Now that the crisis had been averted, Sully was going to make sure the one-key situation no longer existed.

"Hey, Dad. Wanna take a quick ride with me?" Sully asked.

"Sure," Marc said, and followed Sully out the back door and into his car.

Marc hadn't missed the calm manner in which Sully had dealt with what appeared to have been a crisis to Lovey, and was in silent admiration. Sully didn't immediately assume what he'd been told was the whole truth, and he didn't get angry or lay blame. But it was his last act that said to Marc what kind of a man Sully was. Chet needed to finish what he'd been sent to do, so as not to feel like a failure, and Sully knew it when he gave Chet the key a second time to complete the task.

"You know what, Sully?" Marc said.

"What, Dad?"

"You're a good man, and I don't say that to a lot of people," Marc said.

"Thanks," Sully said.

"On another note, where are we going?" Marc asked.

"To Bloomer's Hardware to get some keys made."

"Yet another good move. What would you have done if the key was lost?"

Sully grinned. "Taken my bolt cutters to the lock, in which case I'd still be on my way to Bloomers to buy a whole new lock with multiple keys."

Marc grinned.

They arrived at Bloomer's, where Sully introduced his dad to Fred, then explained after they left that was where Melissa used to work.

When they got back to Granny's, they went in the front door. Lovey looked up.

"Did you get it out?" she asked.

Sully dropped two new keys on key rings into her hand.

"These are for you. And it wasn't in the toilet after all. Chet and I had a talk first, at which time we discovered he has a small hole in his pocket. I found the key ring under the shelves beside the bathroom door. Those are extras. Put them wherever you want, just not on the same hook with the first one."

Lovey rolled her eyes and then hugged him. "Thank you for the new keys. You are going to be as handy around here as a pocket on a shirt."

Sully laughed. "I'm going to head back home now. Melissa was making dinner when we left. Dad, do you want to eat with us, or stay here and eat? If you stay, don't miss the biscuits."

Marc saw the look on Lovey's face, and the decision was made.

"Thank you for the invitation, but I'm staying here to see what this place is all about."

Sully waved and left.

Lovey beamed and grabbed a menu.

Two days later, Marc was in the banquet room at Granny's, wrapping up the interview and photo shoot with Lovey and Johnny Pine. Even the two orderlies had come, staying long enough for him to question them a bit and get their names. He had everything he'd come for, and more.

There was a whole new horror in knowing the injured woman in the picture was someone he'd known and loved.

•

But as a documentarian, his personal view did not belong in the piece.

And, knowing it was going to be a two-day drive to get home, he'd already settled his bill at the B and B this morning. His car was packed and he was ready to go, all except saying his goodbyes.

He packed his camera back into the carrying case, the iPad with notes in his bag, and then they all stood.

"Johnny, thank you for the interview and the pictures. When I get a release date from Nat Geo as to when they plan to air it, I'll let you know. I'm sure we'll be seeing each other again, because Blessings is going to become a regular stop-off for me."

"It's been an honor to meet you, sir. I'll look forward to seeing your documentary," Johnny said. They shook hands, and then Johnny was out the door.

Marc turned to Lovey and smiled as he cupped the side of her face.

"Finding you has been the gift of a lifetime. You know I'm not going to fade out of your life again. And you also know I'm expecting all three of you to come meet the family, so please be figuring out a way to make it happen."

Lovey felt the love in his touch and let it settle in her heart.

"I will, and there's something I've been wanting to say ever since you appeared. Having you and Sully back in my life was a gift I never saw coming, but it's the best thing that's ever happened to me. I belong in Blessings. It's where I'm happiest, and where my heart is. I don't really belong to anyone here. I have many good friends, and Ruby is my best friend, only none of these people knew the real me. But you did. I once read an article on aging and there was a sentence in it I never forgot. *When the last person who knew you as a child has died, when there's no one left to say 'remember when' to, then you've lost that part of your life.* I feel whole again. Thank you for forgiving me… Thank you for understanding why I gave our baby away."

Marc frowned. "There is nothing to forgive. Everything you did, you did out of love. You were protecting me from the threat your parents laid down, and you protected our baby the best way you knew how. It was a good thing. Sully's parents were good to him. They loved him. And they raised a good man. Yes, they lied to him, too, but people react differently to fear, and I know Dolly Raines feared losing the baby to you."

Lovey threw her arms around him and hugged him tight, then gave him a quick pat on the back.

"I'd better get back to work or the boss will fire me. I'll see you in a few weeks."

Marc gave her a quick goodbye kiss. "I wish fate had been kinder to the both of us."

Lovey shrugged. "Life happens. The good part is we're both still here to live it. Drive safe. Text to let us know you got home okay."

"I will, and I'll be in touch." And then he packed up his things and left.

When he stopped at the house to tell Melissa and Sully goodbye, Melissa answered the door. "Marc! Come in. Sully is out back."

"I don't want him to stop what he's doing. I just came to say goodbye for now."

"Then I better get a hug," Melissa said.

Marc obliged, adding a quick kiss on her cheek. "You're going to be my favorite daughter-in-law. You know that, don't you?"

Melissa grinned. "Duly noted. Now follow me, and I'll let you out through the kitchen door."

Marc gave the Elliot Graham painting one last look as they passed it, then followed her through the house and outside onto the patio.

"Sully!" Melissa called. "Your dad's here!"

Sully turned and waved, then leaned his rake against a tree and loped back to the house.

"Hey, Dad. Are you leaving?"

"Yes. I finished the interviews. I already have a promise from Lovey that she'll come with you guys to meet the family."

"I can't wait," Sully said. "You just say the word and we'll be there."

"I never knew what I was missing until I found out you existed. After that, it was a physical ache. Thank you for being so accepting of letting me into your life," Marc said.

"I understand that feeling," Sully said. "Once I learned I was adopted, it created such a hole in who I thought I was that I knew I wouldn't be happy again until I had some answers."

"And thanks to a huge twist of fate, the impossible happened. Just prepare yourself for all kinds of hugging and kissing and crying and laughing...because that's what big Greek families are all about," Marc said.

"Something to look forward to," Sully said, then walked his dad back to his car and stood on the front lawn waving until he was out of sight.

Two and a half weeks later, Sully was on I-70 with the two most important women in his life, driving back into Kansas City to meet his dad.

Melissa was in the seat beside him, and his mom was in the back seat, quietly looking at everything they were passing.

"Mom, how does it feel coming back after all this time?" Sully asked.

"I don't exactly know how it feels. I hadn't thought about this place in so long, but I do know that I left here without you, and the fact that you're the one bringing me back makes the whole thing come full circle," Lovey said.

"Oh, Lovey, what a perfect way to think," Melissa said. "Sully is the common denominator between us. I knew him after you were gone, and loved him. Then you and I met years later, unaware of the connection we already shared, and now we're coming back together to where it all began. That's not coincidence. That's karma, and I for one am happy to close the circle on that."

"Where it all began," Lovey said, and kept looking at everything they passed.

"Sully, where is it we're going again?" Melissa asked.

"Dad made reservations at the Fontaine. It's a really nice hotel near Country Club Plaza. He arrived last night. Our rooms are supposed to be near each other and on the same floor."

"And tonight is 'meet the family night,'" Lovey said. "I brought the same thing to wear that I wore for the big reveal. It may be too fancy, but it makes me feel good and I need that. I left this city with my tail between my legs, but I'm coming back a survivor and proud of it."

"It's going to be good, Mom. Dad and I will make sure of that for you," Sully said.

"And I will sing your praises loud and long," Melissa said.

Lovey laughed. "Then sing then loud enough for me because I only hear half of everything that's being said these days."

A short while later, Sully reached the hotel and stopped at valet parking. He sent a quick text to his dad that they had arrived, and within minutes a bellhop had their luggage and was leading them in to registration.

Marc was grinning as he met them in the lobby and then walked them to the front desk. When the clerk asked for their names, Marc took charge.

"The reservations are all in my name," he said, and produced his photo ID and the same card he'd used to make the reservations.

"Yes, sir," the clerk said. "And you have two more rooms reserved beside the one you're in now?"

"Yes, and please make sure this beautiful lady is registered into the room next to me," Marc said as he took Lovey's hand. "Our son and his fiancée will be on the other side."

The clerk smiled at Lovey. "So, beautiful lady, I will need your photo ID."

Lovey was trying not to grin at all the attention, but she failed miserably as she handed over her driver's license. As soon as Sully and Melissa were registered, too, the bellhop got their room numbers and went to take up their luggage as they headed for the guest elevators.

Marc had his arm around Lovey's shoulders and they were talking like the two old friends they were, leaving Sully and Melissa to follow.

"Do you think Lovey and Marc could ever be a couple again?" she whispered.

"I think that ship has sailed," Sully said. "Dad is planning a whole other trip on his own soon, and Mom isn't budging from Blessings. I get the feel that they're united by friendship and me, and I'm good with that."

That conversation ended when they all reached the elevators, and a whole new one began about meeting the family tonight.

"Sully, are you nervous?" Marc asked.

Sully shook his head. "Never. You have no idea what an affirmation it will be for me to see myself in other people's faces. Mom and I have already discovered we have the same smile. And seeing myself in your face was the best."

Marc beamed. "Your mom and I never got to be the proud parents with the new baby, so tonight we get to be the parents of a very awesome man. Prepare yourself to be doted upon and bragged about."

Then an elevator arrived, and as soon as it emptied they stepped in and headed for the seventeenth floor. Their luggage was in their rooms when they arrived.

"It's about three hours until we go to Aunt June's. Did you guys eat lunch?" Marc asked.

"We ate a late breakfast on the road," Sully said.

"We can go down to the bar in a few and share a couple of appetizers with a glass of wine if you want, or lie down and rest if you'd rather."

"I've rested more in the last two days than I have in the last twenty years. As soon as I get unpacked, I would like to go to the bar," Lovey said.

"So would I," Melissa said.

"Sounds good to me," Sully said. "Give us about fifteen minutes, then knock on our door. We'll be ready."

The time passed quickly with wine and snacks, and when it was time to go back to get ready, Sully asked, "How long will it take to get from the hotel to the party?"

Marc thought a moment. "Oh, I'd say with rush-hour traffic and me taking shortcuts, somewhere between thirty and forty-five minutes. Just text me when you're ready, and we'll head that way."

CHAPTER 20

A SHORT WHILE LATER, MARC TURNED DOWN A BLOCK lined with long-established homes and the kind of land-scaping it takes years to achieve. As he turned, he pointed to a big two-story Craftsman in the middle of the block ahead.

"See all those cars lining both sides of the street? They belong to family, and the two-story blue Craftsman-style house with gray trim belongs to Aunt June." As he neared the house, he suddenly laughed. "Ha! Looks like Aunt June made sure there was a parking place for us in the driveway. Being the guests of honor in a family this size does have its perks."

Sully was excited and grabbed Melissa's hand as they stopped.

Marc looked across the console at Lovey. "Have I told you how beautiful you look tonight?"

"This makes three times, but who's counting?" Lovey said.

"Then let's go do this. Janie…sorry…Lovey, you and I are going in first together because I want it understood that we're a team. Are you okay with that?" Marc asked.

Lovey sighed. "Yes, and thank you."

Marc caught Sully's gaze in the rearview mirror. "And you, my son…just prepare yourself for the impact your appearance is going to have. Melissa, don't try to remember all the names tonight. We have a lot of family years ahead of us, okay?"

"Okay," Melissa said.

"Sit tight, ladies. We'll help you out," Marc said as he and Sully exited, then circled the car. After they'd paired up, Marc led the way into the house.

"Knock, knock," he called out as he and Lovey walked in.

For a split second the room was silent, and then everyone began talking at once and shouting out greetings from all over.

They were still absorbing the fact that the elegant gray-haired woman on Marc's arm was the Janie Chapman they'd known as a girl when the second couple walked in behind them and closed the door. At that point, there was an audible gasp of disbelief.

Marc took it as his cue to begin introductions.

"I know most of you remember the young Janie, and this is my beautiful Jane Cooper now, who prefers to answer to Lovey." Then he and Lovey stepped to the side. "This man is our son, John Sullivan Raines, who goes by Sully, and his fiancée, Melissa Dean."

And then a voice shouted from somewhere in the back of the room.

"Marco!"

"Polo!" Marc shouted back.

At that point, Lovey knew who it was, and tensed when she recognized Marc's brother, David, coming toward them. But she immediately relaxed when he greeted her with a kiss on each cheek.

"Welcome to the family, Lovey Cooper. You grew into a most elegant woman. It is so very nice to see you again." Then he punched Marc lightly on the shoulder and pointed at Sully. "Of course, you would produce a son in your own image!"

The family laughed as David continued. "Sully, I am your uncle David, your father's younger, shorter brother whose hair did not turn an attractive shade of gray but has chosen instead to fall out."

Sully grinned as once again the family laughed.

David poked Marc on the arm. "And, as if it wasn't hard enough to grow up with such a handsome older brother, now I see I will be going into old age with his clone as my only nephew. But the good news is that my nephew is much smarter than my brother, because it didn't take him nearly as long to find such a beautiful woman."

At that point, laughter rocked the house, and they were all engulfed by the family crowing around them. Introductions began, starting with Aunt June, who was their hostess, and after that there were so many others that Sully gave up trying to remember who they were.

Lovey had already been reclaimed by her old schoolmates—Sophia, Marlee, Tina, and Rachel—who were taking credit for reuniting her and Marc.

"You're absolutely stunning, and we're so happy you've all found each other," Sophia said. "I hope this is the beginning of many Adamos family dinners together."

Lovey's voice was shaking a little. "Thank you, and I'll be honest, I'm still pinching myself that this has happened. I never dreamed I would see Marc or our baby again."

Marlee hugged her. "Dreams do come true, and you're living proof. So tell us about Blessings. Marc said you own and run a restaurant called Granny's Country Kitchen? That's amazing."

Finally, Lovey was on familiar ground. Her eyes began to sparkle.

"It belonged to my husband and me. I took over the running of it after he died. As for Blessings, it's one of those places that you can't believe still exists. I've lived in a lot of places, but Blessings has my heart."

While family was being reunited and old friends were reminiscing, Melissa left Sully in the midst of a horde of Adamos men and made her way into the kitchen.

As they began to visit, June mentioned the recent loss of her husband, and Melissa felt an immediate rapport.

"I lost my husband when we were young. He's been gone for a good twenty years. I consider myself blessed to have reconnected with Sully."

June's eyes widened. "Reconnected? You mean…you two knew each other before…like Marc and Jane?"

"Yes, I grew up in Kansas City, too. Sully and I went to the same school. He was my first love, and the first boy I kissed. We spent one year as boyfriend and girlfriend, and then they moved." She laughed. "I thought my life was over."

June kept shaking her head. "This is powerful. Two Adamos men…reconnecting in this way with their first loves, and in the same small town."

"Pretty strong karma, for sure," Melissa said. "So what can I help you do? I'm used to staying busy. Give me a job."

June beamed. Without knowing it, Melissa had just earned a place in the family before she even bore the name.

Marc and Sully were in the den, talking to more family, when one of them asked, "Hey Sully. You said you live here… What do you do?"

"I've been a firefighter with the Kansas City Fire Department all of my adult life. I just recently retired and moved to Blessings. Melissa has a business there, and I fell in love with the place."

Always ready to brag, Marc jumped in to add what he would have called *color commentary* to the story.

"When I was searching for Sully online, I saw evidence of his heroism before I ever met him. But then I met him, and one of the first things I learned was that he saved Melissa's life from a burning car less than an hour after his arrival in town."

The quiet murmurs of disbelief, followed by a solemn silence, said more than words could have expressed, but everyone in the family was eyeing him with new respect.

"Once a fireman, always a fireman," Sully said. "I've carried a lot of people I didn't know out of fires, so you can imagine my shock in the ER when I realized she was a girl I'd grown up with."

"Straight out of one of my wife's romance books," David said.

Sully looked at Marc and then casually put a hand on his shoulder when he added, "The biggest shock was finding out I was adopted, which I did not know until a couple of months ago when my adoptive mother passed. But as I told Dad, it finally made sense out of something that had bothered me all my life."

"What's that?" David asked.

"I didn't look like my parents. Not any of them or the relatives. I'd ask why my hair was black when they were both blonds, and they'd make some offhand remark about recessive genes. They had small features, and they were both short. I'm over six feet tall, and with this face."

The men laughed and then began pointing at each other

and making fun of who had the bushiest eyebrows or the most prominent nose.

Sully sighed. "Just sitting here looking around this room and seeing familiar features is the most gratifying feeling of my life," he added.

Then Marc added a stroke of poignancy to the story that they could all appreciate.

"You can imagine how I felt when I first saw his picture! It was like looking at a younger version of myself. He was my blood, and I didn't know he existed until the family gathering the night before Uncle Wayne's funeral."

"I knew something was wrong then," David said. "But you didn't say, and I would never have guessed."

And then the subject shifted to Sully and Melissa and the big ring she was flashing on her finger.

"Nice move," one of the men said.

"I'd have to take out a loan to put one like that on my wife's finger," another said, and more laughter ensued.

Sully was absorbing these people and their energy through every word and action—and trying to remember who was who, and how they were related—when his uncle David spoke up.

"Have you two set a date?"

"We've spent the last two weeks in planning, and we're looking at the first week of November."

"An exciting time, for sure," Marc said.

A short while later, the men dispersed to other areas of the house. Sully went looking for Melissa, while Marc went in search of Lovey. When he saw her happily laughing and talking with old friends, it felt good knowing they'd already forged a bond beyond that of the son they shared.

She caught him watching her and winked just to let him know she was okay. Satisfied all was well, Marc went into the kitchen to talk to his aunt again and found Melissa writing down a recipe for one of the snacks June had made, while Sully stood there eating it.

Sully glanced up and saw his dad watching him, and in that moment a swell of emotion washed over Marc so strong that his vision blurred. None of them could change the past, but they had the rest of their lives to make a family out of what was left.

The next morning after breakfast, Sully decided to take his family to his fire station to introduce them. As soon as his car was brought up from valet parking, they drove away.

"This is going to be a surprise for the guy I talked to when I was trying to track you down," Marc said. "He thought I was running a scam of some kind and was certain you weren't adopted."

Sully braked for a red light. "Rick is great. He's always the one with the answers, but this time he got them wrong and the guys are going to ride him about it."

"I'm looking forward to meeting them," Lovey said. "The more people I meet who knew you when I didn't, the more I learn about the man you became."

"Aw, Mom… I'm sorry," Sully said.

Marc reached for Lovey's hand and squeezed it.

"It's not a sad thing. It's a good thing," Lovey said, but Marc's presence on the way was appreciated.

When they finally reached the station and parked, Sully breathed a quick sigh of relief.

"Good. They're not on a call. Let's do this," he said, and they all got out. Sully reached for Melissa's hand and they led the way inside.

The men were all busy at different tasks, but the moment they saw Sully walking in, they began sounding off. "Hey guys! Sully's here! Sully's here."

Captain Lawson heard the shouts and got up from his desk and went out into the dining area where they were gathering. He walked up to Sully with a grin on his face and shook his hand.

"Hey, Sully. I knew you wouldn't be able to stay away. Want your old job back?"

Sully laughed. "No thanks, Cap. I found a better gig. You know my mother died right after I retired, right?"

They all nodded and began offering condolences again, but Sully stopped them.

"No, guys. That's not where this is going. When I was going through her papers for the lawyer, I found my adoption papers and a letter from my mother saying she was sorry she never told me."

Now every man in the place was quiet, listening in disbelief.

"I had exactly the same reaction," Sully said, "and to make a long story short, I went looking for my birth mother. I'm won't go into how it happened, but I brought her to meet you. And there was an added bonus in my search," he said, as he put his arm around Melissa and pulled her close. "I found this pretty lady in the same place. We were teenage sweethearts, and now I've got a ring on her finger. This is my fiancée, Melissa Dean. The pretty lady to my right is my birth mother, Jane Cooper, but we all call her Lovey. And this is my birth father, Marc Adamos."

"Oh shit," a small voice said from the back of the room.

Sully laughed out loud. "Yeah, Rick. I already know my dad called here looking for me and left his number… but since you were so sure it was a scam, you didn't pass it along."

All of the men began crowding around them, congratulating Sully on how his life had taken such a remarkable turn.

Lovey got a hug from every man in the room, and was in tears before it was over.

Marc kept fielding comments about cloning himself, and how much he and Sully looked alike, when Captain Lawson spoke up.

"I'm sure this is a coincidence, but I watch Nat Geo all the time and began noticing some years back that there was a Marc Adamos credited as the documentarian."

Marc grinned. "That's me."

Now Lawson was in awe. "Oh man! You have my utmost admiration. I don't know how you survived some of those shots you got, but my hat's off to you, and it's a pleasure to meet you."

"And by the same token, you have my utmost admiration…all of you do…for helping keep my son alive until we could find each other. It's been a pleasure meeting all of you," Marc said.

Before anyone could ask another question, the alarm went off. Sully gave them all a thumbs-up, and then they were gone, with the captain right behind them.

Melissa watched, in her mind seeing Sully as one of these men, and took a slow, shaky breath, grateful that part of his life was behind him.

"And that's how you clear a fire station," Sully said, as two of the three trucks left with sirens screaming.

They got back in the car and returned to the hotel, only to say their goodbyes to Marc again an hour later.

"We have a wedding coming up soon," Melissa said. "Don't go so far on your next trip that you can't make it back."

"I promise," Marc said.

Sully waved. "See you soon," he said, and drove away.

Marc stood at valet parking, waiting for his car as he watched them leave.

"Nice family," the attendant said.

Marc looked at him and smiled. "Yes, they are, and thanks."

During the next two weeks, Sully and Melissa finally cleared the wedding date with the pastor. She made a solo trip to Savannah and found a wedding dress she liked, then hid it in the closet of another bedroom. She found someone in Savannah who agreed to make their cake and deliver it to Blessings, and had Myra Franklin on notice for the flower order.

When she asked Lovey if she'd be her matron of honor, Lovey beamed.

"I've been a few too many brides, but I've never been in someone else's wedding. I am honored!"

Sully called his dad to ask if he would be his best man, and Marc quickly said yes, without letting on there were tears in his eyes when Sully asked.

They'd both agreed they wanted to keep the whole service simple. They weren't sending out invitations, just a blanket invitation to any of their friends who wanted to come.

———————————

While Sully and Melissa were making plans for their future, Hoover Slade's plans were being made for him. He'd been released from the hospital and was on his way back to prison in a wheelchair. The only good part was they weren't taking him back to Coastal State.

He didn't know how the rest of his life would play out, or if he'd even survive prison in this handicapped state. What he did know and accept was that it was every bit his fault.

While he was in the hospital, he'd written a letter to Truman, telling him what had happened. About a week later, he got a reply. All Truman had to say was "That's tough," and that he was moving to Oregon.

Now that Hoover was being moved to another prison, he had to accept that he and Truman were going to lose each other, and from the tone of Truman's reply, Hoover didn't think he was going to care.

———————————

The week of the wedding, Melissa put the wedding invitation to the citizens of Blessings in the paper, because when someone got married in Blessings, everyone was invited.

All of Sully's belongings had arrived safe and sound from Kansas City some time back, and now that he had all of his clothes here, he was wearing his best suit, which just happened to be black, with a white shirt and a black tie to go with it. He was still in the dark about Melissa's dress, but that only added to the excitement.

The days flew past until they were finally down to the wire. The big day was tomorrow, and Melissa had worn herself out today making sure everything was in place.

She was in her nightshirt when she came out of the bathroom into the darkened bedroom. Sully was already in bed watching TV, and she dropped on the bed beside him.

"I am so tired."

"Poor baby," he said, and when she laid her head on his bare shoulder, he put his arm around her and pulled her close.

Melissa sighed. "Don't get me wrong. I'm tired, yes, but I'm so happy where our lives are going. You. Me. Us. I never thought I would be part of an *us* again, and then you walked back into my life, and the familiarity and comfort I felt was so immediate that I knew it was meant to be."

"I know. We were so young, and to be able to pick up right where we left off is a gift. I didn't realize how solitary my life had become. Now I can't imagine my life without you. Thank you for your faith and trust in me. Thank you for saying yes to spending the rest of your life with me. I won't fail you, Missy. I won't ever let you down."

He nibbled his way up her neck, then behind her ear, then centered his mouth on her lips and groaned when she opened them ever so slightly for him to come in.

That one kiss turned into more, and then more, until it

morphed into a game of strip poker. For every kiss she gave him, he took off another article of her clothing, stroking the spot he'd just bared until she was naked beneath him.

Foreplay was over.

He moved between her legs and took her, with passion and purpose in every motion. The heat between them set a flash fire burning. Within a minute, they were lost in the feelings, chasing that ever-building surge toward the lightning-fast climax that hit—leaving them sated and weak.

They fell asleep in each other's arms.

They woke the next morning to the alarm going off on Sully's phone. He turned it off and then looked at her and smiled.

"Let's do this," he said, and they were out of bed and laughing.

Melissa showered first, and then dressed in jeans and a shirt because she still had a trip to the beauty shop to make. And as soon as Sully had shaved, showered, and dressed, they quietly left their room and made it to the kitchen.

"Cereal?" Sully asked as he moved to the pantry.

Melissa was making coffee, and nodded. As soon as she started it brewing, she got bowls and spoons from the cabinet while Sully got the milk and took it to the table.

They sat across the table from each other, fixed their cereal, then scooped up the first bite.

"To first love and sweet kisses," Sully said.

Melissa grinned as they toasted each other with spoons dripping milk.

"To us," she said, and then the cereal went in their mouths.

She kept watching him, thinking how beautiful it was going

to be to share breakfast with him for the rest of her life, while Sully was thinking he wanted to take her back to bed, then reminded himself that their future would be filled with days like this, when the wedding was nothing but a sweet memory.

"So what's the plan?" he asked as they were carrying their bowls to the sink.

"I get my hair done at ten. I'll come home afterward to gather up my stuff and get dressed at the church. If there's food here, I'll eat a bite before I leave."

"Since I'm dressing here, I'll make sure there's food," Sully said. "We'll leave for the hotel in Savannah after the reception, but Dad's just an hour outside Blessings now, so I'll be catching a ride to the church with him, and you drive my car today, okay? It has more room for our bags."

"I will," Melissa said, and then threw her arms around his neck. "This is happening, isn't it? It's really, really happening."

He grinned. "Yes, ma'am, it sure is."

After that, the time flew. Before Melissa knew it, it was time to leave for the Curl Up and Dye.

"My car keys are in the hall," Sully said. "I'll be here with food when you get back. What do you want me to bring for you?"

"I don't care. I won't want much. You and Marc please yourselves, and I'll be happy with whatever is here."

She blew him a kiss and then waved as she went out the door.

Ruby was waiting for her when she walked in.

"Hey, girl. Those green eyes of yours are flashing. Someone might think you were getting married today." Melissa laughed, and Ruby began. "So what are we doing today?" she asked.

"I want the sides pulled back, but the rest of it left down and curled under, like you do it sometimes."

"You do rock that old-time pageboy look, and your hair has gotten so long it will still be brushing the back of your neck. Is that what you're wanting?"

"Yes," Melissa said, and relaxed into the chair.

It was after eleven thirty when Melissa left the beauty shop, her hair elegant and her nails done.

She smelled fried ham and biscuits when she walked in and guessed Sully had gone to Granny's for some of Mercy's biscuits.

"I hope you saved me one," she said as she walked into the kitchen.

Marc got up and greeted her with a quick kiss, but it was Sully who pulled out a chair. "Here, sweetheart, sit down. I'll get a plate and some iced tea for you."

"Thank you," she said.

"Your hair is beautiful," Marc said. "Are you nervous?"

"Not about getting married," she said.

Sully brought her a paper napkin, a paper plate, and a glass of sweet tea, then pushed a platter of ham biscuits toward her.

"These are the best biscuits I ever ate in my life," Marc said.

"We know," Melissa said. "Mercy Pittman is one of the gems in Blessings." She took one from the platter and took a bite. "Umm, nothing better than honey-cured ham on a buttermilk biscuit."

"Is that a Southern thing?" Marc asked.

Still chewing, Melissa gave him a thumbs-up and nodded.

She ate with an eye on the clock, listening to father

and son trading stories and remarking on similar likes and dislikes.

Then all of a sudden the time was upon them, and Melissa was running up the stairs to get her suitcase and the two garment bags, one with her wedding dress and the other with the clothes she was wearing to Savannah for their overnight honeymoon.

Sully carried it all down for her, and she came down with her purse over her shoulder and her veil on a hanger covered in a clear plastic bag.

Marc followed them out.

"Are you sure you have everything?" Sully asked.

"Both garment bags, one suitcase, and my veil. Yes," she said, and took the keys he dropped in her hand. She waved at Marc, then put her hand behind Sully's neck and kissed him senseless. "See you at the altar!" she said, and then she was gone.

"You are so done for," Marc said.

"Yes, and thank you for calling that to my attention," Sully said as they went back inside.

Melissa was driving to the church with her heart pounding, excited and a little bit anxious that she might have forgotten something important.

She arrived at the church and then parked at the back so she and Sully wouldn't get caught up in other traffic. Before she could get out, she was swarmed by a host of friends from church who carried everything inside and escorted her to one of the classrooms that had been set aside for them to use.

"Is Lovey here yet?" she asked.

"She just got here and is in the adjoining classroom getting ready. Ruby is doing her hair, and Mabel Jean is doing her nails."

"Have the flowers been delivered?" Melissa asked.

"Yes, honey. They're all in the big refrigerator in the kitchen to stay fresh. Myra said she'd come back near time to get them to you, and the bakery from Savannah called about twenty minutes ago from the road so they'll be showing up here soon."

"All of a sudden I'm nervous," Melissa said.

"Don't be. We've got this for you. One of the girls will be at a table at the door with your guest book. We have two ladies who will be serving punch. The bakery said they're staying to cut and serve the cake, that it's part of their service. All you have to do is calm down, get dressed, and go get married."

Melissa sighed. "I've already said 'I do' a thousand times in my heart, but today will make it official."

While the women were helping her, Sully and Marc had been taken to a room at the end of the adjoining wing.

Marc knew Sully was wearing a black suit and tie with a white shirt, so he'd brought a gray suit and tie to go with his white shirt, and now they were mostly pacing the room, waiting.

"Thank you again for being my best man," Sully said.

"Are you nervous, Son?"

"Not a bit. Why should I question the fate that threw us all together like this?"

They sat, waiting in companionable silence until the pastor came into the room and hurried them down to the place where they would enter the nave. Myra Franklin had arrived and was waiting to pin a small boutonniere on each of their suit coats.

"You both look very handsome," Myra said, and hurried away.

Sully could hear people filing into the church and down the aisles, talking quietly as they took their seats.

Melissa was still in her dressing room when Lovey came in. She'd made one last run to the Unique Boutique and, in honor of her son's wedding, had broken down and bought a dress—a pale-blue chiffon with a scoop neck, long sleeves, and a slightly flared skirt. Her necklace was her only jewelry, and the heels she was wearing were pearl gray and comfortable. She felt good, even pretty, and then she saw Melissa and stopped.

"Oh, honey. You are stunning. Your hair. Your dress. That sweetheart neckline is beautiful, and the slight flare in the skirt is perfect. I love that there's not a trace of lace anywhere on you except for your veil. I love it. Turn around. I want to see the back."

Lovey nodded her approval at a bit of bare expanse, and then the door opened and Myra was standing in the door.

"It's time, ladies," she said, and handed a bouquet to Lovey as she walked out, then gave the bridal bouquet to Melissa, who followed behind.

Melissa clutched the flowers in front of her, barely glancing at the white calla lilies with their stems bound tightly in green ribbon, as they walked all the way to the vestibule, bringing her closer and closer to Sully.

They stopped just out of sight, waiting for the music to begin. Melissa got a quick glimpse of Sully and Marc walking out with the pastor as they took their places in front of the altar.

At that point, the organist struck a chord, the signal for the congregation to rise. And as they did, they also turned toward the entrance. When the organist began the traditional wedding march Melissa had chosen, Lovey appeared in the doorway with her shoulders back and her chin up, just as she'd done the night she left her baby behind, and started slowly down the aisle. Only this time she wasn't crying. She looked neither to the right nor to the left, but to the two men standing at the pulpit as peace flowed through her.

And then Melissa appeared, pausing in the doorway until Sully saw her. Only then did she take her first step toward him, then had to fight the urge to run into his arms.

Sully remembered her arrival at the altar, then taking her hand and turning toward her. After that, everything faded except her and those bright-green eyes looking straight into his soul.

The rest of their lives had just begun.

Not ready to leave Blessings, Georgia?
Read on for a peek at Sharon Sala's novella,

count
your
blessings

RUBY DYE SHOWED UP IN BLESSINGS, GEORGIA, TWELVE
years earlier with nothing to her name but her divorce
papers and a cosmetology license. She had just enough
money from her divorce settlement to set up a beauty shop
she called The Curl Up and Dye, with very little left over. It
was a simple plan. If she didn't cut enough hair, she wouldn't
eat. But as it turned out, she had arrived in Blessings to provide a service that had been missing. Before the first week
was out, she was booked solid. Considering it was the first
good thing that had happened to her in a long time, she was
grateful.

She made it a practice to change her hair color and style
on a biyearly basis as a means of advertising her own skill,
and last night had been the night for another change. She'd
gone home with shoulder-length brown hair and auburn
highlights. This morning her hair was chin length and red.
Audacious Red was the color on the box, and she considered it a good measure of her attitude. She came in the back

door, unloaded the box of doughnuts fresh from the bakery, and started coffee.

Vesta and Vera Conklin, her fortysomething identical twin stylists would be here soon, and neither one of them was fit for conversation until they'd had something sweet and a cup of coffee in their bellies. Ruby loved the both of them, but they were the most opinionated women she'd ever met, and their confrontational attitude was probably why neither one of them was married.

At thirty-two, Mabel Jean Doolittle was the youngest employee. She did manicures and pedicures at The Curl Up and Dye and, when they were extra busy, helped out on shampoo duty, as well.

She was a feisty little blond with a scar on her forehead from going headfirst into the windshield of her boyfriend's car when she was only sixteen. It was a daily reminder to never make stupid-ass choices in men again.

Ruby was proud of what she'd accomplished. The one thing she hadn't expected was for the shop to become the local confessional, which it had. Eventually, every secret in town came out at The Curl Up and Dye.

She was running the dust mop over the black and white tiles when the back door opened. Vesta and Vera entered, both wearing pink smocks and the same pissy scowl on their faces.

"Morning, girls. Coffee is hot. Doughnuts are fresh. Help yourselves," Ruby said.

"Morning, Sister," they echoed, then stopped. "Nice hair color," they added, and headed for the break room.

Ruby smiled as she headed for the register to count out the money for the till. Nearly everyone in town called her

"Sister," and she liked it. It made her feel like she was part of a great big family. Once the money was in the drawer, she moved to the front door. She was just about to turn the Closed sign to Open when she saw Alma Button pull up in front of the shop.

The fact that it was August 15 and Alma was driving the family van made Ruby wince. It must be time for back-to-school haircuts for Alma's six boys. When she saw the side door open and boys spilling out like puppies turned loose in a barn full of chickens, she took a deep breath and yelled out, "Girls, grab your scissors! Here comes Alma and her boys."

The twins stepped out of the break room. On a scale of one to ten, their tolerance for children was a three, and judging from their expressions, that had just plummeted to a one.

Vera was muttering beneath her breath as she brushed powdered-sugar crumbs off her smock.

Vesta frantically stirred a second packet of sugar into her coffee.

Ruby turned the sign to Open and unlocked the door.

"Morning, Alma. Y'all are here early."

She smiled at the boys trailing in behind their mother.

From the looks on their faces, they were no happier to be here than Ruby and her girls were to see them coming.

"Morning, Ruby," Alma echoed, and gave the boys a warning look. "You know Joe down at the barber shop is still in the hospital from his hip replacement, and I didn't want to have to drive all the way to Savannah with six boys just to get their haircuts. I figured if we came early we could avail ourselves of your 'walk-ins welcome' offer."

Ruby pointed to the three open stylist chairs. "Yes, I heard about Joe. They say he'll be out of the hospital in another couple of weeks but won't open back up for a while yet."

"That's what I heard, too," Alma said.

Ruby pointed at the chairs. "Okay, boys, who's first? Three of you grab yourselves a seat and we'll get this over. My goodness, you all have grown. Looks like no more booster seats for the Button boys, right?"

"I'm six now and tall for my age," Cooter announced.

Billy Joe punched his little brother on the arm.

"Big deal, Cooter. I'm almost eight."

"Shut up, the both of you," Larry muttered. At ten, he considered himself beyond that.

Ruby heard what sounded like a slight whistle, followed by the scent of an odorous fart. She turned on the ceiling fan and pretended not to notice, but was guessing it was either Jesse or James, the twelve-year-old twins, who were suddenly interested in the display of hair gel.

"*Madre*, someone farted!" Cooter yelled.

Alma glared at her son. "Hush your mouth," she hissed. "He's learning Spanish from *Sesame Street*," she added, hoping the use of a second language overrode her other child's social faux pas.

Vesta's nose wrinkled in disapproval, both for the smell and the task ahead.

Bobby Button, who had been nicknamed Belly before he started first grade, took a seat in Ruby's chair, refusing to acknowledge the boys he'd come in with. He would turn fifteen in a week and eyed his hair with regret. He'd been growing it all summer and was pissed at having to give it up. When he saw his mother watching him, he glared.

She glared back. Whether they liked it or not, part of getting her six boys ready for a new year of school meant buzz cuts, and they had Belly's entrance into second grade to blame. Before his first month in second grade was over, he had been infected with head lice and proceeded to share the infection with everyone else in the family before Alma knew that he had them.

By the time she had the scourge under control, she'd quit having sex with her husband, claiming it was partly his fault for giving her nothing but boys; burned every piece of bed linen she owned; and shaved the boys bald. Her skin had crawled for months afterward. Although it had never happened again and she finally went back to her wifely duties of submitting to her husband's sexual advances, she was thoroughly convinced the scourge remained under control because of her due diligence to cleanliness and the removal of most of her sons' hair.

The twins climbed up in the other two chairs, somewhat fascinated by the fact that the women who were about to cut their hair were also twins. They looked in the mirror, then at each other, and giggled. Then they looked at the expressions on the hairstylists' faces and frowned. Obviously, Vera and Vesta were not as amused.

"The usual?" Vera asked, as she put the cape around a twin.

"How short?" Vesta asked.

Alma folded her arms across her bosom. "The usual. Very short."

When the clippers began to buzz, Cooter covered his eyes. Billy Joe fell backward onto the floor, pretending he was dead, and Larry was picking his nose.

It was an auspicious beginning to what would turn out to be an eventful day.

Also by Sharon Sala

Blessings, Georgia
Count Your Blessings (novella)
I'll Stand By You
You and Only You
Saving Jake
A Piece of My Heart
The Color of Love
Come Back to Me
Forever My Hero
A Rainbow Above Us